STRIPPED

BY JASINDA WILDER

STRIPPED

ISBN: 978-1-941098-08-0
Copyright © 2013 by Jasinda Wilder

Cover art by Sarah Hansen of Okay Creations. Cover art © 2013 by Sarah Hansen.
Interior book design by Indie Author Services.

"A friend is like a good bra: hard to find, comfortable, supportive, always lifts you up, makes you look better, never lets you down or leaves you hanging, and always close to your heart."
—Author unknown

To Leah, Tara, and Nyree,
For being my good bras

CHAPTER ONE

"No DAUGHTER OF MINE will engage in any such lewd and sinful behavior as *dancing*," Daddy says to me, his blue eyes blazing. "It is gross and immodest and entirely sexual. I've seen the kind of dancing those... those *harlots* engage in at that so-called academy. You will not attend."

I screw my eyes shut and restrain the urge to scream and stomp my foot. I'm sixteen and a lady. Stomping my foot does not become a lady. At least, that's what Mom tells me. "Daddy, please. *Please*. I won't do anything like that. I'll be modest, I promise. You can okay each dance, each outfit. Just...please. Please, please, let me dance." I clasp my hands in front of me and dip at the knees, giving him my best puppy-dog eyes.

He's wavering. I can sense it in him. "Grey, I don't approve of dancing. God does not approve of dancing."

Mom to the rescue: "Now, Erik, you know that's not what the Scriptures say. You're just being a cantankerous old dinosaur. David danced before the Lord. The Psalms mention dancing to honor the Lord in several passages." She glides to Daddy's side and presses up against his arm, resting her hand on his shoulder. "Our daughter knows right from wrong, and you know it. She just wants to bring glory to God by using the talents He's given her."

"Please, Daddy. I won't allow any choreography that's lewd or sexual." I can barely breathe from the burning weight of hope in my chest.

He glances from me to Mom and back. I can see him chewing it over in his head. "I'll allow it...*for now*. But at the first sign of anything sinful or ungodly, I'll pull you out of there so fast you won't even have time for your head to spin. You hear me, child?"

I hug him, squeal with joy. "Thankyou thankyou*thankyou*!"

"Don't disappoint me, Grey. You are a pastor's daughter. You have to set a fitting example for the entire community."

"I will, Daddy. I'll be the best example. I promise, I promise." I spin away from him and dance a few flowing steps away, then settle into an arabesque, which I hold for a moment. I turn back to him. "See? Nothing wrong with that, is there?"

He just narrows his eyes at me. "I have to finish preparing Sunday's sermon."

Daddy is the founder and executive pastor of Macon Contemporary Baptist Church, one of the largest churches in the entire state of Georgia. Granddaddy Amundsen was the hellfire and brimstone pastor of a tiny Reformed Baptist church in the backwoods of Georgia, so Daddy grew up a pastor's kid, was groomed for the pulpit his whole life. Granddaddy was even more strict than Daddy, impossible as it seemed. He didn't even approve of me wearing pants or shorts, even as a little kid, but Daddy let me get away with that as long as the shorts weren't too short or the pants too tight. To Granddaddy, women stayed in the kitchen, wore dresses, and were seen and not heard. He was a bit of a fossil, Granddaddy. He never approved of the fact that Daddy taught the more modern and contemporary Baptist theology.

I grin at him and dance out of his study.

Mom is waiting for me in the kitchen. "There you go, Grey. Now you can dance all you want and not worry about either of us getting in trouble."

I've been dancing in secret since I was fifteen, watching Internet videos, teaching myself, watching *So You Think You Can Dance* on my laptop and trying to imitate the choreography. Mom helped me out a bit this past year, taking me to dance classes on Saturday mornings, telling Daddy it was manicure-pedicure appointments. He approved of mani-pedis as little as he did everything else, but he had a hard time saying no to me and Mama, so he let us go. He didn't need to know about the secret dance classes as long as Mom was driving me. Now that I've gotten my license and a car, he'll expect to keep tabs on me everywhere I go. Of course, Mom and I really do get mani-pedis after dance, but that's beside the point.

I hug Mom and give her a kiss on the forehead. "Thank you, Mom. I know you didn't like lying to Daddy—"

She glares at me, silencing me with a finger over my lips. "I never lied. Not once. He asked if we were going to get our nails done, and that's what we did. If he didn't ask where *else* we went, that's not lying. If he had ever asked me directly if I was taking you to dance classes, I would have told him. You know that."

I don't argue with her, but as I head up to my room to email Mrs. LeRoux that I can officially join the troupe, I wonder at my mother's evasions. Wasn't it lying by omission if we didn't tell Daddy what we were doing? He wouldn't have let us go at all if he'd known. If he finds out now, I'll never be allowed to leave my room again. I don't know what kind of trouble a wife can get in, but I know Daddy would be mad at Mom for her complicity.

I glance through the videos Mrs. LeRoux has uploaded to the website since last week. She's taken to setting up a video camera during every lesson, and then, at the end of the day, uploading the content to her website. Or rather, she has her daughter Catherine do it. If we haven't been there for that class, Catherine and Mrs. LeRoux go through the video of the day and cut out most of it, leaving in bits that are supposed to teach us something. No one knows this but Mrs. LeRoux started this practice mainly for my sake.

She saw some kind of potential in me that very first class I attended at the beginning of this year. She loved the way I danced and applauded the fact that I was self-taught. She gave me a scholarship so I could attend for free. Since I couldn't attend as many classes as everyone else did, she started taping the lessons, rehearsals, and group practices so I could keep up. Other students started watching them and found them useful as well, so they stuck.

When the first midweek group lesson rolled around that Wednesday, I'd practiced the group choreo, as well as the solo piece I was working on. Daddy had watched me practice in the basement, sitting on the stairs with his fingers pressed together in a steeple, eyes following my every move. It was nerve-wracking, honestly. He was watching me just to see if I'd mess up, to see if this plié was lewd, or that leg extension was improper and unladylike.

Group on Wednesday after school is split into two parts, forty-five minutes each. The first section is group choreo, going over the eleven-girl piece Mrs. L designed, making sure each of us knows our individual parts and that the whole piece flows properly. The second part is instruction, where Mrs. L teaches us a new move or technique, demonstrating and having each of us try it in front of the class. She corrects as needed. I'm struggling a bit with the group work, since I've never danced in a group before today. I keep messing up the *pas de chat* in the middle, missing a step and knocking into Devin, the girl next to me.

Finally, Mrs. L stops the practice and brings me forward, having everyone else line up on the barre along one wall. "Grey, you're doing great, my dear, but you need to get this part down. You can do the *pas de chat* perfectly on your own, but for whatever reason, when you try it with the other girls, you mess up. Why do you think this is?"

Mrs. LeRoux is a tiny woman, barely over five feet tall, with iron-gray hair and pale gray eyes set shallow in her beautiful face. She's French, having moved to Georgia twenty years ago with her husband, who died suddenly, leaving her in debt. She opened a dance studio with the last of her cash and fought her way to prosperity, one lesson at a time. I've seen her dance before, and she isn't one of those teachers who can't do what they teach. Mrs. LeRoux can make you cry with a two-minute routine. As a teacher, she's fiery and fierce, demanding yet fair, and compassionate in all things. She's never mean in her criticism but she expects you to do your best and she refuses to let you get away with less. I love her dearly.

I stand in front of the class and consider Mrs. LeRoux's question. "I've never danced in a group before."

"It's the same as dancing alone, my dear. You must merely be more aware of your surroundings. This *pas de chat* is simple. Child's play. You are talented enough to have no problems. Try again alone, please." She gestures with her hand for me to do the move.

I take a deep breath, set myself into the crouch that leads into the pas de chat. It's a ballet move, since Mrs. L's training is primarily ballet, although the studio also focuses on contemporary dance, jazz and modern. Every piece she choreographs tends to have a balletic bent to it, I've discovered, which is fine with me. I love the flowing nature of ballet, even if I don't like the stiffness of it. I dance to be free, to express myself.

I go through the series of steps and leaps, and I know I nail them. Doing them alone was never the problem.

"Very good, Grey. Perfect. Now, Lisa, Anna, Devin, take your positions around her. Aaand… begin." Mrs. L nods as the four of us perform the section of the routine together.

I get through the first two leaps with no problems and this time, I focus all my attention on Lisa to my left and Anna to my right as we pirouette together and begin the second series of leaps. Devin is behind me for the beginning of the series but ends up in front of me after we pause, readjust our lines, pirouette, and leap again. This switch, the pirouette, is what I'm having trouble with. I'm always too close to Devin, and my arms smack against hers as she and I spin in opposite directions, with Lisa and Anna spinning to either side of us in opposing directions. It's a beautiful sequence, or at least it will be if I can nail it this time.

It's not technically a pirouette, according to the balletic definition, since our arms aren't domed above our heads, but rather are spread apart to create a kind of vortex effect in the center of our four bodies. If it was a simple balletic pirouette I wouldn't have any trouble, as my arms would be contained within the sphere of my elbows and knee, but with my arms extended like this…

I feel the knife-edge of my left hand brush Devin's forearm, and although I finish the maneuver, I know I've messed it up yet again.

"Better, Miss Amundsen, better. But now again. This time...*focus*. Watch Devin. Your hands should pass above hers each rotation. Again, go." Mrs. LeRoux gestures imperiously and steps back.

We return to the beginning position, leap, leap, leap...pause, set, spin...

I nail it perfectly, grinning in exultation. The next series of leaps flow naturally, and at some signal from Mrs. L that I don't see, the other girls join us without so much as a whisper of interruption. The rest of the piece is effortless. We do it through three more times, and now it's smooth as silk as it should be.

Instruction period is easy. We learn some basic tumble/floor jazz sequences. After everyone demonstrates the moves to Mrs. LeRoux's satisfaction, she dismisses us. She calls me aside as I gather my things.

"Grey, a moment?"

I set down my bag and curtsy as I stand in front of her. "Yes, Mrs. LeRoux?"

She smiles at me. "You did well today. I'm proud of you."

"Thank you."

"How is your solo coming?"

I bobble my head from side to side, an unsure motion. "Pretty well, I think," I say. "I'm kind of stuck near the end, though. I can't make the transition go smoothly from one part to the next."

"Show me."

"From the beginning, or…?"

She waves her hand. "Yes, yes. From the top. Let me see it."

I slide my gear bag to the edge of the room with my foot, and then take position in the center of the room. I'd do better with my song playing, but that's not how Mrs. LeRoux works. She expects you to know the steps and the moves cold, with or without the music. She says the music should add soul and expression to the piece, but it shouldn't be a crutch.

I pause for a few beats, sinking into the mental place where I can call up the rhythm and let it move through me. I bend at the knees, extending my arms to either side, then sweep my hands around in a circle, sliding one foot out and putting my balance on the other foot. My extended leg rises, my arms slicing forward to put me into a flat-footed arabesque. I hold it, rise up on to my toes, and then bend at the waist and point my toes skyward, letting momentum pull me into a head-toe-head-toe diagonal spin. At the end of three rotations, I plant my palms on the floor and let the energy of the spin carry me over into a handstand. My feet droop slowly, and I arch my back until I'm doing the bridge, feet planted, hands planted, spine arched, head between my arms. I lower myself to the floor and twist onto my stomach, crawling forward, trying to express desperation. This is a piece that is meant to speak of my desperate need for freedom, my sense of confinement. Parts of the piece are wild and energetic, arm-flung spins, floating across the floor. Other parts are contained, limbs close to the body, gliding across the floor in tripping steps. I near the end of the piece, coming to the place where my choreography is stuck.

I'm in the center of the room, upright, coming off a pirouette, arms clutched against my chest. My palms turn out and push as if against a wall, an invisible barrier in front of me. The barrier gives way suddenly and I topple forward, stumbling as if taken by surprise.

"This is where I'm stuck," I say, huffing for breath in the middle of the dance floor. "Originally, I'd intended to fall forward, but it just doesn't feel right."

"Show me the original move, please."

I do the pirouette again, the pushing against the wall, the deliberate stumble forward, and let myself fall forward. I stand up and wipe the sweat off my upper lip. "See? It just…it doesn't work."

Mrs. LeRoux shakes her head, scratching the back of her neck. "No, your instincts are correct. It's not quite right." She peers at me as if seeing me moving, though I'm still. I can tell she's working through the choreography in her head.

"Ah, I have it. Instead of falling forward, stumble, sway, and spin in place, but off balance. Like this, yes?" She demonstrates what she wants me to do.

"Through the rest of the piece, you're battling the forces containing you, struggling to find your equilibrium and your freedom. So here, at the end, you must be victorious. It is the purpose of this piece, yes? It's an expression of your sense of entrapment. I see this. So now, you must break through. The wall gives way. So, when you end the pirouette, which is beautifully done by the way, instead of just pushing against it, act as if you're beating it down. Smash and flail against it. Let your anger bleed through. You're holding back at the end, Grey. You're ending weak. This must finish strongly. You must feel the power in yourself, yes? This could be a breakthrough. Not just in your dance, but in your head. In your soul. In yourself. Batter against the wall.

"I think I understand some of your struggles in your life. I fought them, too. My father was very demanding. He put me into ballet when I was only four years old. I danced every single day for my entire life. I had few friends and fewer social activities. There was only ballet. Only ballet. Then I met Luc. He swept me away. He was a dancer, too. He was so fluid, so strong. Every thing he did was beautiful. We met in a vineyard in *le Midi*. I don't remember exactly where. Near Toulouse, perhaps." She gazes into the middle distance, remembering. She shakes herself. "No matter. I understand. You must break free, in yourself. In this dance."

She waves her hand in the gesture that means *again, again*.

I run through the piece from the top, and this time I think of each rule I have to follow, each party my school friends go to that I can't, each time I'm told that a pair of jeans is too tight, a top too low-cut, that I'm wearing too much makeup. I think of the expectations of me to be a perfect little southern belle, the perfect little pastor's daughter, the expectation that I'll marry a godly man headed for the seminary, some boring young man with no aspirations beyond the pulpit and the flock.

I put all that into the dance. When I leap, I fling myself into it. When I spin in place, I let all my muscles pull me into the spin with all my energy. When I crawl across the floor, I claw at the polished wood planks as if pleading for my life. When I begin to batter at the walls surrounding me, I see my father's face, hear his voice and his harsh criticism, and his strict, dictatorial ways demanding perfection, I pound and pound and pound at it. Finally, I feel the walls give way and stumble forward, spinning in place, flailing, intentionally off-balance, wobbling, spinning around the floor as if finding joy in the unscripted dance of free steps. I end standing with my head hanging, hands loose at my sides, chest heaving, breathless.

I look up to gauge Mrs. LeRoux's reaction. She's leaning against the wall, hand covering her mouth, eyes wet.

"Perfect, Grey. Just…perfect. I felt it all. Perfect."

Her gaze flicks over my shoulder, and I turn in place to see my mother watching from the doorway to the foyer area. Her eyes reflect her emotions, and I know she's seen it all. I know she saw what I felt in that dance.

The corners of her eyes are tight, her forehead wrinkled. I turn away from her, back to Mrs. LeRoux.

"You think it was good?" I ask.

She nods. "I think it was an example of your potential. You can be a magnificent dancer, Grey. You must keep putting all of your emotions into your dance. Don't allow yourself to hold back."

I bend to grab my bag, rummaging through it for a towel. I join my mother at the door, wiping at my face with the rough white cotton. We leave and neither of us speaks as Mom drives us through Macon and out to our house in the suburbs,. I turn to glance at her, confused by her uncharacteristic silence. Usually she's chatty as a blue jay after dance class. She was a dancer, too, until she met Daddy and had me. She likes to talk about what I'm learning, the various techniques and such. Talking shop, reliving her days as a dancer. Now, however, she's slumped toward the window and she's driving with one hand. Her other hand is pressed to her forehead. Her eyes are narrowed, her features screwed up tight.

"Are you okay, Mom?" I ask.

She shoots me a faint attempt at a reassuring smile. "I'm fine, honey. I just have a headache."

I shrug and let the silence hang.

"Your dance was beautiful, Grey." Her voice is quiet, as if to speak too loud would cause further pain.

"Thanks, Mom."

"What did it mean?"

I don't answer right away; I'm not sure how to. I shrug. "Just…sometimes I feel…trapped."

Mom is the one to hesitate this time. "I know, honey. He just wants the best for you."

"*His* best. Not necessarily *my* best."

"He's your father."

"That doesn't mean what he thinks is right for me is always the only option."

Mom rubs at her forehead again with her knuckle, then holds out her hand, shaking it as if it's asleep. "I don't want to get into this right now, Grey. He's your father. He loves you, and he's just doing what he thinks is right. You need to be respectful."

"He's not respectful to me."

She shoots me a sharp, warning glare. "Don't, Grey." She winces, and then turns her eyes back to the road, blinking hard. "Goodness, this is the worst one yet," she mutters, more to herself than out loud.

"Worst one?" I stare at her in worry. "You've been having a lot of these headaches?"

"Here and there. Nothing too bad. They hit me in the morning, and they usually go away on their own." She clenches her hand into a fist and releases it, shakes it again.

I'm not sure what to say. Mom is tough. She's never sick, and the few times she is, she rarely complains and never takes the time to rest. She just powers through it until she's better. For her to visibly be in pain isn't a good sign. She must really be hurting.

"Should you see a doctor?" I ask.

She waves her hand in dismissal. "It's just a headache."

"What's wrong with your hand, then?"

"I don't know. It just…it feels numb. It's fine now."

We're home at this point, and she pulls the BMW into the garage and is out her door and into the house before I've even hauled my bag out of the back seat. I wave at Daddy as I pass his study on my way up the stairs. After I've showered, I head down to the kitchen, expecting to find Mom making dinner, but the kitchen is empty.

Daddy is still in his study, typing away at his computer, preparing for Sunday's sermon.

"Where's Mom?" I ask.

He looks up over the rim of his narrow reading glasses. "She's lying down. She's got a migraine, I guess."

"Is she okay? She said she's been having headaches."

He leans back in his chair. "I know. If they don't stop soon, I'm going to take her in to see a doctor whether she wants to or not."

"I'll make dinner then."

"Thank you, Grey. When you're finished, see if Mom wants something. She may not." He turns back to the computer. "I'll eat in here."

I retreat to the kitchen and start making dinner. I'm not as fancy a cook as Mom, but I can make a few good dishes. I rummage in the fridge and see that she'd gathered the ingredients to make chicken cordon bleu, so I make that, bringing Daddy his plate and can of Diet Coke. I head upstairs to check on Mom but she is asleep with the curtains drawn against the evening light. Even in sleep, her forehead is wrinkled and tight with pain.

Worry shoots through me, but I dismiss it. I leave the plate of food in case Mom wants it later, taking my plate and Coke into my room to eat as I finish my homework. Except for Mom's headaches, life is good.

So why do I feel a gnawing sense of unease?

CHAPTER TWO

THE LAST OF THE SCHOOL YEAR passes without incident. Mom's headaches have subsided or she hides them. I've danced in several recitals, with Mom and Daddy in attendance. Daddy still doesn't quite approve, and he definitely glares during the other girls' more overtly sensual solos. He knows I'm talented, though, and this pleases him. I dance over the summer, and I get to know Devin and Lisa and a few other girls from the studio. Daddy lets me go out with them as long as I check in regularly. For the most part, we don't do anything except hang out at the mall and watch girly TV at Devin's house. Boys come over a few times, but none of us says anything to the adults. Devin is a pixie, barely five-one and not even a hundred pounds soaking wet. She's got

auburn hair and brown eyes and she's a spitfire, energetic and fiery and outspoken. She pretty much has
the run of her house since her parents work all the
time. As far as Daddy knows, it's just me and Devin
and Lisa and cheesy '80s movies like *Flashdance* and
Footloose and *Girls Just Wanna Have Fun.*

He doesn't know about the occasional party
Devin throws on the weekends while her parents
are in Atlanta or elsewhere for business. Compared
to the stories I hear at Central High School, these
parties are usually pretty tame, It's mostly the same
twenty or so people, a few girls from Mrs. LeRoux's
studio, some guys from the football team, and some
girls from the dance program at Central. The others
sip beer and do shots of whiskey someone brings, but
I don't. Daddy would smell alcohol on me before I
even got into the house. I tried beer once, but it's
nasty. I took a tiny sip of whiskey and nearly choked.
I stick to Coke and have fun watching the others act
like idiots.

At one of these parties, near the end of the summer, I find myself sitting on the deck behind Devin's
house, watching as six or seven drunk boys play a
rowdy pickup game of football, girls cheering and
getting in the way. One of the Central dance girls has
her shirt off, her pink bra bright in the late evening
darkness. I'm embarrassed for her. How she could
be okay like that, half-naked, knowing every single

guy at the party is watching her? I want to cover her. Several guys hit on her, try to get her to go inside with them, but she seems to effortlessly fend them off without hurting any feelings. She's clearly intoxicated, dancing to the music playing from Devin's portable iPod speakers. She's got her hands in her hair, bunching it up at the back of her head. She's writhing her hips to the beat of the music, turning in place slowly, hips gyrating, skin flashing tan under the light of the moon and the pale yellow glow from the house. Everyone is watching her. Everyone. She's a dancer; she knows what she's doing. She knows she's got their attention. She glides her hands over her belly, over her hips, pushing at the waistband of her skintight blue jeans. Her dance has taken on a life of its own, spinning in place, flinging her hair around, pushing out and shaking her hips. Each move is provocative. The guys are frozen, and I watch as one affected guy adjusts himself. Even though I'm in the darkness of the deck, I blush hard.

A low, husky voice comes from my left. "Can you dance like that?"

I jump, startled. I peer into the shadows and see a boy frequently at Devin's parties, a football player named Craig. "No," I say, shaking my head. "Definitely not."

He laughs, leaning on the railing of the deck. "Sure you can." His finger brushes over my shoulder, and I shiver, edge away. "You should try. You'd be hot. She's okay-looking, but you? You're fine as hell, girl."

I blush so hard my face is hot. I giggle nervously. "You're crazy."

"No, I'm not. I just know what I like." His tone indicates he's referring to me.

I still can't quite see him. He's in the shadows, on the grass beyond the deck. I've seen him before. He's tall and blond, the kind of guy most girls go gaga for. He's wearing a red tank top that shows off his burly arms and a pair of low-hanging tan shorts. He's good-looking, that's for sure. My stomach flip-flops. He likes me. He's leaning forward to see me better, his eyes pale and wide in the darkness.

Abruptly, he plants his hands on the railing of the deck and vaults over so he's right in front of me. I give a quiet shriek of surprise and move back away from him. He swaggers toward me. He's so tall, and I'm afraid of what I see in his eyes. Desire. Hunger.

I don't know how to deal with it, with him. This is new territory. I know I'm pretty so boys are always interested. I'm tall for a girl, standing five-nine in bare feet. I've got honey-blonde hair that's long and fine and straight. My eyes are gray, the dark iron color of an approaching storm, or so Devin says. I've got a dancer's body: thick, powerful thighs, hips wider than I'd like, a fairly slim waist, and a generous bust line. By "generous," I mean I've got huge boobs, even for my height and build, which is kind of a challenge when I'm dancing. I usually wear sports bras just because I bounce too much without them, even when I'm not dancing.

It's there that Craig's eyes are glued right now. I'm wearing a loose blue T-shirt and a flowing, floor-length gray skirt. Completely conservative. No skin shows but my arms and a slim rim above the high scoop neck of my shirt. Even still, Craig can't take his eyes off my chest. I'm suddenly irritated by this. But then he closes in with another step, and he's close enough that I can smell the beer on his breath and see the lust in his eyes.

"Come on, Grey, show me how you dance." He puts his hands on my hips, low, and grinds against me.

I'm frozen, because no one has ever touched me like this. Should I react? Part of me likes it, but that part is sinful. The lustful sinner in me likes it.

With a sharp intake of breath, I yank myself out of his grip. "I don't think so, Craig."

He just laughs, as if I'm playing a game. Following me so his body is hard against me, he doesn't let an inch between us, Before I know what's going on, his mouth is on mine, sour beer breath and faint body odor. It's a split second of contact, but I'm revolted. I push him away and stumble backward, then slap him, hard. I don't bother speaking, but storm into the house, closing the sliding glass of the patio door behind me.

Through an open window, I hear Devin's voice calling out from the yard. "She ain't like that, Craig. You can't pull that shit with Grey Amundsen. Don't you know who her father is?"

"Who? Should I know?" I hear him reply.

"Erik Amundsen. Pastor of Macon Contemporary Baptist Church."

"Isn't that the huge church out off of seventy-five?"

"Yeah. That's her father. She's a pastor's daughter, C. She ain't the kind of girl that's gonna make out with you at a party. So forget it. Forget her."

"Sucks," Craig mutters. "She's hot as hell."

"Well, she's off-limits. Go hit on Amanda."

Craig laughs. "Yeah, right. Every guy in Macon under the age of twenty-five has banged Amanda. I don't want on that train."

Devin laughs with him. "Which means she's a sure bet, don't it?"

"Sure bet for herpes, you mean." I hear a shift in Craig's voice. "What about you, Dev? What kind of girl are you?"

Devin doesn't answer right away. I can't believe she'd fall for a tactic like that, but her voice is low and breathy. "Get me another drink, and you surely just might find out."

I retreat into the house, not wanting to hear anymore.

I skip the next party Devin throws, and I think she gets it. The exchange runs through my head for the rest of the summer, though. I'm the girl who's off-limits. I'm the pastor's daughter. I'm not off-limits because they respect my beliefs on marriage, or because of who I am, but because of Daddy. Devin was right that I'm not that kind of girl, but that doesn't mean I entirely minded Craig's advances—at least, until he assaulted me with his mouth. I liked feeling desired.

I've taken a lot of AP classes my first three years of high school, so my senior year schedule has some large open blocks where I can take electives. I'm trying to choose some classes that interest me, but there's nothing. I've already taken photography, theater, journalism and the dance elective. I don't want to repeat any of them except maybe the theater class. It was fun getting up on stage, pretending, and acting. It was even more fun watching the others. We even got to each direct our own scene, and that was where I shone.

I settle on an introduction to film class, taught by Mr. Rokowski, who had worked in Hollywood as a cameraman for most of his life before retiring to Macon with his wife. He's a short man with a round belly and long gray hair bound back in a ponytail.

The semester flies by. Most of my classes are boring, hard but dull. All except film. We watch movies, dissect them, talk about cinematography, camera angles, the reason for a dozen takes for every scene. Something about the process hooks me. Hearing Mr. Rokowski talk about being behind the camera for movies like *Ghost* and *Dirty Dancing*, being a part of making something so lasting, so iconic…I love it, I love every story he tells. I drink in the films. I love to see the different things a film can make you feel, just by the music in the background or the angle of a close-up, or how a shot sweeps from one place to another. It's manipulation of light and sound and emotion. Each film is a piece of magic. It's just like dance for me. When I dance, I lose myself. I can be anyone, do anything. I can say what I think, what I feel. With films, I can get lost in another world, in the lives of other people with problems different from mine.

At the end of the last day of the semester, Mr. Rokowski pulls me aside. "Grey, I just wanted to say what a pleasure it was to have you in class this semester. Every once in a while, this class ignites something in a student, and those are the moments I live for. I teach film because it's what I know and what I love, but when I'm able to show a student the magic in films, that's the best part." He pulls a brochure from his briefcase. "I teach at The Film Connection. It's a film institute with a branch here in Macon. It's an awesome program that really teaches you the ins and outs of the industry. You go through the process of producing your own film, and it even connects you to execs in Hollywood. I think you might be a great candidate for the program. It's something to think about. You could possibly even get in as a co-op. I could make the recommendation for you."

I feel something like hope blossom inside me. "It's a real film institute?"

"Absolutely. It's a great way to get experience and make some contacts in the industry."

"I'd learn how to really make a film? Like, for real?" I want it so bad I can taste it, until I remember Daddy. "My father wouldn't let me," I hear myself telling Mr. Rokowski.

"Why not?"

I shrug, not wanting to have to explain. "He's… very strict. He doesn't approve of Hollywood."

"But if it's what you want? I mean, what if you get a scholarship? It's entirely possible. I know people. You really showed a passion for film this semester, Grey. I think you could really go places."

I shake my head. "I'll think about it. I'd like to, I really would. But…I just know Daddy."

Mr. Rokowski wipes his face with his hand, his brown eyes glancing at me and then away. "Your relationship with your father is your business. Just think about it, okay? I'd hate to see talent go to waste."

I think about it…oh my, do I think about it. I'm sitting at the bar in the kitchen, twirling a pencil in my fingers. I'm working on an idea for a film, writing the screenplay and thinking about the script. I try talking to Mom about it, but she doesn't think it's a very good idea.

"You know how Daddy is, Grey. Hollywood is immoral and the whole film industry is full of sharks. You'd be exposed to so many unclean things. It's a glorification of all that's sinful about our society."

She's borrowing directly from Daddy's lexicon.

"I don't think you've really thought about what you'd be getting into, honey. Pursue dance. Find a good, godly man."

"You mean a pastor, so I can be like you."

"Is there something wrong with that?" Mom asks, her voice sharp.

"No, but it's not what I want. I love films. I love dance, but I love it for me. I don't want to dance professionally, since it wouldn't be fun anymore. I want a career in film." *I don't want to be a pastor's wife*. I think it, but I don't say it.

"I just don't think that's a possibility, sweetheart." She pushes her carefully curled blonde hair away from her face. Two fingers pinch the bridge of her nose, and she breathes out slowly. "Just think about it again, Grey, honey. Is it worth alienating your father over? He would be so disappointed."

She stumbles, then, as if dizzy or disoriented. I lunge off the bar stool and catch her against me. "Mom? Are you okay?"

"I'm fine, dear. I just got dizzy for a moment. I haven't had much of an appetite lately, so I might just be hungry."

That doesn't make any sense to me. "Mom, seriously. Are your headaches back?"

"They never really left, honestly." She leans back against the counter of the kitchen island. "I'll be fine. I'll take some Tylenol, and I'll be fine."

I let it go, but the worry is back.

The following week, I approach Daddy in his study. It's a Tuesday, which means he's just starting his sermon for the week, which is the best time to talk to him. After Wednesday he gets cranky if he's interrupted.

I plop down in the leather chair on the opposite side of his huge oak desk. "Hi, Daddy. How's the sermon coming?"

He sits back, pulling off his glasses. He brushes a hand through his fine blond hair. "Hi, there, Grey. It's going pretty well. It's a discourse on the reality of practicing grace in a graceless world." He peers at me. "I sense a 'Daddy-can-I' coming."

I smile as charmingly as possible. "Maybe."

He grins at me and takes a sip from a tall glass of sweet tea. Ice clinks, and a bead of sweat runs down the side of the glass as he sets it back down. "Well? Out with it."

"So, I took a film class this last semester. I really, really liked it, Daddy. It was so fun. We learned a lot about movies. The instructor used to be a cameraman, and he worked on *Ghost*, you know, the movie with Patrick Swayze and Demi Moore?"

"You mean the one about the man who haunts his wife? Ghosts are minions of the devil, Grey. Tools of the Evil One. It's no subject for crass entertainment."

"It's *romantic*, Daddy. He loved her. He didn't want to leave her alone."

"He couldn't accept God's plan for his life."

I sigh. "Well, regardless, I liked the movie, and I loved the class. Mr. Rokowski thought I might be a good candidate for The Film Connection."

I show him the brochure and he leafs through it slowly, reading the explanation and the testimonials.

"I would love, love, *love* to do this. It would be an opportunity to really learn the industry. Mr. Rokowski thinks he could even help me get a scholarship so you wouldn't have to pay much, if anything, for it."

Daddy slips his glasses back on and reads the brochure from front to back, then wakes up his computer and types in the website's address. I sit in silence, hoping against hope. After long, silent minutes, he removes his glasses again and leans back. "You're serious about this?"

I nod vigorously. I'd thought long and hard about the best tactics for presenting this. I had to make him think it was about ministry. I had to show him how I could be different from Hollywood. "Absolutely. It's what I want to do with my life. I don't want to be an actress or anything like that. I want to tell stories. There are so many ways to tell a good story, to move people, and film is one of those ways. It could be my ministry. Like Kirk Cameron and *Fireproof*."

He blows out a long breath. "I expected better from you, Grey." His voice is suddenly hard, whip-sharp, and I flinch. "I really did. Film school? That's worse than any lewd dancing. You would be working with the scum of the earth. People who think it's okay to glorify murder and dishonesty and sexual perversion."

"But Daddy, it doesn't have to be like that—"

"It would be, though. They would take advantage of you. An innocent, beautiful girl like you in Hollywood? They'd eat you alive."

"But that's what's so great about this program. It's here in Macon. I wouldn't have to move to L.A. to do it."

He doesn't respond for a long moment. When he does, his eyes are hard as flint. "This conversation is over. You will not be a part of that industry." He swivels his chair away from me, toward his computer screen, a clear dismissal.

I fight back a sniffle. "You don't understand."

"I do, all too well." He's not looking at me, now. Dismissing me. "You're the one who doesn't understand what it's like. What people are like, what they'll do. They'll pervert you. It's my job as your father to protect you, to shelter you from that."

My fists clench and tremble, my throat closing with hot, impotent anger. "But that's all you do! Shelter me! You don't understand me! Not anything. You never have. This is what I want. Just because you're a pastor doesn't mean I can't live my own life and like my own things. Not everything is sinful, and that's how you act, like every single thing that's not a Bible study or a prayer meeting is sinful!"

I'm standing up, crying and shouting. "God, you're just so…so damn close-minded about everything!"

Flushed with anger, Daddy stands up and knocks over a mug of pens. "Don't you dare take the Lord's name in vain in that manner, Grey Leanne Amundsen." He points a finger at me, and now he's in full-out preacher mode. "I am your father, and God has given me the responsibility of taking care of you. I am responsible for your soul."

"NO! You're not! I'll be eighteen soon. I can make my own decisions." I'm torn between fear and pride. I've never, ever spoken back to Daddy before.

This moment in time changes everything, somehow.

"For as long you live in my home, you'll follow my rules and do as I say. And I say you'll not do that program." He sits down and rights the mug of pens. "For your rebellious attitude and foul speech, all dance privileges are revoked."

I sink into the chair. "No, Daddy. I'm sorry. Don't…I'm in a performance on Monday. If I don't dance, they'll have to re-block the whole piece."

"Then they'll have to re-block it." He doesn't look at me again after that.

I leave his study in tears, retreating to my room. Eventually Mom comes in and sits on the bed. I roll toward her, and sit up immediately. She looks pale and thin, her face pinched. "Mom? Are you okay?"

She shrugs. "I'm fine, baby." She pats my hand. "I told you not to push it, sweetheart. I'll talk to your father and see if I can convince him to let you be in Monday's performance. But…you really should let go of this silly film thing. I know…I know you may not want to be a pastor's wife, and I understand that. But film? It's not for you."

I don't answer. I know they won't get it, not even my mom. When it's clear I'm done talking to her about it, she stands up, patting my hand again. "I'll talk to him. Just…think about your choices, okay? Think about God's plan for your life. Does this sudden obsession with sinful movies glorify Him?"

I only sigh, realizing the futility of arguing with

her about the difference between their ideas of God's plan for my life and *my* plan for my life. She leaves, and I'm alone again. I lie on my bed and stare at the ceiling, honestly trying to think through it. I could understand their reaction if I said I wanted to move to L.A. and be an actress, or to Nashville to be a musician. But I'm proposing that I stay close to home and in their circle of influence after high school. All Daddy cares about is his own idea of what's right and wrong. Everything is in black and white for him, and most things are black. There's more that's sinful and wrong than there are things that are okay.

I find myself wondering how he knows that God disapproves of all the things Daddy claims are wrong. I know he'd have Bible verses to support everything he believes. I just…I just can't help wondering if that's manipulating the Scripture to fit what he doesn't like or isn't willing to understand. And honestly, he's never left Georgia. He grew up here in Macon, got his degree in theology from Trinity Baptist Seminary in Jackson, an hour north. He can't know everything.

The more I think it through, the angrier I get.

I start imagining all the smart and witty and thoughtful arguments I could have made to Daddy. I'll never say any of them, but that's the way I am. I'll chew on an argument for days afterward, thinking about what I could have said, what I should have said, how I could have made it come out differently.

I'm surprised when my door opens and Daddy stands in the opening. I expected it to be Mom, but instead he's standing there looking scared.

"Daddy? What's wrong?"

"Your mother…she—she fainted. An ambulance is on the way. It's these headaches she's been having. She just fell over, Grey. She hit the edge of the stove and broke her wrist. Pray for her, Grey. Pray that the Lord will protect her."

I tremble, unshed tears closing my throat. This is bad. Very bad.

CHAPTER THREE

I SIT WITH MY HANDS FOLDED on my lap, eyes downcast. I can't look at her. A machine beeps steadily,
monitoring something. My eyes burn, but they're
dry. I've cried all my tears over the last few months.
She went from bad to worse, and now she's a skin-
wrapped skeleton in a hospital bed. Her hair is gone.
Her cheeks are ridges of sharp bone. Her fingers are
limp, frail and tiny. She's barely breathing. I've cried
and cried, and now I can cry no more.

I begged God to spare her. I stayed awake night
after night, pleading, on my knees. And still Mama is
dying.

Mama. I haven't called her or thought of her as
"Mama" since I was ten and Ally Henderson made
fun of me in front of the entire class for it. She's

been "Mom" ever since. But now…she's "Mama" again.

Undaunted, Daddy remains resolute in his faith that God has a plan.

God Has a Plan.

Those four mighty words that solve everything for him.

I don't think He does have a plan. I think sometimes people just die. Mom is dying. She's only got days now.

Two days earlier, I'd stood outside the hospital room while Dr. Pathak told my father to prepare himself for the worst.

Daddy just repeated his mantra. "The Lord's will cannot be subverted."

Dr. Pathak grunted in irritation. "I respect your faith, Mr. Amundsen. I truly do. I am also a man of deep faith, although I know you would not agree with what I believe. So I understand your faith. Sometimes we must be prepared for the plan of our God to not be what we would like it to be. Perhaps your God will not work a miracle. Perhaps He will. I hope for your sake and for your daughter's sake that He will do a great miracle and heal your wife as I have seen such miracles happen. I, too, pray, in my own way, for miracles to happen. But sometimes they do not. It is simply a fact of life."

Now I hold Mom's hand with its parchment-paper skin in mine, and I watch her breathe. Each breath is a slow process. She struggles to suck in air over long seconds and at last she lets it out again as slowly as she drew it in. Something in her chest rattles. Her body is giving up. She isn't, but her body is. Mom fought. God, did she fight. Chemo, radiation, surgery. There are scars and lines of stitches on her scalp where they drilled and cut. She wanted the tumor out. She wanted to live. For Daddy. For me.

She made me live my life. Made me keep going to high school, keep studying. Made me apply to colleges. She even let me send out an application to USC, the University of Southern California. One of the premier film schools in the world. She helped me get scholarships. She kept Daddy off my case and convinced him to let it all go. She didn't want us to argue, so we didn't. Daddy never agreed, never approved. But when I got the acceptance letter from USC and stopped even pretending to look at any other colleges, he realized it was for real. It was happening. Maybe he thought Mama being sick would change my mind. Maybe he thought he could just put his foot down and have his way, regardless of what I wanted. I don't know.

But now…she's losing the fight.

And all I know is that I'm going to USC. Mom understood my passion, before the cancer took her soul. I used my allowance to buy a Flip camera and started making my own films, artistic pieces about me, about life. I made friends with a homeless man living in Macon and did a piece on him. Mr. Rokowski helped me edit it and put a soundtrack on it using some pro programs.

I showed that piece to Daddy. He said it was a moving piece but if I went to school in L.A., my intentions wouldn't matter. I would get sucked into sinful lifestyle of Los Angeles. I let him rant, and then walked away. Film is my art, as much as dance. I don't need his approval.

I've filmed Mama's fight with cancer. She let me film every moment of it. I even skipped classes to go to film the chemo with her. She said it was her legacy, that she would beat it, and my film would record her victory.

My Flip is on a tripod in the corner, watching her die now. Recording her struggle for breath. It recorded her last words two days ago: "I love you, Grey." It's recording every beep of the machine monitoring her heartbeat.

They've said she's going to die any day now. They don't understand why she hasn't yet. I know, though. I think she's still fighting. For us.

Daddy is gone getting coffee and something to eat. I glance at the door, closed but for a crack letting in a thin stream of fluorescent light from the hallway and the occasional squeak of sneakers. There's the distorted squawk of the overhead PA: *"Dr. Harris to OR seven…Dr. Harris to OR seven, please…."*

I gently squeeze Mama's hand. She squeezes my hand back, a breath of pressure. Her eyes flutter but don't open. She's listening.

"Mama?" I sniffle and fight for breath. "It's okay, Mama. I'll be okay. I'll miss you every day. But… you've fought so hard. I know you have. I know how much you love me and Daddy. I'll take care of him, okay? You…you can go now. It's okay. You don't have to fight anymore."

That's a lie: I won't take care of Daddy. She needs the lie, though, so I tell it. A sob breaks free from my lips. I rest my face on her frail chest, listen to the faint *thumpthump…thumpthump…thump…* of her heart beating.

"I love you, Mama. I love you. Daddy loves you." I hear the faint beating grow fainter, slower. A few seconds between beats, then almost a minute. "I love you. Goodbye, Mama. Go be with Jesus."

Those words are the worst lie. I don't believe them. I don't believe in God.

Not anymore.

Someone is sobbing loudly, and I realize it's me. I choke it off. I have to be strong for Mama.

A faint patter from her heart, her chest rises… falls. A breath of pressure on my hand, once, twice, a third time, strongly. Then nothing. Silence from beneath my ear. Stillness.

I'd tuned out the monitor. Now I hear it flatlining. A team of nurses flurries in, begins the scramble of resuscitation.

"STOP!" I yell it at the top of my lungs. I don't even rise from my chair. "Just…stop. She's gone. Please…just leave her alone. She's gone."

Daddy is in the door, a white little Styrofoam cup of coffee in his hand. He sees the commotion, hears the flatline, sees the tears on my face, and hears my words. The cup slips from his fingers and hits the floor. Scalding, burnt-smelling coffee splashes up onto the legs of his expensive jeans and shiny leather shoes.

"Leanne?" His voice cracks on the last syllable.

I'm mad at him still. But he's my father and this is his wife and he's lost now. "She's gone, Daddy," I say.

"No." He shakes his head, pushes through the flock of nurses in red scrubs. "No. She's not… Leanne? Baby? No. No. No." He brushes at her forehead, kisses her lips in a broken, silent plea.

She doesn't kiss him back, and he crumples. Slides to the linoleum, clutching the metal bars of the bed railing. His thick shoulders quake, but he remains silent as he weeps.

His grief is awful to witness. As if something inside him has been broken. Shattered. Sliced apart by the knife of an uncaring God.

"Why did He let her die, Daddy?" I can't stop the words from escaping my lips.

They're cruel words, because I know he doesn't have the answers. I've always known the reality: his God is a charade.

He's on his knees beside her bed. The nurses quietly and respectfully watch. This is the oncology ward; they've watched this scene play out time and again.

"God…my God, why have you forsaken me? *Eli eli lama sabachthani?*" He pulls away from me, covers his face with his hands.

Really? He's spouting Aramaic now? Is he putting on this pious show for the nurses? He's really grieving, I realize that. But why does he have to act so damned holy all the time? I turn away from him. I lean over Mama and kiss her cooling cheek.

"Goodbye, Mama. I love you." I whisper the words low enough so no one can hear.

I leave the room. It's number 1176. The route to the elevators is one I could walk in my sleep now: turn right from room 1176, down the long hallway to the dead end. Turn left. Another long hallway. Right at the nurse's station, through the doors that open in opposite directions, one away from you and the other toward you. The elevators are at the end of that short hallway, a double bank of silver doors. The button lights up pale yellow, the up and down arrows blurred from a thousand thumbs pressing against them. I have no visual memory of the elevator ride down or leaving the hospital, only stumbling out into the sunlight. It's a beautiful, gorgeous fall day. No clouds, just far, endless blue sky and a bright yellow sun and cool October air.

How can it be a beautiful day when my mother just died? It should be a black, awful day. Instead, it's the kind of day I should be cruising around downtown in Devin's convertible Sebring, listening to Guster.

I find myself on my hands and knees in the grass, surrounded by parked cars. I'm sobbing. I thought I'd cried all my tears, but I haven't. Not by a long shot.

I feel Daddy's presence in the grass beside me. For the first time in my entire life, he's something like real. He sits down in the grass next to me, heedless of the moisture from the sprinklers from an hour ago. It's early morning, just past dawn. I'd been beside her bed for forty-eight hours, waiting. I hadn't moved, not once. Not to eat, not to drink, not to pee.

Mama…Mama is dead. I ignore my father and weep. Eventually, he picks me up off the grass, walks me to the car, and settles me in the back seat of his BMW where I lie down. The smell of leather fills my nose, tangy and damp from my clothes. He drives slowly, and I hear him sniffle and snort. I hear the soft *skritch* of his hand passing over his week's worth of stubble as he wipes his face, clearing away the tears, making room for the next wave of hot salt grief.

I can't breathe for the sobs, for the raw weight of grief. Mama is dead. She was the only one who understood me. She was my intercessor between me and Daddy. When he wouldn't listen, she would talk to him for me. Sometimes I wonder if Daddy even likes me. I mean, he's my father, so I know he feels the patriarchal emotion of protective love, but does he *like* me? For who I am? Does he understand me? Has he ever tried?

And now the only person who's ever understood me is gone. Gone.

"Pull over, please." I'm scrambling to a sitting position, scrabbling at the window button, at the locked door. "I'm gonna puke—"

He's over the rumble strip and on the gravel shoulder and slowing enough for me to lunge out of the still-moving car and into the tall, scratchy grass at the roadside. Vomit pours from me like a hot flood, burning my throat, convulsing my stomach. My eyes water as wave after wave gushes through me, and my nose drips. Daddy doesn't help me, doesn't hold my hair back. He just watches me from the driver's seat, the engine idling. A Michael W. Smith song plays softly from the speakers, floating to me from the open door. "The Giving." I hate that song. I've always hated that song. He knows I hate that song.

I kneel on the gravel and the grass, heaving, panting. I stare over my shoulder at him. The grief in his eyes is like knives. But it's lonely grief. He's in his own world.

So am I.

I spit bile, wipe my face on my sleeve, and kick the back door shut. I slide into the front passenger seat, click my seat belt in place, and then angrily punch the stereo off.

"Grey, I was listening to that."

"I hate that song. You *know* I hate that song."

He calmly taps the CD player back on and touches a button to skip the song. "It's my car. I'll listen to what I want." He hasn't skipped the song, it turns out. He skipped back to start it over. Even in the midst of grief, he still has to be completely in control.

The car is still stopped, so I unlatch my belt and shove the door open. "Fine. Then I'll walk."

"It's five miles, Grey. Get in."

Something explodes inside me. I turn to him and snarl; it's an animalistic, guttural, wordless growl. "Fuck you," I say.

He actually gasps. "Grey Leanne Amundsen—"

I ignore him and start walking. A car passes by with a loud *whoosh* and a belated gust of cool wind. He gets out and cajoles and pleads and commands. Then he tries to manhandle me into the car. His arm goes around my waist, and he drags me to the passenger door. I stomp on his instep, jerk free from his grip, and then—before I know I intend to do so—I punch him in the jaw. My fist clenches on its own and flashes out, connects with his cheek. He stumbles backward, more surprise than hurt. My hand aches. I don't care.

"What's God's plan now, Daddy? Why? Why did he let this happen? Tell me, Daddy! Tell me!" I'm slamming my fists on his back.

He catches my hands in his. "Stop, Grey. Stop. STOP! I don't know! I don't—I don't know. Just get in the car and we'll talk about it."

I wrench my hands free. "I don't want to talk about it. Just leave me alone." I say it calmly. Too calmly. "Just…leave me alone."

And…he does. He drives away, leaving me on the side of a highway, miles from anywhere. In that moment, I hate him. I didn't think he'd just leave me here even if I did get out of the car. Another sob slips from me, and then another, and then I'm bawling again. Miles pass under my feet slowly, so slowly. Eventually I call Devin, my closest friend, and she comes to pick me up.

She's my closest friend, other than Mom.

Who's dead. It hits me all over again.

I slip into Devin's car and slump forward against the dashboard. "She-she-she's gone, Devin. She died. Mama died."

"I'm so sorry, honey. I'm so sorry, Grey." She leaves the radio off and pulls away off the shoulder, back onto the highway heading away from the Medical Center of Central Georgia and out to where we live.

Devin lets me cry for a long time before she speaks. "Why were you walkin' on the side of the highway?" Devin has the perfect southern belle accent down pat. She cultivates it, I think. I'm always trying to sound less like a mid-Georgia hick, but the accent creeps in sometimes.

"I got in a fight with Daddy. He…he always has to be in charge. You know? Everything, all the time. I can't take it anymore. I can't. Everything has to be *his* way. Even when we were fighting, he had to control what I did and what I said and what I felt." I sniffled. "I…I think I hate him, Dev. I do. I know he's my Daddy and I should love him, but he's just…he's a jerk."

"I don't know what to tell you, Grey. From every-thing you've told me, he is kind of a jerk." She glances over her shoulder as she changes lanes, and shoots me a sympathetic smile. "You want to stay with me for a while? Momma and Daddy won't mind."

"Could I?"

"Let's grab your stuff," Devin says, trying to be cheerful.

Daddy is in his study with the door closed. That tells me a lot; Daddy never, ever closes the door to his study unless he's really upset or "deep in prayer."

I pack a bunch of clothes and my toiletries in a bag, grab my duffle bag of dance gear, my stash of allowance cash from the drawer of my desk. I look around my room, and it feels like it's for the last time. On impulse, I snatch my iPod and charger off the desk along with the charger for my phone. I go back to my closet and shove all my clothes into the suitcase, bras, panties, dresses, skirts, blouses, heels, sandals, all of it shoved into the Samsonite case until it's overflowing and I have to sit on it to get it closed. I had planned to pack more thoroughly but for some reason I just know. This is it. The end.

I take in the posters of various dancers on my walls, the Broadway playbills from the trip to New York Mom and I went on for my sweet sixteen…it all seems juvenile. The room of a child. A little girl. There's even a shelf in one corner full of American Girl dolls from my childhood, all dressed neatly and sitting in a row.

One last glance. My framed photo of Mom and me in Times Square goes in my purse. She looked so happy there, and so did I. That trip is what inspired my love of dance.

My dance bag is slung over my shoulder as I pull the suitcase down the stairs. The wheels thump from step to step until I'm on the landing. The front door is before me and the closed French doors of Daddy's study to my left. One of them swings open and Daddy fills the space, eyes red-rimmed, face haggard.

"Where are you going, Grey?" His voice is hoarse.

"Devin's." I hold up the acceptance letter for USC, the envelope with my room assignment, my new roommate's information, check-in instructions. "And then L.A. I'm leaving for college next week."

"No, you're not. We're a family. We need to stick together during this trying time." He tries to step closer to me, and I back away. "Your mother just died, Grey. You can't leave now."

I huff a disbelieving laugh. "I *know* she died. I was *there*! I watched—I watched her die. I have to go—I have to get out of here. I can't stay here. I don't belong here."

"Grey, come on. You're my daughter. I love you. Please…don't go." His eyes are wet. Watching him cry hurts but doesn't change the fact that I hate him.

"If you loved me so much, why'd you leave me on the side of the highway?" I know it's not fair, but I just don't care.

"You refused to get in the car! What was I supposed to do? You *punched* me!" He slumps to the side against the closed door, resting his head on the wood. A tear slides down his cheek. "She was my *wife*, Grey. I've been with her since I was seventeen. I lost my *wife*."

I tip my head back, trying not to cry again. "I know, Daddy. I know."

"So stay. Please stay."

"No. I…can't. I just can't." I hold the strap of my purple-patterned Vera Bradley purse in my hands and twist.

"Why not?"

I shake my head. "I just can't. You don't understand me. You don't know anything about me. I know she was your wife, and I know you're hurting just as much as me. But…without her, I don't know what to do. She made this family work. Without her…we're just two people who don't understand each other."

He seems so confused. "But…Grey…you're my daughter. Of course I understand you."

"Then why do I like to dance?"

He seems puzzled by the question. "Because you're a girl. Girls like to dance. It's just a phase."

I have to laugh out loud. "God, Daddy. You're such an idiot. Because I'm a girl? Really?" I groan in disgust and hike my dance bag back on my shoulder. "That's exactly what I mean. You don't understand the first thing about me. I'm just like Mama used to be before she married you. You know that. And that's what bothers you about me. She was this free and wild dancer, and she married you and she changed for you. I won't do that. That was her choice, and that's fine. For her. But it's not my choice. I don't want to be a pastor's wife, Daddy. I don't want to go to prayer meeting every Wednesday, two services on Sunday mornings and small groups on Mondays and women's Bible study on Thursdays. That's not my life. I don't even *like* church. I never have." I let that sink in, and then I drop the real bomb: "I don't believe in God."

Daddy's lip curls in horror. "Grey, you don't know what you're saying. You're upset. It's understandable, but you can't say these things."

I want to scream in frustration. "Daddy, yes, I'm upset, but I know exactly what I'm saying. This is stuff I've wanted to say for *years*. I just haven't because I didn't want to upset Mom. I didn't want to fight. I'm basically an adult, and I…I don't have anything else to lose."

"Grey, you're eighteen. You think you're an adult, but you're not. You've never worked a day in your life. Your clothes, your manicures, your dance classes, everything, it's all paid for by the generosity of the congregation…the church that *I* built on my own. I started with six people in the back of a restaurant in 1975. You wouldn't last a day on your own."

Wrong thing to say. "Watch me." I pick up my suitcase and extend the handle, tip it onto its wheels, grunting as the weight nearly topples me over.

Daddy moves in front of the door. "You're not leaving, Grey."

"Get out of the way, Daddy."

"No." He crosses his arms over his chest.

I set the suitcase upright and rub my forehead with the back of my wrist. "Just let me go."

"No." He seems to swell, to take strength from defying me. "You're not going to that Babylon. Los Angeles is the home of…of…prostitutes and homosexuals. You're not going there. You're not leaving."

"Daddy, be reasonable." I try the cajoling method. "Please. You've known this is what I've wanted since before Mama got sick."

"You're not leaving. That's final."

I do scream then, an enraged howl. "God, you're so mother*fucking* stubborn!" I want to shock him with my vulgarity; I don't like swearing, but I want to make him angry. "Just move out of the way!"

I shove at him, and he moves. I'm a tall girl, strong from dance. He stumbles to the side and I throw open the door so hard it smashes into the wall, cracking the plaster and knocking off-true a framed picture of Mama and Daddy when they were young, before me.

He grabs the frame of the open front door, sagging against it. "Grey…please. Don't leave me."

I want to love him. I want him to be the daddy I need, the kind that hugs me and holds me close. The kind that comforts me. My mother, his wife, is dead. We've both lost her. But instead of bringing us together, it's fracturing us.

Devin stands there horrified, just outside the door. She grabs my suitcase and hurries to the car, pops the trunk, and heaves in the heavy black case. I follow after her, stopping as I stand in the open door of the car, about to duck in. I stare back at my father over the blue fabric of the ragtop convertible roof. He stands in the doorway, looking lost. I almost go back. Almost.

"Goodbye, Daddy." It's the last attempt.

He rallies, takes a step toward me, resolve hardening in his eyes. "Grey, please. Don't break us apart like this. Don't do this to us."

"How can you turn this back on me? I'm not going away forever. I'm just going to college, Daddy. I…I'm just doing what's right for me. Please try to understand."

"If you leave this house, you've made your choice. If you leave, you'll be willfully choosing sin."

"It's not sin! It's my life. Why can't you be reasonable?"

He clenches his fists, straightens his back. "I am being reasonable. Come back in and we'll discuss your options."

"I have to go, Daddy. I have to." I go back, stand in front of him. "I love you. I know…I know we've had our differences, but…I love you."

"Are you staying, then?" He takes my hand, the iron in his gaze softening every so slightly.

I pull my hand away. "No. I have to go."

"Then you've made your choice. "Goodbye, Grey." He turns away from me and closes the door without a backward glance.

And just like that, I'm alone in the world.

CHAPTER FOUR

I GO TO THE FUNERAL. Of course I do. Devin takes me. She holds my hand, wraps her tiny arm around my waist, and holds me up when they lower the coffin into the ground. During the viewing I sit with Devin, far away from my father. He doesn't look at me. Not once. He acted so strong during the viewing and the service, like he was a pillar of Godly faith and perfection. I hate him.

I cry again. I thought I'd shed all my tears, but more slip free. I pull my Flip from my purse and film the first shovelful of dirt hitting the oak-wood top of Mama's coffin. People gasp at my temerity, my sheer gall. I don't care. It's the last scene of her film, the final recording of Leanne Beth Amundsen's life.

When it's all over, I cling to Devin's arm and try to breathe as we pick our way carefully through the grass and between the headstones. My heels stick in the ground, wet from a recent rain.

"Grey, wait!" I hear my father's voice.

I stop and turn. I nod at Dev so she continues to her car. I wait for Daddy to run up to me. He's fighting tears as he puffs to a stop in front of me.

He wipes his face with his palm. "I hate the way things are. You're all I have left."

His parents both died when I was nine, and Mama's parents died before I was born. He's all I have, too. "I hate the way things are, too, Daddy."

"Then you'll stay?" He sounds so hopeful.

I laugh/sob. "No, I'm not staying. I could stay if you could accept me for who I am. Support my decisions, even if you don't agree with them."

"You're really going to move to Los Angeles, whether I want you to or not?"

"Yes, Daddy. I'm going to L.A., no matter what. You're my father, and I want to love you. I want to have a relationship with you. But if you can't understand that I'm going to live my life *my* way, why bother trying? You've never understood me and never wanted to try. You've never approved of anything I do, anything I like. You don't understand why I dance. You don't understand why I want to make movies. And the worst thing is, you're not even going to try to understand." I shift my purse higher on my shoulder and meet his eyes, pleading with him one last time.

He just stares at me. "Grey, can't we compromise a little?"

"Compromise how? You mean I give up film school to make you happy?"

He rolls his shoulders in a half-shrug. "Well…not give up what you want, just meet me in the middle."

"There *is* no middle in this, Daddy. I'm going, one way or another. Whether or not we have a relationship when I leave is up to you. Our relationship is on you."

His eyes harden, and he stuffs his hands in his pocket. "Fine, then. Be a prodigal."

I laugh. "God, you're so dramatic. I'm not a prodigal, I'm doing what's right for me. You just can't accept that." I straighten my back and harden my heart. "Goodbye, Daddy."

"'Bye, Grey."

Neither of us says "I love you." There are no hugs. I wait for him to change his mind. He doesn't. I turn away then, walk over to Devin's car and slide into the passenger seat.

Devin asks, "Are you—"

"I'm fine." I clench my jaw to keep from crying again.

"Well, that's some bullshit, but whatever helps you through it." Devin glances at me, eyes concerned.

"He doesn't…he just won't let it go. He doesn't have any give to him." I rub my eyes with the heels of my palms, trying to push away the burning. "He won't accept what I want to do, and I ain't—I'm not gonna let him run my life anymore."

The tears come then. I can't help it. Just a few trickling down, and I don't bother wiping them away. I don't care if my makeup is running.

"So now what?" Devin asks.

I shrug. "Now? I move to L.A."

"Alone?"

I nod. "I guess so."

The rest of the drive to Devin's house is quiet. She doesn't know what to say, and neither do I.

Devin walks me to the security gate at the airport. Everything I own fits in a suitcase and a duffel bag, which have been checked in. I've only flown once before, two years ago for my sweet sixteen New York trip with Mama. She had helped me through the process. I hug Devin, tell her goodbye. I'm alone now.

I turn and wave one last time to Devin, and then focus on the security checkpoint. An older man with thick glasses sits at a desk, his uniform shirt bright blue. In my hand I have the boarding pass Devin's dad printed out for me.

"Driver's license?" he says without looking at me.

I dig through my purse, find my license, and show it to him. He glances at me, at the ID, scribbles something onto my boarding pass, and then waves me through. Around me, people seem to know what they're doing. I don't. I watch the woman ahead of me step out of her heels, pull a thick black laptop from her carry-on bag and place that in a white container. In a separate one goes her purse, license, boarding pass, and shoes. I follow her lead, stepping out of my dance flats and putting them in a container with my other belongings. I wait my turn to step into a thing that looks like something from Star Trek, a spinning wall in a circular glass enclosure. I'm told to lift my arms over my head, and the machine spins around me.

What if they want to search me? I don't have anything to hide, but I'm anxious anyway. They pass me through without a second glance, and I retrieve my things. The whole process seems…embarrassing, strangely intimate. Businessmen in suits traipsing around in dress socks, women in bare feet, juggling their belongings and trying to keep out each other's way, and all the while the blue-shirted TSA men and women watch apathetically, shouting instructions and looking stern.

I find my gate after passing bookstores, duty-free shops, restaurants, and groups of travelers with backpacks and headphones, rolling carry-on bags with extended handles. Everyone is with someone else. I see one other solo traveler at my gate, a man in his thirties with a carefully trimmed goatee and an expensive-looking briefcase. He has three cellphones on his belt and a suit coat draped over his arm, and is reading a precisely folded *New York Times*. He glances at me, looks me over, and dismisses me. No one else even seems to see me.

I've never in my whole life felt so alone. I have my iPod and a paperback copy of *Breath, Eyes, Memory* that Devin gave me. I'm not sure why she thought I needed this book, but it's something to pass the time. For the hour that I wait, I set aside my own life and lose myself in the struggles of other people.

The flight is long and boring. I finish the book halfway through and then I'm stuck with nothing to do but listen to my iPod on "repeat." I leaf through a Skymall catalogue. The landing is rough and jouncing, and the airport in L.A. huge and confusing. It still feels like this could be a dream, like I can wake up in my bed at home, and Mama will be there, alive, and she'll make me lunch. Eventually, I find the luggage claim and wait for my bags. There's a new rip in the side of my duffel bag.

I follow the signs to the exit, and when the glass doors slide open, I'm assaulted by a wave of dry heat. Suddenly, it all seems more real. I have four hundred dollars in my purse; half of that is mine, saved from my allowance. The rest is a gift from Devin's parents. It's all I have. Four hundred dollars. A cab ride from LAX to USC costs $40, and I'm left with $360 dollars to my name. I haven't eaten since I left Devin's house, so my stomach rumbles. I'm too nervous and scared to eat. The cab driver is a huge, burly, silent black man with thin dreadlocks hanging to his shoulders. He doesn't say a word. When we arrive at USC, he simply points at the fare meter and waits expectantly. I pay, parting with the money reluctantly.

USC is huge. I follow other young-looking people around my age, some equally as scared. Most of them have their moms or dads with them, some both. No one notices me. I follow the crowd to an office swarming with people. There's an orientation, a tour of the campus. Maps are handed out along with cheap day-planners. My dorm room is a box with bunk beds on one side; a thin, shallow closet; and a tiny computer desk, which I assume belongs to my roommate. It's off-white, and there's a thin window in one corner with dirty white blinds tilted to one side, letting in a dull glow from outside.

My roommate is already there, sitting on the bottom bed, flipping through an issue of *Vanity Fair.* She's a few inches shorter than me, several sizes smaller, and model-gorgeous. Her makeup is perfect. Her platinum blonde hair is sleek and polished and perfectly coiffed in a French twist. Her clothes are expensive, and perfect. Her nails are French manicured, and a Dooney & Burke purse sits on the bed near her, an iPhone peeking out of the top. She smiles at me, takes in my outfit, off-brand but not cheap clothes—a knee-length skirt, a fitted but modest V-neck T-shirt, much-worn dance flats—and her smile dims a bit. She's clearly unimpressed.

"So, are you an actress?" she asks. She sounds like a movie version of someone from "The Valley."

"No. I'm going into production."

"Oh, like, those *behind*-the-camera people?" She oozes disdain as she says this.

"Yeah, I guess."

"You're from the South," she points out.

"Yes. I'm from Macon."

"Is that, like, in Alabama?"

I stare at her, and I wonder if she's joking. "No, it's in Georgia."

"Oh. I'm Lizzie Davis." She doesn't offer to shake my hand.

"Grey Amundsen."

"Grey. Like the color?"

"Yeah, well…except it's spelled with an 'e.' G-R-E-Y."

"Oh. Like *Fifty Shades.*"

I shrug, not wanting to admit I don't know what she's talking about. She smirks self-righteously and goes back to reading her magazine. Her phone chimes, and she sets the magazine aside, crossing her legs and tapping at the phone. This goes on the entire time that I'm unpacking. I have no posters, no decorations at all except the photograph of Mama and me in New York. I don't have a laptop, or a phone. I see a laptop on Lizzie's desk, a big silver MacBook.

When I'm unpacked, I'm at loose ends. Lizzie is still texting or whatever she's doing. It's four o'clock in the afternoon on Wednesday, and classes don't start until Friday, and then we have the weekend off before the semester really gets under way. I climb the ladder then lie on my side and stare at the wall, missing my Mama. She'd tell me to stop moping and find something to do. Explore the city, dance. Make a film.

Instead, I lie on the top bunk and wonder if I've made a mistake coming here.

CHAPTER FIVE

THE RUMBLING OF MY STOMACH becomes a constant over the next year. The stipend my scholarship gives me to live on is tiny, barely enough for the meals at the cafeteria, which are generally awful and far between. My classes take up most of my day from morning to evening, and I often only have time for a bagel in the morning and something quick and nasty in the evenings. I make good grades, a 4.0 for the first semester, 3.9 for the second. I study film, and I dance. My haven, my sanctuary away from everything, is a quiet room on the top floor of one of my lecture halls. I've never seen anyone else there, since the floor is primarily faculty offices. The room is large enough for my purposes, and empty except for a lone filing cabinet in one corner, so I can dance freely. There's a window to let in daylight, and an outlet near the floor where I can plug in my portable iPod speaker dock.

I retreat there between classes, keeping the music turned low and the door locked. I find a song that hits me in the place within where movement lives, and I let go. I just move, just let my body flow. There's no choreography, no rules, no expectations, no hunger or grades or homework or loneliness. Just the extension, the leap and the roll and the pirouette and the power of my legs, the tension in my core. I can be totally me there.

My first year goes fine. I've gotten a lot of the prerequisite courses out of the way, the English and the chemistry and the two semesters of a foreign language. My second year begins with my first mid-level courses and a few introductory film production classes. The absence of funds means I rarely leave the campus. I spend my days in lecture, taking notes, or in my dorm room doing homework. Lizzie is gone most of the time, often coming back at all hours, reeking of alcohol. She invited me to a party once, but I declined. I'm not interested.

My father never contacts me.

My twentieth birthday passes unnoticed. I spend it writing an essay on an old silent film, *Metropolis*, on the use of camera angles and shot length. I'm not making any friends. I don't know how to make the effort.

The only thing keeping me sane through this whole process is school. To most people, college is work. It's something they have to go through to get on with their lives; for me, this *is* my life. For me, it's not just about sitting through lectures and writing essays, it's about learning a craft, a trade. I'm soaking up everything I can about film, about the process of taking an idea from some notes scrawled on a legal pad to a film on a big screen. I watch films in every spare moment, and I dissect them. I have my Flip camera everywhere I go, making short films about anything and everything. Most of those pieces are vignettes, just momentary slices of life set to music. They're as much expression to me as dancing.

I'm halfway through my sophomore year when I get summoned to the financial aid office. It comes by way of a letter written in vague language saying there's an issue with my status. Or something. I barely read it. I find my way to the office with its gray tile floor and gray pillars and red leather ottomans and partial cubicle offices. After a thirty-minute wait, I'm summoned by a woman in her mid-thirties with mocha skin and short, kinky black hair.

"Hi, Grey. I'm Anya Miller."

"Hi, Mrs. Miller. I got a notice from this office about my financial aid."

"Call me Anya, please." She takes my student ID card and brings up my file, reading it with an increasingly blank expression, the kind of look that says she has news I won't like. "Well, Grey. Your scholarships have been covering nearly all of your tuition and your book costs, as well as room and board. Unfortunately, you've used up most of the scholarship funds. You have enough to finish out this year, fully covered. Or you can stretch it out and it'll cover some of your tuition, but not all. You're listed as an independent, which means you're capable of supporting yourself. If you were listed as a dependent on your parents and their income was low enough, you would qualify for financial aid. But since you're an independent, you can work to support yourself."

"How can it just run out? I thought it was a loan? Like, it would just keep piling on? I mean…what am I supposed to do?"

Anya just gives me a sympathetic look that says she doesn't have much in the way of answers. "It was a grant, and it was a finite amount of money. This should have been explained to you. You might qualify for a work-study program, but the job fair was held a week ago, and the positions are all filled, I'm afraid. As far as staying on campus? Most students in your position end up finding a job of some sort to pay their way." She says this as if that much should be obvious.

I suppose this was explained to me, or to Mama, but I was so absorbed by Mama's fight with cancer that I didn't pay much attention. And I suppose it should have been obvious, but I've never had a job before. I have no clue how to go about finding one. I absently thank Anya Miller and leave the office of financial aid in a daze. I spend the rest of my time between classes that week asking around campus about work, but there are no openings. Even the laundry facilities are fully staffed. I receive an official letter from the university delineating how much scholarship money I have left, laying out the exact tuition, and how much I'll have to pay every semester if I use my scholarship to pay half. It's an extraordinary amount of money. I have thirty dollars to my name.

I start filling out application after application for nearby restaurants and bars, shops and stores and boutiques, No one is hiring. A week passes, and then two. I get a map of the L.A. bus routes and start filling out applications farther and farther afield from the university.

Maybe I'm not asking the right questions, or maybe all the jobs really are filled, but I have zero luck. I think have a lead on a job at a bar, but then the manager conducting the interview finds out I have no experience and that fizzles out. The end of the semester closes in. If I don't come up with a job soon, I'll have nowhere to live, and my reason for being in L.A.—my film degree—won't happen.

I ride the bus line farther and farther away, asking anywhere and everywhere if they're hiring. No one is.

And then I see a "NOW HIRING!" sign.

My stomach sinks when I see the name of the establishment: Exotic Nights Gentlemen's Club. The hiring notice says, *"Now hiring exotic dancers. Inquire within for details."*

I may be a naïve pastor's-daughter and a hick from Macon, Georgia, but I know what a gentleman's club is, what exotic dancing means.

I keep riding the bus. I stop in at a drive-through taco joint and ask about jobs, no luck. I even find a dance studio, do an audition and ask about working there but the owner just laughs.

Weeks pass. The end of the semester is drawing near. hiring notice haunts me. I dream about it. It's work. It's income. It's the ability to stay on campus. But…it's a gentleman's club. A strip bar.

It means taking my clothes off in return for money. I get sick to my stomach just thinking about it. I've never even worn a bikini before. No one has seen my naked body since I started bathing myself at the age of nine. I can't. I just can't.

Can I?

I can't ask Daddy for money. I can't go back to Georgia.

I don't sleep, can't eat. I miss a class, and I fail a test. I receive an official notice that my dorm funding is gone. A week after that, I get the letter reiterating how much I'll have to pay in tuition for the next semester, assuming a full-time class load of at least twelve credit hours. Books are extra.

I cry myself to sleep at night.

I put quarters into a battered, graffiti-covered payphone and dial Daddy's number, listen to it ring once, twice. I hang up before it rings a third time.

Then, a break. I land a job as a hostess of an Italian restaurant. It's a job, it's work. I stay long enough to pull two full paychecks, and that's enough to make me realize hostessing won't even come close to paying tuition. I beg them to give me more hours, let me wait tables, anything, but the manager stonewalls me, pointing at my lack of experience. In a few months I might be able to start taking some tables, but not yet.

It's not enough. I don't have months; I need income *now*. I keep hostessing, and keep looking for something better paying.

Again and again the gentleman's club crops up in my thoughts. I know enough to know I'd make good money.

Finally, the semester is over and I have two weeks to come up with tuition, room, and board. It's a staggering amount of money. Thousands and thousands of dollars.

Decision time.

I shoulder my purse, shove the nausea down, and get on the bus. It's one of the new red and futuristic-looking ones. I have my earbuds in, and I'm listening to Macklemore, "Ten Thousand Hours," a song I came across online by accident. I bob my head to the beat and focus on the words, the smooth, passionate flow of his rhythm and the beauty of the lyrics. I try not to think about what I'm about to do.

I'm nearly successful in pretending I'm just applying for any other job. But then the bus rumbles to a stop and I get off, stepping into the blistering heat. My wedge-heel Mary Jane shoes *clack* on the cracked sidewalk, and I follow the broken squares the three blocks to the door of the club. It's a low red-brick building with a faded white awning. The name is written across the blacked-out windows in yellow neon tubes: *Exotic Nights Gentlemen's Club*, and next to that is the hiring notice. There's no phone number listed, no address, no notice of hours of operation. Just a single door, through which is visible a short hallway/foyer. It's broad daylight, and the tiny parking lot off to the left is empty except for a single car, a white early-nineties Trans Am, the T-top open. My hands tremble as I clutch the sun-heated metal of the door handle. I taste bile, but I force it down.

There's no chime when the door opens. The hallway, which is barely ten steps long, ends at another door, this one a basic black wooden slab with a round brass knob, which squeaks as I turn it. I can barely breathe as I take my first step into the club, into the first and only bar establishment I've ever been in. The lights are all on, illuminating fifty or so small, round black tables clustered around a semi-circular stage. A silver metal pole extends from the stage to the ceiling, and a bank of lights, currently turned off, point stage center. A bar runs the length of the club on one side, and there are booths along the other wall, cracked red leather and tacky-looking Formica with battered metal napkin dispensers and salt and pepper shakers.

A man sits at the bar, in front of him a short glass full of amber liquid and ice despite the fact that it's barely three o'clock. He's short, even sitting down, and he has black hair slicked back, movie mobster style. He's wearing a shockingly bright Hawaiian-pattern button-down shirt and tight black slacks.

He hears me come in and turns toward me, throwing out a perfunctory, "We're closed—" But then he sees me and cuts himself off, stands up.

My eyes are drawn to the pointy-toed snakeskin shoes, and then the bulging belly visible beneath the shirt, and then the gold rings on six of his ten fingers. He has a scruffy, scraggly goatee, a round face, and quick brown eyes.

"Well, hey there, darling. What can I do for you?" His voice is high-pitched but smooth and suggestive.

His gaze travels blatantly from my face down to my breasts, lingering there for a long time, and then moving down to my hips and back up. I'm dressed as I normally am, in a pair of fitted but not skintight jeans and a button-down green sleeveless blouse.

My voice won't work. I can't make the words come out. I take a deep breath and force them. "I saw the sign…and I—I need a job." The southern twang in my voice has never been more pronounced.

The man comes forward and shakes my hand. His palm is clammy, his fingers thick and his grip weak. "I'm Timothy van Dutton. I'm the manager. Why don't you come sit down here?" He pats the back of the high swivel chair next to his. "Can I get you something to drink?"

"Just some ice water, please." I try to smooth the twang out, but it doesn't work. I'm too nervous.

He scurries around the bar, scoops some ice into a glass and squirts water into it from a soda gun, then slides it across the bar to me before coming back around and taking his chair once more. "So. What's your name?"

"Grey. Grey Amundsen."

"Grey. That's a pretty name."

"Thanks."

"So, Grey Amundsen. You're here for the job opening?"

I nod. "Yeah. I…I'm at USC, and I…I need a job."

He rubs the mustache on his upper lip and then his chin, perusing my body yet again. "Have you ever danced before?"

"Danced? I thought—I thought this was a…you know. A strip club." I whisper the last two words, barely able to get them out.

Timothy laughs. "Most of my girls prefer the term 'exotic dancer.' So, I can probably safely assume you've never danced before."

I really need this job, so I'd better put some effort into getting it. I have to make him think I can do it, even though I'm not at all sure I can.

"I'm a dancer. I've been trained in ballet, jazz, and contemporary. So…I'm a dancer. Just…I've never danced like—like that before." I gesture at the stage, the pole.

"I see. So why would you want to do this, then? It's not for everyone. It takes…a certain kind of skill. You can't just get up there and take your clothes off. It doesn't work like that. You have to make them want you." Tim's eyes haven't really left my breasts the entire time he's talking to me.

I ignore it.

"I know how to perform. I've done several recitals before. So…I know how to perform."

He laughs. "This is a whole different type of performance, sweetheart. Now, don't take this the wrong way, but you look like you're about to piss yourself. So why don't you be honest with me?"

"I really need this job." I stare at the sticky bar top, refusing to meet Timothy van Dutton's eyes.

"This may not have been my first choice of job, but…I'll learn."

Timothy doesn't answer right away. He lifts the glass to his lips and takes a sip, hissing slightly after he swallows whatever is in the glass. His gaze sweeps up and down me again.

"Stand up."

I obey, and he twirls his finger in a circle. It's the same gesture Mrs. LeRoux used to have us do a pirouette, so I do one.

"That was pretty-looking, but do it more slowly."

I turn slowly, arching my back, pushing out my chest. I feel his eyes on me, and my flesh crawls.

"Unbutton a couple buttons for me."

I come to a stop facing him and stare. "What?" It comes out as a horrified whisper.

"Your shirt. Unbutton a few of the buttons. I need to see a bit of skin." I hesitate, and he leans forward, his eyes narrowing. "Listen, sweetheart. You're applying for a job as an exotic dancer. This means you have to take your clothes off. We serve alcohol here, so this is a semi-nude club, which means you won't be completely naked, but you have to be comfortable in your own skin. Okay? So either unbutton your shirt or get out."

He's right so I swallow hard, even if I'd rather kick him hard between his legs. I close my eyes briefly and then lift my right hand to my shirt, pinch the clear

plastic button, hesitate again, and then push the button through the hole. I feel layers of innocence being
ripped away as each button slips through the hole in
the fabric of my shirt. I do it again, and then a third
time.

This isn't how I imagined it would feel disrobing
for a man for the first time. I'm sick, and scared, and
disgusted.

My cleavage is spilling out over the top of the
shirt now, and hints of my black bra show. I'm breathing hard, and each breath makes my breasts swell.
Timothy's eyes are glued to my chest. He lifts an eyebrow and flicks a finger at me, which I take to mean
one more button. I do it and feel tears prick my eyes.
I blink them away and keep my gaze down. A tear
drips off the end of my nose and hits my big toe,
quickly joined by a third. I blink hard and breathe
deep and focus on keeping the wave of sobs blocked
in my throat. His face twists in clear lust. I steal a
glance at him from under my eyelashes, and I see
him shove his hand in his pocket. He adjusts himself,
and my gorge rises. I may be a virgin, but I know the
basics. I know why he had to adjust himself.

I swallow it back, bitter and acidic and burning.

"Nice. Very nice. You've got a great body, and the
air of innocence you've got going on will have the
guys going crazy," Timothy finally says.

He's talking *to* me *about* me. It's weird and dis-
concerting. I desperately want to button up my shirt,

but I don't. Timothy is right in that I'll have to learn to be comfortable being stared at. And this is the least of what I'll have to do if I get this job. I have no idea what it pays, but I have the idea that strippers get paid a lot. All I know is that I desperately need a job, and if I'm going to get naked in front of men all night, it had better be worth it.

"Plus," Tim continues, "you've got that sexy southern accent. You'll draw a hell of a crowd."

"So do I get the job?" There's no elation, no excitement. Only disgust mixed with horror and relief.

"You've got the job."

"How…how much does it pay?"

Timothy shrugs. "It depends. I've got a feeling you'll have a huge desirability factor, which works in your favor. If you do private rooms, you'll make a killing. Here's the way it works, basically. The club itself don't pay you directly. You get paid in tips, and you give the club a percentage out of that. Not much, just fifteen percent, which is industry average. You do two or three song sets on stage. Most girls make anywhere between fifty and a hundred per set. If the guys like you, you could do three, four, or five sets in a night. In between sets onstage you'll work tables, which are ten bucks each table, and guys will tip you on top of that. Then there are VIP rooms in the back, four of them. Most girls will get, like, two or three hundred

per VIP room visit. You'd work three nights minimum, but we're open seven days a week. Obviously,
weekends are biggest money." He lifts an eyebrow.
"Since you've never done this before, I'll tell you this.
Most girls supplement what they make here in the
club by doing private parties, birthdays and bachelor
parties, shit like that. They don't have to tip us out, so
they keep it all."

"What—" My voice breaks, and I have to try
again. "What do you mean by doing private parties?"

Timothy laughs. "It just means you do what you
do here, but for a private party. Look, you set the
rules for private parties. Minimum, you do lap dances
and stuff, maybe a striptease for the group." He winks
at me. "I know what you're thinking, and it's not like
that. Unless you want to, of course. But that's up to
you. That's got nothing to do with the club. Guys'll
ask you if you do private parties, and you need to
decide if you do or not."

I have to take a few deep breaths. "Okay. Okay. I
can do this."

Timothy laughs again, a low, amused chuckle.
"You convincing me or yourself?"

"Both, I guess," I admit.

"Why don't you come in tomorrow evening,
maybe seven or eight, and we'll work up a dance
for you. My best dancer, Candy, will be here, and
she'll help you. Give you some pointers and shit." He

stands up, tosses back the whiskey or whatever it is, and then extends his hand toward me, and we shake. "Welcome to Exotic Nights, Grey. Oh, and you may want a stage name."

He walks me out, and in the act of reaching past me to open the door, his hand grazes my bottom. It's not accidental, because I feel his hand squeeze along the way. I scoot forward out of his reach and turn back to glare at him. He just waves at me.

I officially have a job. The relief is tempered by my nauseating horror at what the job is. I haven't done anything yet, which means it's not too late to back out. I can just not show up and hope something else comes up.

I button my shirt back up as soon as I'm out of the club and make my way back to the bus stop. Once I hit campus, I'm more aware than ever of guys checking me out as I head back to the dorm. I'm not a girl who won't admit she's pretty. I'm used to getting looks and glances wherever I go; I just tune them out. But now…after enduring Timothy's lusty perusal and crotch adjusting, I don't want men's eyes on me yet every pair I pass seems to be looking at me. My jeans feel tighter than they did when I put them on this morning, and suddenly my blouse is more revealing than I'd imagined. I wish I had a pair of sweatpants and a hoodie on now.

I make it to my dorm room and into my bed on the top bunk before I let myself cry. The tears come in a hot flood along with embarrassment, guilt, horror, nausea, and doubt. Daddy was right. He said I'd fall into a sinful life, and I have. I just got a job as a stripper. I'm not going to glorify it by calling it "exotic dancer."

I don't even want to know what Mama would say.

I'm going to do it, though. I won't go crawling back to Macon, Georgia. I just won't. I'm going to finish my degree.

I've been working my ass off to get an internship with Fourth Dimension Films, so I edited the piece on my mom and showed it to Mrs. Adams, my film program advisor. She saw real potential in my work, and Fourth Dimension is one of the biggest private production studios in L.A. Getting an internship there would be a *huge* foot in the door. But for that, I can't be homeless. I have to stay in school and have somewhere to live. I need a professional wardrobe.

In short, I need a job, and this is the only opportunity I've found in months of looking.

Still, I cry myself to sleep. Lizzie doesn't come back until after three, and she's got a guy with her. They roll into her bunk, and I hear noises that keep me awake for hours—moans, grunts and giggles.

CHAPTER SIX

I SQUEEZE MY EYES SHUT AND PRAY, but then feel guilty about it; God wouldn't approve of what I'm about to do, that's for darn sure. I clench my hands into fists to stop them from trembling, but they shake like leaves in a Georgia thunderstorm.

"Gracie, you're on in five." Timothy pokes his head into the door of the dressing room, and I certainly don't miss the way his beady little eyes rake over me.

My flesh crawls and I want to tell him off, but I can't. After all, I'm about to get a whole heck of a lot more perused in about five minutes. I'm barely clothed, at least as far as I'm used to. I grew up wearing ankle-length dresses and skirts with loose T-shirts. Nothing low-cut, nothing above the knee. Nothing revealing or immodest. Nothing sexy or sensual. Nothing ungodly or irreverent.

Right now, I've got on a pair of cut-off jean shorts, the hems frayed into white threads. Back in Macon, they would've called these shorts Daisy Dukes, since they're cut so short the bottom of my backside is hanging out. I mean that quite literally. My butt is actually hanging out the bottom of the shorts. They're tight, too, squeezing my thick dancer's thighs like spandex. I'm wearing a flannel shirt, but it ain't—I mean, it *isn't*—much better as far as modesty goes. It's unbuttoned down to my cleavage, which isn't contained by anything at all. There's only four buttons done up, and my boobs strain those four buttons fit to burst. That's the point, after all. The buttons are supposed to pop. There's a whole row of shirts similar to this one in the corner of the dressing room, since part of the act is to pop the buttons as I rip the shirt open.

It's supposed to be sexy, Timothy says. "It'll drive 'em wild." He's the expert, I guess. The rest of the flannel shirt is tied up in the front just beneath my boobs, so most of my midriff is bare. The last bit of the outfit—the costume—is a thick leather belt with a big sparkly buckle, and a pair of knee-high boots. Hooker boots, I've heard them called. Seems appropriate, I guess, since Daddy would call what I'm about to do whoring myself out. They're suede boots, the material loose and bunching, with a spindly three-inch stiletto heel that makes me stand a full six feet tall, since I'm five-nine in my stocking feet.

My blonde hair is brushed to a shine so glossy Candy asked me if I was wearing a wig. My face is caked with a garish amount of makeup. Whore paint, Granddaddy would call it. I never wore more than a bit of lip gloss and some eye shadow growing up, so all the foundation and the lipstick and the mascara and all that feels like a mask. Which helps, in a way, as if the mask of makeup could hide me.

I take a deep breath and force myself out of the chair, swaying on the unfamiliar heels. Timothy shoves the door open and holds it for me, but it isn't for the sake of being a gentleman. He stands in the door so that I have to squeeze past him on my way out. I stifle the urge to deck him when he "accidentally" palms my backside.

"Don't do that, Tim," I say, proud of how steady and calm my voice is. It's not the first time I've asked him not to touch me.

"Do what?"

I fix him with the glare I learned from Daddy, the one that makes most men quake in their boots. Or, in Tim's case, pointy-toed snakeskin loafers. "Just 'cause I'm doing this doesn't mean you can go touching me whenever you want, Timothy van Dutton. Keep your slimy little paws off of me." I hate the twang, but

I'm nervous and upset, and it's part of my "Gracie" persona.

Tim leers at me. "Listen to you, Gracie. You sound like a southern belle. I love it. Keep that attitude, it's good stuff. Now get out there and do what I'm paying you to do."

"You don't pay me, the customers do," I retort.

His eyes harden and his voice goes low. "Don't you ever talk to me that way again or I'll fire you." He smacks me on the backside so hard my eyes water, but I don't give him the satisfaction of a response. It may be sexual harassment, but I need the job too much to argue.

He strolls past me, leaving me to gather my wits and my courage about me. When he's out of sight, I rub my bottom where he smacked it, realizing with dismay that he can very well fire me if he wants. Then I'd be up a creek without a paddle.

I wend my way through the backstage area, ascend the three small steps to the stage, and stand behind the curtain. My heart is pounding like a jackhammer, my throat closed so tight I can barely breathe, and I'm on the verge of tears. I don't want to do this.

My "training session" with Candy was awkward and horrible. Swinging around on the pole is a lot harder than it looks. I fell several times before I got the hang of wrapping my knee around the cold metal and spinning around it. There was no one watching but Candy, but I still cried when I took off my shirt for the first time. Candy saw my tears, but didn't say anything. She just critiqued the way I strutted from the pole to the end of the stage.

I don't have a choice, though. Not if I want to finish my degree and get my dream job as a film producer. I got the internship, and I start next week, but I need appropriate clothes.

The generic pop music fades from the house speakers, and the buzz of conversation quiets. Surely the crowd of men on the other side of the curtain can hear my heart, since it's beating so loud.

"Gentlemen, are you ready?" Tim's voice echoes over the PA system, reedy and breathy and dripping suggestion. "I have a very, *very* special treat for you tonight. A brand-new act. She's fresh from Macon, Georgia, a real corn-fed southern girl, and boys… she…is…*hot*."

Catcalls and whistles rise to a deafening din, until Tim quiets them.

"Allow me to introduce…Gracie!"

At least Tim had me use a stage name. The girl standing with her back to a stripper pole, hip popped to one side, hands draped around the cold metal high above her head…that girl is Gracie, a performer. A stripper.

She isn't me.

My name is Grey Amundsen. But Grey, she doesn't exist in here, in this slimy, smoky, sex-hazed hole. In here, I'm Gracie.

The curtain sweeps open, blinding me with the glare of stage lights, white and red and purple, and so hot I break into an immediate sweat. I don't move at first. I let them look. That's why they're here, after all. To look at me. To stare at me…to want me.

I've been assured they can't touch me, but that's little consolation.

I've never been wanted, not by anyone. Daddy always wished I was a son, so I could play football and go to seminary like Daddy did. If I was a son, I could have taken over the pulpit of Macon Contemporary Baptist Church. But I was born a girl, and an only child, so I couldn't do any of that. I was told to be seen and not heard, to sit properly and be demure. Be a lady, be proper. Sit up straight, mind your manners, and obey your elders. No rock music, no makeup, no boys. That last one was the one he focused on most strictly.

I've never even been on a date, never been kissed (except Craig, and he don't—*doesn't*—count).

But, for some reason, Timothy van Dutton thought I had some kind of "innate sensuality" that men would go nuts over, and he hired me. Maybe he just smelled the desperation on me.

The men in the audience get over their shock and begin to whistle and cheer and howl.

"Take it off!" a man at a table near the stage yells.

I circle the pole, holding on to it with one hand, taking long, prancing steps, Broadway-dancer steps, runway model steps. It shows them my legs, lets them see I have style. I'm not just going to peel off my clothes and swing around the pole. No, if I'm going to do this, I'm going to do it with some kind of style.

Candy helped me choreograph my routine. Candy is a svelte, black-haired girl a few years older than me, but with a street hardness I'll never have. She's not exactly beautiful, not up close, but with enough makeup and the body she has, you'd think she was. Plus, she can do tricks on the pole that make the guys crazy. I've seen it. I don't dare try the things she does, complicated spins and upside-down twirls. Candy was brusque and business-like as she showed me how to move, how to sway and shimmy, how to spin around the pole and slide down it. She and Tim watched me practice the routine before the doors opened tonight. I saw the evidence of my success with his bulging zipper.

I leap into the air and swing my body around the pole, hooking my right knee around it, tilting my head back so my thick blonde hair hangs behind me. My heart hammers like a drum as I spin around the pole several times, and then land on one foot, the other still wrapped around the pole. I feel myself jiggling and bouncing in the skimpy outfit. I'm fighting tears of guilt, shame and embarrassment, but I have to not only keep them at bay, but plaster on a fake smile. I get closer and closer to vomiting with every move.

I've choreographed this dance to keep me clothed as long as possible, but the moment comes all too soon. I've swung and hung backward and upside down, I've slid my spine down the pole so I was crouched with my knees spread wide, giving them a tantalizing glimpse of my crotch.

Now…

Now I have to start actually stripping. I swallow hard, disguising my nerves with an unchoreographed swing around the pole, and then land to stand as I was when the curtain opened: my back to the pole, legs shoulder-width apart, hands over my head. Then, with shaking fingers, I slip the top button through the hole, stride forward to the middle of the stage, untie the knot at the bottom. Now the shirt is loose, and the inside of my cleavage is exposed. Then, just to tease them, I button the bottom buttons. The men groan and lean forward, and I can see hunger and lust in the leering of their eyes.

Then, as the club music rises to a crescendo, I grasp the lapels of the shirt and rip it open, scattering buttons with a dramatic flourish. My breasts bounce free, and I stand topless in front of a hundred and fifty men.

A single tear drips free to mingle with the sweat on my upper lip.

I'm officially a stripper.

CHAPTER SEVEN

I'M DRESSED IN A SLIM NAVY pencil skirt, a basic ivory button-down shirt, and a pair of heels to match the shirt. My hair is tied up in a bun, and I've got minimal makeup on. I've never worn a lot of makeup, but I wear even less now since I started dancing at the club.

Dance.

Yeah, I've started thinking of it that way. I've been there three months, and I'm the most popular dancer by far. All the VIP rooms request me. I do five stage sets a night, and I always pull in at least a hundred dollars per set. I charge twenty per table dance, five for lap dances, and VIP rooms start at one-fifty.

I still get sick before each performance, and I still cry myself to sleep some nights. I hate being a stripper. An "exotic dancer." It's not dancing; it's lewd provocation. It's performing to make men lust after me. I've been groped more times than I care to count, and propositioned even more. I've been offered a thousand dollars to "entertain" a celebrity in private for one hour. I turned him down.

Now I'm going in for my first real assignment with the Fourth Dimension internship. I've been learning the ropes so far, filing papers, working in the office, taking dictation, following the real producers around. I worked my ass off to get the internship, and I worked even harder for Fourth Dimension as an office assistant, hoping to get noticed and given work on an actual project. Apparently it worked.

John Kazantzidis is an important producer, known for having a good eye for strong, compelling scripts. He's worked on some of the best-selling films of the last ten years, including the recent blockbuster film adaptation of *The Sun Also Rises*. He's always been polite to me, and he seems to take me seriously as a production student. He's a partner in the studio, so working with him directly is a huge deal. My classmates are crazy with jealousy.

I wait outside his office until Leslie, his secretary, answers the intercom and sends me through. Mr. Kazantzidis, or Kaz, as he likes to be called, is tall and broad with thick black hair and dark brown eyes. He exudes authority and power and wealth, although he's not ostentatious. For an older man, he's very attractive and charming.

He waves at the deep leather chair in front of his desk, a phone pressed to his ear. He listens for a few moments, then interrupts in Greek before hanging up. "My apologies, Grey. That was my mother." He grins at me, showing white teeth.

"No problem, sir. I think it's nice that you talk to your mother."

He nods. "Mothers are important. Do you see your family at all?"

I shrug. I've tried to avoid talking about myself or my family. "Not really. My mother passed away, and my father and I…well, we don't really get along, unfortunately."

Kaz frowns. "I'm sorry to hear of your mother. How did she pass?"

"A brain tumor." I pull my new, company-issued iPad out of my purse and open Pages, ready to take notes. "What's my assignment, sir?"

Kaz leans back and fiddles with a pen. "You can put that away." He waves at the iPad. "It's very simple. You'll be working as the direct liaison between Fourth Dimension and the lead actor on our newest film. We're partners in the remake of *Gone With the Wind*, and I know I don't have to tell you how important this project is. The original is an iconic part of American culture."

"Yes, sir." I slip the tablet back in my purse and cross my leg over my knee, listening carefully

"I've emailed you all the pertinent files on the film, including the bio on your assignment. Before you come in tomorrow, study all aspects of the project. Filming begins next month, so there won't be much to do until then, but your assignment begins as of now." Kaz leans forward and sets the pen aside. "Grey, you've proven yourself thus far. I like you. If you do well on this assignment, I'll bring you on board full-time when you graduate. Until then, you'll receive base-level salary."

I try not to squeal. This has been an unpaid internship so far. If I get paid, I can quit stripping.

"Thank you, sir! I won't let you down, I promise." I can't help grinning.

"I know you won't, Grey." He leans back and slides his phone from his blazer pocket, tapping a message. "I believe Leslie has some paperwork for you to file, and then you may go."

The paperwork for the assignment only takes a few minutes, which is good, since I have to get back to my dorm, finish a paper for my lit class, and then change for work tonight. This internship is a godsend, but it's kept me busier than ever. I work four nights a week on top of five classes every semester and thirty hours per week at the internship. I barely eat, barely sleep, and haven't had time to dance for my own enjoyment in weeks.

It'll be worth it all if I can get hired full-time by the studio.

I get back to my dorm and finish the paper as quickly as possible. I start going over the files Kaz emailed me. Fourth Dimension is the primary production studio for the project, along with Orbit Sky Films and Long Acre Productions. Jeremy Allan Erskine is directing, and I spend the rest of my study time going over Kaz's notes on Mr. Erskine's body of work and his overall ideas for the project. He's best known for *Red Sky*, a post-apocalypse drama that won six Oscars, including Best Picture. He worked with Fourth Dimension and my boss Kaz on *The Sun Also Rises*, so a film adaptation isn't new to him. The intent with this remake—according to Mr. Erskine's notes in my file—is to stay true to the novel and pay homage to the 1939 film, while rejuvenating it with a more modern aesthetic.

Kaz isn't just treating me as an assistant because I know it's not normal for a lowly intern-assistant to a lead actor to have this kind of project file. He genuinely understands my passion for film and hopefully is grooming me to work with him on future projects. Still, he has to answer to the spirit of the internship, which means a low-level assistant assignment to complete the grade.

I don't have time to get to the cast list before I have to leave. I peel out of my skirt and blouse, put on a pair of yoga pants and a T-shirt, and head out to catch the bus to the club. Once there, I change into my costume, the booty shorts and flannel shirt. I cake on the makeup, tease out my hair into glossy honey-colored waves, and then check myself in the mirror.

As always, I barely recognize myself. My hair is huge, hanging down past the middle of my back and brushed out for maximum volume. Makeup turns my gray eyes stormy and, if I'm admitting it, hypnotic. Bright red lipstick, rouge, thick foundation, mascara…

I'd have expected to lose weight, seeing how infrequently I eat and how much I'm running around, but I'm still me. I'm still thick through the hips and bust. I see my body differently now. I'm not just a woman with clothes on. I see the body beneath the clothes, which I never looked at before. Not really. I'm not just a person, just like anyone else. I'm an object, a thing to be desired. I'm aware of my breasts and backside and of the fact that men enjoy those parts of me.

I sigh as I loosen the knot in the shirt a bit, adjust my breasts and retie the knot so my cleavage is more accentuated. I brush some foundation over my hip where I bumped into the desk in my dorm room. Guys don't want to see bruises.

I'm delaying. I always delay. I never want to go out there. I thought I would get used to it, but I never have. My heart still hammers and I still feel ashamed, still feel nauseated. When the moment comes that I have to peel my shirt off and bare my breasts, I always want to crawl into a hole and pull dirt over me. I hate the lewd gazes and the pawing hands and the whistles and the suggestions.

I'm about to reach out to open the dressing room door when Timothy barges in. "Grey. Glad you're here early." Excitement gleams in his eyes, which worries me. "Tonight's your lucky night, Grey. Some bigwig actor rented out the whole club! And guess what? He wants a private dance in the VIP room with just you and him. I told him you don't do nothing extra, so you don't have to worry about that. But this is big, Grey. Big, big money."

I nod and try to calm my nerves. It's just another night. I've done celebrity VIP rooms before. We're a tiny little club *way* off the beaten path, and most of our clientele are lower-middle-class working men, and sometimes a few Hollywood types out to "slum it up." But every once in a while, an actor or sports star will show up, hoping to get a night out away from the paparazzi. One thing Timothy is adamant about is no photographers and no journalists, ever.

I touch up my makeup a bit, recheck the knot in my shirt, and make sure my cleavage looks right, and then I go out there. Lydia is on the stage at the moment, dancing to a Ludacris song. She is a short, big-breasted Iraqi girl working her way through nursing school. Lydia's sweet and a good dancer, and like me she refuses to do private parties outside the club, and never does extras of any kind. I walk the club floor, assessing the guys. They're all Hollywood, sleek and attractive and polished and oozing faux-charm. Most are already drunk, and I do half a dozen lap dances before I've even gotten from one side of the club to the other. I haven't seen the actor who rented the place out yet, but he's in a VIP room. This is just the hangers-on, the sycophants and the assistants. I do a few tables, then do my turn on stage. Part of my draw is that the only time I'm actually topless is during dances. I do the tables and work the floor in costume. Guys are into it, I guess. They like the mystery. Of course, the flannel shirt is opened far enough that I'm basically topless, so it makes the guys nuts.

I do my basic routine, spinning and twisting around the pole, teasing by unbuttoning the shirt but not letting them see anything, then re-buttoning and popping the buttons. The topless part I've nearly gotten desensitized to. Nearly. Meaning, I don't actually start to cry until I have to take off the shorts and they're next. Since they're tight, it's actually quite a feat to get them off gracefully.

Then I'm dancing in nothing but a skimpy thong. I'm close to tears the whole time. They can see my bottom, all of it. The thong is little more than a minuscule triangle over my privates, and barely covers that much. When I dance and move around the stage, they can see everything.

I finish my stage set and retreat to the backstage area to re-gather my nerves. The guys in the club are hammered, and they're tipping like crazy. I pull a hundred and fifty from the first set on stage, and I had another eighty from the lap and table dances. And I haven't even been to the VIP rooms yet. But the stage number…oh, god. The catcalls and the suggestions were worse than they've ever been. The reaching hands, which is technically against the club rules, but really up to the individual dancers to discourage… they grab me and touch me and try to peel the thong off. They ask me to go home with them. They shout in crude detail what they'd do to me. I blush when they shout those things. I can't help it. I don't think they can see the blush underneath my makeup, but it's there. I blush and I cringe and I swat away the hands playfully but firmly, and I avoid their eyes.

When I'm backstage and Inez is up for her set, I feel my stomach revolting. I hurry into the dressing room and barely make it to the little toilet, where I heave my stomach empty. Tears mingle freely with the sweat on my face. When I'm done heaving, I slump to the cold floor and rest my face against the cool porcelain, and I let myself sob for a moment. I let myself wish I was back home in Macon. I can't help but picture Mama's face if she could see what I'm doing to survive.

A fist pounds on the door, and then it opens. "Grey, goddammit, you don't have time for this!" Timothy is pulling me away from the toilet and dabbing at my mouth with a paper towel. "They want you in the VIP room. Right now. Room three. Brush your teeth and then go!" He doesn't cop a feel this time, just shoves me toward the sink and then once I'm done, out of the dressing room and through the doorway leading to the VIP rooms.

I catch my balance and my breath, and then shoo Timothy away.

My heart is pounding and my skin is crawling, tingling. I stand outside room three with my hand on the knob, but I hesitate. Something inside me is rebelling, telling me to run, to go back, to leave. But I can't. I'll lose the job, and I'm not guaranteed the full-time spot at Fourth Dimension, not yet.

I twist the knob and push the door open. A scarlet leather couch runs in a semicircle around the room, which is lit by a pair of lamps with shades to match the couch. The walls are matte black, and side tables endcap the couch. A bottle of Johnny Walker Blue Label sits on one end table, surrounded by bottles of

Coors and Bud Light, some empty, some full. The room is hazy with cigarette smoke, and beneath that is the acrid scent of marijuana. One of the end tables has a pile of white powder on it, with some divided into thick lines.

There are four men in the room. Three of them are stunningly gorgeous. The fourth?

He's a god of the big screen.

The three men are off to one side, near the pile of cocaine. I recognize them all. One is Armand Larochelle, who won Best Actor for his role in *Name of Heaven*. Armand is tall and slim, with shoulder-length blond hair and sculpted features. The second is Adam Trenton, a character actor and supporting actor in action movies. He recently did a role in a sci-fi action adventure that landed him his first leading role. The third is Nate Breckner, mostly known as a romantic comedy lead, but he's been doing roles to get him out of that typecasting.

The fourth man is Dawson Kellor. My heart stops, my breath catches. I've seen pictures of him, I've seen him in his latest films. But none of that does him justice. Not even close. Onscreen he's breathtaking. Sharp features, penetrating hazel eyes, dark hair somewhere between brown and black. Tall and ridiculously ripped, with sculpted arms and a broad, hard chest. He's Brad Pitt and Henry Cavill and Josh

Duhamel and so much more. That's just how he seems on screen.

In person…he's beyond perfection. I can't look away from him, but his beauty burns me, like staring into the sun.

And now he's in my club, and he's staring at me expectantly, and I can't move. His eyes are quicksilver, a changeable hazel. He's too beautiful for words, and I'm not sure what to do. My body won't work.

Music thumps from the speakers, a Jay-Z song. Armand is watching me, a small tube in his fingers, head bobbing to the music. The other two men have beers in their hands and are staring at their phones. They look drunk. They glance at me and then dismiss me by looking away.

"Are you gonna dance or what?" Dawson asks. His voice is darkness, deep and enveloping.

The song ends, and a techno dance beat comes on. I can't take my eyes off Dawson, but I force my hips to move. I let the music take over and flow through me. I lose myself in his eyes, which seem to darken as I sway closer to him. I know there are other men in the room, but all I can do is focus on Dawson Kellor and hope to get through this night.

I'm in front of him now, nearing him. His knees spread apart, and his hands come to rest on my hips, his palms brushing the bare skin above the denim of my shorts. I've never let a client touch me before, but

I can't seem to find the strength push his hands away. My skin burns where he touches me. His eyes are on mine, despite my cleavage in his face.

I'm shimmying to the music, slight, small shakes of my hips, enough to set my breasts bouncing. My arms are over my head in that awkward pose men seem to love. His gaze flickers down to my jiggling breasts and then back up to my eyes. I can't read his expression. Men always wear their desire on their faces, in their eyes. Dawson doesn't. But his hands are curled around my waist, possessive. I should make him let go of me, but I don't.

I've never been touched like this, never had a man's hands on my body, anywhere. Not like this. It's always been stolen touches, brushes across my back-side or pawing fingers at my breasts as I dance on stage.

This…it's a connection. His hands touch me and I'm sucked in, and I'm not a stripper, for a moment. I'm clothed, and he's looking at me. At *me*. Almost as if he's seeing Grey, instead of Gracie, even though he couldn't possibly know the difference.

The song shifts to "Just Give Me a Reason" by Pink and Nate Ruess. I'm not sure why the song filters through my awareness. I force myself out of his grasp and into the center of the room. I dance, and I find myself dancing more like a dancer than a stripper. I know I have to take my clothes off. I can't get away with just dancing. That's not my job. But now, more than ever, I don't want to do that. I want to talk to this man. Not because he's a celebrity. Not because he was *People*'s Sexiest Man Alive last year. Not because he's a phenomenal actor, although he is. There's something in his eyes that's drawing me in.

I make my fingers unbutton the top button of my shirt, and I see Armand and the others shift on the couch. I ignore them and spin in place, bend at the waist facing away from them, straighten, turn again, untie the knot and unbutton my shorts. Dawson never looks away from my eyes.

I wonder what he sees in my gaze.

Nausea blasts through me as I slip another shirt button free. I hate this part. My heart pounds with the familiar sense of shame. Now the shirt is open, and my moves are sinuous, silky and serpentine. I roll my shoulder, and the flannel slips, dipping low on one side. Another shimmy and shake of my shoulders, and the shirt falls down around my back. My arms pin the shirt in place, but the tops of my breasts are bared, my crossed arms covering my nipples. My hips sway and rock to the music.

I'm caught in his gaze again, and everything fades away except his eyes.

And then I force my arms away, let the flannel fall to the floor. Armand sucks in a deep breath, and I hear one of the other men groan in appreciation.

Dawson doesn't move, and his expression doesn't shift except for a widening of his eyes. His gaze rakes over me then, from head to toe and back. I go back to dancing, accentuating the bounce of my breasts, running my hands over them, lifting them and posing, all the things I've learned get me tips.

This is harder than stage dances, harder than lap dances or other VIP room work. This is personal. Other men look at me and they clearly want me, but something in Dawson's gaze speaks of more than desire. There's possession in his eyes.

I toy with the zipper of my shorts, glancing down at my front and back to Dawson, the calculated coy glance that I don't feel. I lower the zipper and pull the edges away, showing the triangle of red fabric and the pale skin beneath.

I'm struck then, apropos of nothing, by the memory of Candy, on my first day, telling me I had to get my privates waxed. It hurt, and I nearly died of shame.

The song shifts again, to another nameless dance beat, and I begin the swaying shimmy that leads to my shorts sliding off. Before I can push the denim over my backside, however, Dawson voice fills the room.

"All right, boys. Out."

"Aw, come on, Dawson. It's just getting good," Nate says.

Dawson doesn't answer; he just casts a long, hard stare at Nate, who sighs in frustration. "Fuck. Fine." He gets up, and the other two men go with him.

When the door closes behind them, Dawson stands up slowly. It's like watching a lion rise from the grass, all coiled power and silky grace. He moves toward me, eyes hot and dark, almost the same stormy color as my own somehow. He grabs my wrists in huge, powerful hands.

"Leave them on."

I don't struggle in his grip, and I'm not dancing. Any time I'm at work, I'm dancing. Every move is a dance. From table to table, booth to booth, onstage to offstage, it's a dance. Even if it's just the exaggerated sway of my hips and the bounce in my gait, it's a dance. I'm never still.

But now I'm frozen by the heat in Dawson's eyes as he stares down at me. I'm in the high-heeled boots that make me six feet tall, but Dawson stands easily four inches above me.

"Why?" I ask.

Men always want me to take it off. And I'm a stripper, so I do. But this man is stopping me, and I don't get it. I don't dare think of the raw power in his eyes, the easy strength in his hands, the possessiveness in his touch.

Dawson doesn't answer. He just puts his hands on my hips and gets me moving to the beat. He moves with me. He's dancing with me, swaying with the beat. I let him. I shouldn't, but I do. Something in the vibrancy of his presence erases my capacity to resist him.

Then his hands push at the denim, and fear hits me like a ton of bricks. "No, you can't—" I stammer. In my nerves, the Georgia accent is thick.

"Yes, I can. You want me to." His voice wraps around me, slides over me like blood-warm water.

I shake my head. We're still dancing together, moving to the music. I'm staring up at him, lost. "I don't—I don't do extras. You can't touch me."

"Yet here I am, touching you." His palms slide up to my waist, spanning the space between breasts and denim. His hands are enormous, powerful, yet impossibly gentle.

His touch is fire. I'm trembling, shivering. I gasp when his palms slide down again, and then his fingers hook into the belt loops and tug down. He tugs the denim, tugs again, and then they're off and collapsing around my ankles. I step out of them and try to breathe.

His palms slide like lava over my waist to my naked hips, and I'm trembling, frightened, terrified. Consumed. He's touching me. No one has ever touched me like this. Seeing desire in a man's eyes one thing. Feeling his desire in the raw strength of his grip on my skin—that's something else. Dawson's touch is hypnotism made flesh. I can't resist it. I don't know what's happening to me, but it's terrifying me. I don't want to want this, but he's right. I do want him to. I'm devoured by his hands on my hips. He hasn't touched my bottom, hasn't touched my breasts. Just my waist and my hips. And Lord help me, it's like something is eating away inside me, pushing some kind of desperate need through me.

I don't know what it is I need, except it has something to do with this man in front of me, who has stripped away my clothing and my strength and my confidence in one smooth move. I'm naked in front of him. The thong is no cover. Not for the way his eyes see through me.

"Don't be scared." His voice is warm. Almost kind.

I shrug. "I ain't…I mean, I'm not."

He laughs, a single huff. "You lie, Gracie."

"What am I afraid of, then?" I find my voice somehow, and pretend insouciance I don't nearly feel.

"Me." He caresses my hips. "This."

I suck in a long, deep breath. "Don't touch me. Please. Just let me dance."

He backs away, dropping his hands, and collapses to the couch, grabbing the bottle of whiskey and pulling on it. "Then dance."

So I dance. Naked, afraid, and humiliated some-how, fraught with some kind of desire I don't understand, I dance. Not like a stripper. Not to provoke lust. I dance. As Grey, I dance.

All motion and power and confidence, I dance.
I lose myself in it, in the music and the movement,
heedless of my bared body. When I stop, Dawson is
on the couch still, the bottle forgotten. His eyes are
dark and conflicted, but the bulge at the zipper of
his tight, expensive blue jeans shows me the effect of
my dance. He sets the bottle down and stands up. I
resist the urge to back away from him, but he doesn't
touch me again, although he reaches for me.

"You don't belong here." He gingerly extends his
hand, brushes a lock of hair away from my mouth. It's
a tender gesture, and it confuses me, scares me. Hits
me somewhere deep inside.

His mouth descends to mine, and his lips brush
across mine, hot and moist and soft. I'm not breathing. How can I? He's kissing me. Why? My heart is
frozen. My blood is a scorching river of fire in my
veins, and I'm shaking all over. The black silk of his
button-down dress shirt is stretched taut across his
chest, and as he kisses me, he draws me against him.
Silk is cold against my flesh, sinfully soft against skin
and brushing my bare nipples, turning them rigid.
His tongue slides across the seam of my lips and his
fingers curl into the muscle of my backside, sending
thrills of heat through me.

It lasts a mere moment, and then it's over.

He spins away abruptly, departs with a slam of the door, and I'm left limp. Emptied of everything, gasping for breath and trembling.

What just happened? I collapse back against the couch and struggle to breathe.

When I return to the main club floor, he's gone.

And I'm changed, totally.

CHAPTER EIGHT

I GET HOME AFTER THREE in the morning, so I don't
have time to go back through the project files before
classes the next day. My first class is at eight, and since
I have to be at the Fourth Dimension office immediately after class, I dress in my business attire before
I leave the dorm. There's no time between classes for
anything but hurrying to the next class. I don't even
have time for lunch, like most days. By the time I
leave my "History of Europe from 1700" class, my
stomach has been growling for hours. I shoulder my
backpack full of textbooks and notebooks, sling my
purse across my body, and click in my three-inch
heels to the bus stop.

My stomach is a mess, roiling and growling, waf-
fling between ravenous and nauseous. Today is the

first day the Fourth Dimension team meets the cast of the film. The project has gone through development and preproduction, and now we're getting ready to start actually shooting. I don't know what to expect. I should, but I don't. I should have every aspect of the project memorized by now, but I don't even know who the lead is. I'm jittery, excited, and scared. In my film classes I've gone through the entire process of film making in miniature, from development to sound and electrical, camera to auditions to post-production. But that's all been in-class mock-ups. This is for real. I'll be working with a real actor, dealing with his rider and various other requirements.

The Fourth Dimension parking lot is filled with expensive cars. There's a Ferrari, a Bentley, a stretch limousine, and an assortment of Mercedes and BMWs. And then, in the back by itself, is a low-slung sports car painted a kind of silver-chrome that's almost a mirror. The car looks like it's worth more than all the other cars in the lot combined, although I couldn't tell you what brand it is. And here I am, arriving on foot from the bus stop.

I step into the ladies room before going up to the conference room. I've brought a fresh blouse to change into, knowing I'd sweat through the one I'm wearing. I put on deodorant, my new blouse, touch up my makeup and fix my hair. I'm dressed in my most conservative outfit. It's a plain gray linen skirt that falls to my capri line, a pair of black heels, and a non-revealing white blouse. I look professional, like a businesswoman. There's not a shred of sexy in my appearance at all, and that's exactly how I want it.

I take the elevator up and follow the sound of voices to the conference room. The meeting is in full swing, but Kaz knows I come right from class. I pause outside the door, out of view, and suck in a deep breath, hold it for a ten count. Through that door sit some of the most powerful and influential men and women in Hollywood. And then there's me, a messed-up pastor's daughter from Georgia, a film student stripping her way through college.

I don't know why this thought hits me now. No one knows what I do. Lizzie barely acknowledges my presence, Kaz thinks I work at a bar (which is kind of true), and there's no one else who cares. I'm not friends with any of my classmates. Devin is busy with her own life at Auburn, and my dad doesn't want to know I'm alive. It's better this way. I'm not lonely; I'm too busy for friends.

Then why do I blink away the blurriness, the wet salt at my eyes? The plain beige carpet under my feet wavers.

Deep breaths, long and slow and steadying. I can do this. I can do this.

I blink hard, dig a Kleenex from purse, and dab at my eyes, then check my makeup in a compact.

I push through the door, a tight smile on my face. A dozen heads swivel my way. Kaz smiles at me from his place at the head of the long oval table, and with a wave ushers me toward the table. He gestures for me to take the one empty chair. I'm too nervous to register who's in the room. I take the seat and focus on breathing. I hear Kaz talking in my ear, and realize he's introducing me. I miss several of the names, but I know most of them. I recognize Bill Henderson, the AD; Francine James, the casting director; Ollie Muniz, the unit director. A few others, names I miss, but who will be listed in the files. I force my attention on Kaz.

"…Erskine, our director. Across from you, Grey, is Rose Garret, who will play Scarlett. Next to Rose is Carrie Dawes, playing Melanie. Armand Larochelle to your left, who will play Ashley Wilkes…" My breath catches painfully in my chest when I hear Armand's name. He's staring at me intently, a small smile on his lips. But Kaz isn't done with the introductions yet. "And, last but not least, at the head of the table is Dawson Kellor, who has the role of Rhett."

I'm dizzy—the world is spinning, my heart crashing in my chest. No. No way. I force my eyes up to Dawson's. His face is blank and carefully expressionless, but his mouth is turned down slightly, tight at the corners.

Kaz is clearly oblivious to the sudden tension. "I'm sure you're familiar with Dawson's work, Grey. You will be his assistant for the duration of the film. Anything he needs, you will provide. Anything." Kaz's eyes flick to mine, and I force myself to breathe in before I pass out. Kaz addresses Dawson. "Grey is the best intern I've ever had, Mr. Kellor. I have complete faith in her abilities."

Dawson rubs his upper lip with his finger. "Grey, hmm? Do you have a last name, Miss Grey?"

I swallow hard. "Am…Amundsen. Grey Amundsen."

I'm two seats away from Dawson, but we might be the only two people in the room. He's staring at me intently, as if he could glean my secrets through my eyes. Only, he already knows my secret.

I flash back to last night, to his hot gaze on mine, his hands on my skin, his eyes raking over my naked body. I feel his lips against mine. I stumble to my feet and lurch to the door.

"I'm sorry," I mumble to Kaz. "I'm not—I'm not feeling well. Something…I ate." I put my hand over my mouth and rush to the ladies room, where I bend over a toilet and vomit, a burning acid flood.

This can't be happening. It's not real. I know for a fact Kaz will fire me in a heartbeat if he knows I'm a stripper. I watched him fire an assistant secretary when he discovered she'd stripped in college. He fired her, not for having been a stripper, but for having lied about it. I've lied about it. Not directly, but by omission. It's enough. I can't work with Dawson. Not now. He knows my dark secret. He has power over me.

Never mind all that. Dawson himself is the problem. The way he looks at me, the way he touches me. Even in the public business atmosphere of the conference room, his eyes burned into mine, quicksilver gray and hypnotic. His mere presence sets my blood racing and my body trembling.

I hear the bathroom door open and a pair of heels click across the tile. Carrie Dawes pushes the stall door open and touches my back, then pulls my hair away.

"Grey? Are you okay?" Carrie is young and beautiful, with naturally red hair and fair skin, and she's gotten a lot of notice recently for her leading roles in some of the best-reviewed dramatic films of the last three years.

I nod and force myself upright. "Yeah, I'm okay." I wipe my mouth and inch past Carrie to the sink. "Thank you. Something I ate didn't agree with me."

Carrie leans back against the counter, and I see her doubt. "Uh-huh. It looked to me like you'd seen a ghost."

"I had a late night and some bad food. I'm fine." I have a travel-size bottle of mouthwash in my purse, and I rinse my mouth with it.

Carrie rolls her eyes. "If you say so." She leaves then, and I'm alone once more.

I turn on the faucet and dip my cupped palms under the cold water, rinse my mouth and spit several times to get the taste of bile out of my mouth. I'm retouching my lip stain when the bathroom door opens. Dawson strolls through the door, and I can't breathe all over again. He's dressed in dark blue distressed jeans and a tight light gray T-shirt that looks softer than clouds. His dark hair is artfully mussed, and a shadow of stubble covers his rugged jawline. His eyes match his shirt, the color of an overcast sky. He doesn't stop, but crosses the bathroom to stand barely an inch away.

I can't meet his eyes. My cheeks feel like they've been set on fire. "Mr. Kellor, sir. What can I do for you?"

"You can explain." His voice is like an earthquake felt from miles away, a low rumble.

I inch away from him, but I can still feel the heat emanating from his huge, hard body as if he's a furnace. I shrug, a roll of one shoulder. "There's nothing to explain, sir."

"Quit that. Even if you were just an intern-assistant, you wouldn't call me sir. How are you here?"

"I took a bus."

Dawson grunts in irritation and rubs his hands over his face. "Don't be obtuse."

I try to breathe, but I can't. I've got his reflection in the mirror, and the blinding reality of his presence in front of me. He's too gorgeous for words. Too much man to be real. His cheeks are high and sharp, his jaw like a sculpture of marble. His arms are thick and long and rippling with muscle. The T-shirt is a second skin over his muscles. His jeans cup his thighs and backside, and I just can't look away from him. I close my eyes and try to breathe. I'm nauseous all over again.

"I'll make this easy," Dawson says. "You were at the club last night. You were Gracie. Now you're here, and you're Grey."

I feel a rush of panic, and it comes out as anger. "There's nothing to explain! You've got it all figured out, don't you? You saw what I do. What else do you want me to say?"

I push away off the counter, but my heel slips and I stumble. Strong arms catch me and hold me, lift me upright.

"Don't touch me," I snap, shoving away from him.

"Grey, it's fine. I don't care."

"It's not fine. I care." I'm facing the door, with Dawson behind me.

His fingers touch my shoulder and effortlessly spin me around. I duck my head to avoid his eyes, because his gaze is all too intent, all too knowing. Just the touch of his fingers on my shoulder is enough to set my heart thumping. I was leaving, I was walking out, but I can't move. I can't pull away. He's sucking me into the orbit of his intensity. His touch is a riptide. It sucks me under. It's a catalyst, igniting the fire of need. I need. Him, his touch, something. Anything. I don't even know. Just him.

I panic and scramble away from him. "I have to go."

"Where?"

"Away. I don't know." I yank the door open, but his hand catches my wrist and stops me. I jerk free. "I said, don't *touch* me! This won't work, Mr. Kellor. I'll have Kaz—I mean, Mr. Kazantzidis—assign another intern for you."

"I don't think so."

I don't answer. Arguing is futile. I can't do this. He's too much. He knows. Working with him professionally, when he knows what I am…no. I can't.

I go back to the conference room, and everyone asks if I'm okay. "I'm fine," I say. "Kaz, can I have a word in private?"

He frowns but accompanies me to his office. I sit in the deep leather chair in front of his desk and wait for him to sit. "Is everything okay, Grey?"

I shake my head in a negative. "No, sir. I…I can't accept this assignment."

"Grey, I don't understand. This is vitally important. This is potentially the biggest film this studio has ever worked on. It could gross billions. What's the problem?"

I don't know what to say, how to explain without explaining everything. "I just…I can't work with Dawson Kellor."

Kaz leans back in his chair. "God. I was wondering if this would come up." He sighs and fiddles with his pen, spinning it around his fingers. "I know Dawson has a bit of…a reputation. But I've been assured that his time away from Hollywood has matured him."

I have no idea what he's talking about at first, but then I remember reading a series of articles in various magazines about Dawson. He had a reputation as a hard-partying womanizing playboy. There was a scandal involving a married assistant, and then another one with a famous actress, also already married. And that didn't even touch the endless parade of girlfriends he'd been photographed with. He had a different woman on his arm in every photograph, several of whom sold stories to the media about his predilections in the bedroom. He liked dirty sex, according to the stories. And a lot of it. The scandals mounted and swirled around him like a hurricane, but through it all he kept acting, and each role was better than the last, so he kept getting roles. Then there was an allegation of rape, and that was when Dawson vanished from the public eye for the last few years. This role as Rhett Butler is going to be his big comeback, his reboot of his career and his image.

"Did he make a pass at you?" Kaz asks.

I want to say he did. I want to put it all on Dawson, let his reputation win the fight for me. But I can't. I shake my head. "No, it's not that."

"Well, then, I confess I don't understand. What's the problem?"

I'm near tears. I breathe and try to focus. "It's…I just can't, Kaz. I'm sorry. I just…can't."

Kaz pinches the bridge of his nose. "Grey, I like you. You're hard-working, you're smart, and you really seem to love the business. I want to hire you full-time. I really do. I think you could go far. But… if you refuse this, my hands are tied. Unless you have accusations to level at Dawson, you need to do this. This is the biggest opportunity of your life. It could make your career, but if you don't do it, it will break it. I'm being honest with you."

I do cry then, a few tears leaking out. "I get it."

"Why don't you go home and think about it?"

I nod. "I will, sir. Thank you."

Rising on unsteady feet, I leave his office, ride the elevator down, and walk the two and a half blocks to the bus stop. I don't hear him behind me until it's too late.

"Where are you going?" His voice is right behind me, buzzing intimately in my ear.

I jump, and then hunch forward, away from him, away from his intense presence. "Home."

"What are you afraid of…Gracie?"

I whirl in place and have to restrain my impulse to slap him. "That's not my name. Don't call me that, and don't touch me."

I step back. If he touches me, I'm lost. Something bad will happen. I know what will happen.

He closes the space between us, and despite the scorching early-evening heat, he's perfectly unruffled. His hair is perfect, his clothes are dry. My armpits are sweaty and my forehead is dotted with moisture and my hands are shaking. It's after seven in the evening, and I haven't eaten since six this morning and am getting dizzy. But all this is irrelevant in the face of his proximity. He's not even an inch away. My breasts are brushing his chest. I remember how his eyes looked at me, how he devoured me with his eyes. He wanted me. But he saw me, too. Saw me, saw into me.

You don't belong here, he said.

And then he kissed me. He's that close again, and I'm drowning. If he presses his mouth to mine, I won't be able to stop him.

My stomach growls then, and a wave of dizziness crushes me. I sway on my feet, and I'd fall if it weren't for an iron arm around my waist holding me up.

"When did you last eat?"

I shake free of him. "I'm fine. I just need to get back to my dorm." I stumble again as I try to get away from him. I lean against the bus stop sign, and struggle for steadiness and for breath.

"You're not fine. Let me drive you home," he says.

I wish it was home. It's just a dorm room; it's not home. I don't have a home. I shake my head and cling to the sign.

He glares at me, seeming affronted by my stubbornness. "You're going to pass out."

"I'll be fine."

He shakes his head and spins on his heel. I hear him mutter under his breath: "Stupid ass."

"I heard that," I mumble.

He doesn't answer, just strides away. I can't help watching him; he moves like a predator, like a panther stalking through the grass. I clench my eyes closed. Something in him speaks to me, calls me. It's not just that's he's so beautiful. It's something in him. Some magnetic draw in his eyes and his presence dragging me into him.

Tires squeal, and a sleek mirror-silver car, the one I'd seen in the parking lot, roars toward me. No. No. I have to resist.

He skids to a stop in the middle of the curb-side lane, flings open his door and gets out, heedless of the traffic piling up behind him, unmindful of the horns and the shouts. As he moves toward me, his eyes are different. A blue-gray now, and angry. He jerks open the passenger door, wraps an arm around my waist, and easily and un-gently shoves me into the car. The door closes, and then he fills the driver's side, and I'm assaulted by his scent, cologne and sweat. The car is cool, air conditioning blasting. Rock music blares from the speakers, something hard and heavy. I'm dizzy, so dizzy. The world spins, and all I see is Dawson next to me, a bead of sweat trickling down his tanned neck and under his shirt collar. All I know is the rocking motion of Dawson's driving to the thumping drums of the heavy metal. I'm cognizant of the power of this vehicle, the effortless speed. I glance at the dashboard, and he's doing sixty, weaving through traffic with mad and reckless skill. I remember that he did a movie in which he played a stunt driver, and the rumors were that he did nearly all of the driving stunts himself. I close my eyes as we carve through an intersection, blowing a red light and nearly causing a wreck behind us. I'm pressed against the seat, struggling to breathe.

This car is worth more than I'll see in my life, and he's driving with an absolute disregard for it and our safety. I'm flung forward as we skid to a stop. My door is opened, and the belt I don't remember buckling is unlatched. I'm lifted from the car by Dawon's powerful arms. I smell him, some kind of faint but heady cologne of sweat and man. I recognize the way my body reacts to his presence.

I push against him. "Put me down."

"No."

I look around me. We're on the USC campus, and the entire student body is watching, it feels like. I hear whispers. I see people holding up cell phones and snapping pictures.

"Which building?" His voice is silky and intimate, almost gentle. Almost.

I point, and he makes a beeline for it. I'm nothing in his arms. He moves as if unencumbered. "Please. Put me down. I can walk."

"No." He pushes open the door and pauses.

"Second floor. Two-sixteen."

Word has spread, and doors are opening as we ascend. I hear whispers, hear the electronic click of cell phone cameras.

I hear the shriek of a female voice. "That's Dawson Kellor! Omigod, that's Dawson! Can I have your autograph! Please? Do you want to come in?"

He ignores her, brushes past brusquely. "Not now, ladies. I'll sign a few autographs when I leave." Something in his voice brooks no arguments.

He's at my door, somehow twisting the knob without letting go of me. I hear the telltale moans of Lizzie and her latest boyfriend. "Boy-toys," as she calls them. They are toys to her, too; she goes through boys faster than she does outfits. The door bangs open, thumping against the door and shuddering noisily as it swings back toward the frame.

"Omigod, what the hell—" I hear Lizzie start, and then she recognizes who it is barging through. "Dawson Kellor? Omigod, you're even more gorgeous in person, Mr. Kellor! Grey, what's going on? What's he doing here?

I feel Dawson tense around me, his hands turning to steel around my shoulders and under my knees. "Not now, Lizzie. I'm not feeling well. Can you give me a minute?"

"Leave. Now," Dawson growls, and the sound is pure threat.

I'm twisting in Dawson's arms to see Lizzie fumbling from under the sheet to grab her panties next to the bed. Her current boy-flavor does the same, but he accidentally kicks away the sheet, and they're both left naked. Lizzie squeals, smacks him on the arm, and scrambles into her panties, covering her breasts with one arm. Dawson hasn't put me down, and even though I'm a solid one-forty, he's holding me with complete effortlessness. He just waits impassively while Lizzie tugs on her clothes.

The boy—who really is a boy, a good-looking blond freshman with a big build that he hasn't entirely grown into yet—jams his feet into his jeans and hops out with his shirt in one hand and ADIDAS sports sandals in the other. It's an awkward dance that he does with enough familiarity to make me think he's done it many times. When they're gone, Dawson looks around the room for somewhere to put me. I kick my feet, and he reluctantly sets me down standing, but his hands don't leave my arms.

I wriggle in his grip and move away to sit in my desk chair. "I'm fine, Dawson. Really." My stomach growls again, and his brows furrow.

"When was the last time you ate?" He demands again.

I shrug. "I don't know. This morning?" I don't lie well, or easily, and Dawson just lifts an eyebrow at me. I sigh, and mutter, "Before class. Six?"

Dawson's face contorts. "You haven't eaten in twelve hours? And you walked how many blocks to the office?"

I dig a Powerbar out of my desk and unwrap it, holding it by the wrapper. "I'm fine. See? Dinner. It's fine. I'm fine. I'm used to it."

"Used to it? Meaning you routinely go twelve hours between meals?" When I just shrug again, he growls. "That's not healthy. And a Powerbar isn't dinner."

He rummages in the mini-fridge, but I stop him. "That's Lizzie's. Nothing in there is mine." I open my snack drawer in my desk, where I keep Powerbars, granola bars, a bag of bagels, and some Stacy's Simply Naked Pita Chips.

Dawson just stares at me. "Where's the rest?"

"The rest of what?" I ask between bites.

"Your food. What do you eat?"

I shrug again, and then determine to not do it again. I seem to shrug all too often around Dawson, and I've only known him for two hours, if that. "I eat. Just not here. I have a bagel in the morning, and I sometimes grab a snack from a vending machine between classes. I have dinner at work."

"And lunch?"

I'm getting irritated. I crumple the wrapper and toss it in the little round white garbage can under my desk, which is filled with wrappers. "Why are you so interested in my eating habits?"

Dawson just stares at me. His eyes were a light shade of blue when he was angry, out on the street. Now they're back to a muted hazel. I can't look away, can't take my eyes off his. Off of him. His jaw shifts, and I realize he's grinding his teeth, thinking. He digs a cell phone out of his pocket, and I'm kind of nonplussed to realize it's an iPhone. After the expensive sports car, I expected him to have some kind of space-age gadget from a sci-fi movie, not a basic black iPhone 5. He taps at it a few times and then holds it to his ear.

"Hey, Greg. Yeah, look I'm on the USC campus, and I need some food delivered." He turns to look at me. "Are you a vegetarian or anything weird?"

I shake my head. "No, but—"

He glances away from me and speaks into the phone once more. "Just a spread of food, I guess. Sandwiches, burgers, whatever. Yeah, campus housing—" He gives basic directions to my dorm room. "Oh, and Greg, bring the Rover and the set of spare keys. I'll drive you back in the Bugatti. Cool, 'bye."

Bugatti. That must be the silvery-mirror car.

He stuffs the phone back in his pocket and slumps into Lizzie's desk chair. Before I know what's happening, he's removed my shoes and has my legs on his knees. His hands and fingers are kneading into my right foot. It's shockingly intimate, sensual, and not a little scary. I want to take my foot back, but he won't let go. He holds my foot by the ankle and digs into the arch of my foot with a thumb. It feels so good I can't stop a groan from escaping. It's a loud, embarrassing sound, and I clap my hand over my mouth. Dawson just smiles, and the small, pleased grin on his lips makes him so beautiful my breath catches in my lungs.

His touch on my foot is like…it's sinful. It makes me feel things I don't understand, makes my stomach roil, makes things flip and twist. Something happens down low, near my core. I don't know if this is an unusual reaction to a foot rub or not. Maybe I have sensitive feet. Maybe he's just amazing at rubbing feet. All I know is, it feels incredible and I can't help but relax into my chair as he massages my foot. And then I realize I've been on my feet all day, and they probably stink. I jerk my feet away and tuck them under my leg, keeping the fabric of my skirt modestly draped over my knees.

"Don't like foot massages?" He seems amused.

"No, I just…they stink. That's gross."

"Your feet don't stink." He leans forward and grabs my foot. His hand is on my thigh, near my backside, as he tugs my feet back out. "Now, give them here. I wasn't done."

"Why?"

"Why what?" He resumes his slow, thorough massaging of my right foot.

I start to shrug again and then stop, which ends up in an awkward roll of my shoulder. "Why are you here? Why did you…why are doing all this?"

His eyes are intense, going dark and stormy as he regards me and considers his answer. "Because I want to."

"But why?"

He doesn't answer, but instead returns with his own question. "Why are you questioning it?"

"Because you shouldn't. You shouldn't be here. You shouldn't be rubbing my foot. You should just go home and leave me alone."

"But that's not what you want. And it's not what I want."

Damn him, he's right. I want him here. I want this foot massage. His presence is…intoxicating. I'm drunk on his proximity. This is all a dream I'll wake up from, I'm sure. But I don't want to.

"You don't know what I want," I say. It's a lie, and I'm a bad liar.

He doesn't answer again, just sets my right foot down on his thigh and picks up my left, and his fingers slid along my calf, his thumb rolls into my arch, eliciting another moan from me. And then his fingers slide a little higher, toward the underside of my knee, and it's too much, too intimate. Too sexual.

I tug my foot away, and he doesn't let go, but the motion brings my leg away from his touch. "Don't, Dawson."

"Why?"

"Because…please, just don't."

He only watches me, and now the only contact is his hand around my Achilles tendon and his thumb on my arch and his fingers just above my toes. Silence reigns then, as I struggle with myself. I want to take my foot back and ask him to leave. He sees too much; his eyes pierce my soul and see what I want when I don't even know it myself. But I also want to slide off my chair and onto his lap, and I want to kiss him again. The thought terrifies me. I shouldn't want him.

He's…wrong. Wanting him is wrong. Sex is wrong. That's been drilled into me since I was a small girl. Marriage happens out of chaste, godly love, and children are born out of some kind of pure and holy act. But this is what I want and it's sinful and sexual.

It's a war inside me, and it freezes me into stillness. I watch him, watch his arms flex in his tight gray shirt, watch his eyes shift and roam. My skirt has hiked up to my knees, and my legs are pressed together to present a modest glimpse of calf and nothing else, but I feel like his eyes see through my clothes. He looks at me as if seeing me as I was in the VIP room of Exotic Nights.

"Dawson, listen—" I start.

"Don't. Not now. We'll discuss that later. Greg will be here with the food in a minute."

"That's not necessary. I'm not hungry," I say, just as my stomach growls, showing up my lie.

He just shakes his head, bemused. I close my eyes and lean my head back to rest on my desk, my legs stretched out in the chair and across Dawson's lap. I'm so tired suddenly. The press and roll and rub of his hands on my feet is soothing, amazing, relaxing. I feel myself drifting and can't stop it.

Dawson's phone chimes, and then my door opens. I struggle toward wakefulness, force myself to sit up and blink the sleep away. A middle-aged man, who I assume is Greg, stands in my dorm room, his head shaved into egg smoothness. He's thick and burly, with crow's feet around his dark brown and sharply intelligent eyes. His arms stretch the sleeves of his Lacoste collared T-shirt, and he has a cell phone clipped to a thin black leather belt. He brings in a stack of carry-out containers, which he sets on the desk in front of me. The smell of grilled burgers and fresh french fries breaks my resolve and I rip open the top container. I'm three bites in to the giant bacon cheeseburger before I realize neither Dawson nor Greg has moved. They're just watching me eat.

"What?"

Dawson just wipes at his smile with a palm, then grabs the container beneath the one I'm eating from. "Nothing. Just…this is L.A. You don't often see girls dig into a burger like that around here."

I swallow, suddenly overcome by embarrassment. I was pigging out like I was starving, I realize. "Oh. I—oh. I'm hungry. I just…Sorry."

Dawson frowns. "Don't apologize. It's refreshing."

I force myself to take smaller bites. I haven't had a burger this good since I've moved to L.A., and it's delicious. I want to devour it, but slow down instead. I don't want Dawson to see me as a hick.

I glance up at the man who brought the food. "Thank you…Greg, right?" Greg nods. "Thanks."

"Don't mention it." His voice is gravelly, a smoker's rasp. He has a tattoo on his neck, the "Don't

Tread on Me" snake on the side of his throat. I see the edges of more tattoos peeking out from under his shirtsleeves, and then the myriad of scars on his arms and face and knuckles register. Suddenly, I'm taking in the reality of Greg, and I'm realizing he's a huge, hard, and threatening man, more of a Hell's Angel type of biker stuffed into business-casual clothes. He's a bodyguard, evidenced in the way he moves to stand with his back to the door, hands clasped in front of him in the way only security guards can do and not look stupid.

Dawson is devouring a corned beef reuben, and I feel better about my own appetite. He casts a glance at Greg and says, "Why don't you wait outside? We'll be leaving in a minute."

"You have a dinner meeting with Uri Ivanovich in half an hour," Greg says.

Dawson frowns. "I do? About what?"

"He wants to pitch a script to you. It's a thriller, I think."

"I don't remember agreeing to this."

Greg's lips tighten in a shadow of a smile. "I'm not surprised. You ran into him the other night. You were pretty hammered at that point."

"Cancel it," Dawson says.

Greg lifts an eyebrow. "Sure? Uri is a big-money player. He doesn't go in for shit scripts."

"Just send him my apologies and have him courier the script to me. I'll read through it later. I'm not doing dinner, though." Dawson chews and swallows, and continues, "I'm not sure I want to do a thriller, to be honest with you."

My business mind kicks in. "I don't think a thriller would be a good move for you," I say, before I can rethink my intentions. "You want to reinvent your image, then you need to stick to more serious dramatic roles. Uri Ivanovich does big-money scripts, but they're summer blockbusters, not serious Oscar-contender projects."

Dawson frowns at me. "Really." It's not a question, but his eyes invite me to continue.

"Before you left Hollywood, most of your roles were thriller and action, a few rom-coms here and there. *Gone With the Wind* is a great return role for you. It sends the message that you're serious."

"Serious about what?" Dawson asks.

"Rejuvenating your image. Your reputation."

"What do you know about my image and reputation?" It's a challenge.

I shrug. "Just what's been written about you."

"Just because they wrote it—" Dawson cuts in, but I speak over him.

"Whether it's true or not is irrelevant. The scandals alone, merited or not, gave you a negative image. And yeah, I know what they say about negative publicity being better than nothing, but I'm not sure how accurate that is. For a come back, you need to present yourself as more mature."

I need a distraction to keep myself from falling for how sexy he is. Thinking thoughts I shouldn't. Even eating, he's beautiful. Rugged and godlike. His jaw shifts and rocks and glints in the evening light as he chews. He licks dressing off his lip, and I remember the way his lips touched mine, the way his tongue traced my lower lip.

I shake myself, and focus on my burger, half gone, focus on the grain of the fake wood of my desk, focus on anything but him.

Greg slips out, and I hear voices chatter outside, see a few camera flashes, and his low growl as he pushes back the crowd. Dawson shoots a tense glance at the door. A crowd is waiting for Dawson to come out. He's in here with me, eating corned beef, and out there are dozens of people waiting, clamoring for a mere glimpse of him. My head spins a little.

I finish the burger, muffle an embarrassing belch, which brings a grin out of Dawson, and I wipe my mouth with a napkin. The voices outside grow in volume, and Dawson's expression turns serious once more.

"I'm sorry," I say, gesturing to the door, and by extension, the crowd beyond it. "Now you have to deal with that."

"I made the choice. It's part of the deal." He shrugs, acting nonchalant. "Not your worry."

I frown. "Are they going to write about me?"

"Probably. They'll make up lies. Just ignore it. They'll go away."

Possibilities and potential ramifications flit through my head, and panic begins to set in. "But… what if they follow me?"

Dawson shrugs. "Don't answer. Do what you have to do and ignore them."

He doesn't get it.

"I'm not a famous actress, Dawson. I'm a student. An intern." I keep my eyes downcast. "You know where I work. What I do. What if they follow me there? People will find out."

Dawson closes the Styrofoam lid and wipes his hands and mouth, then he places my feet back on the floor, leans forward and takes my hands in his. "And that's a problem?"

"Yes!"

"Are you ashamed of what you do?"

I don't answer, don't look at him. I just tug my hands free and stand up. "You should go."

He stands up, too, but only to tower over me, body close to mine. His index finger touches my chin and forces me to look up at him. I do, and I'm breathless. His eyes are the bluish-gray of upset now, intense and conflicted.

"Grey."

"What?" It's a breath, a quiet whisper.

"Why do you do it, if you're ashamed?" His gaze burns into me, and I know he can see my secrets, see my shame, see my need and my fear. His finger and thumb gently hold my chin so I can't turn away.

I refuse to answer. "Please just go."

"Fine." He lets go of my chin and turns toward the door. My skins burns where he touched me. "I'll see you at the office tomorrow."

"No."

He stops and turns back. "What? No, what?"

"I can't do it."

"Grey, what are you talking about?" He scowls at me.

"I can't work with you. I just can't do it."

"I was under the impression that you had to, if you wanted to finish your internship." He scratches his jaw. "I don't know what you're so afraid of. Despite my *reputation*, I'm not that bad."

I shake my head. "It's not that."

"Then what? Explain it."

"You wouldn't understand. You couldn't."

"You'd be surprised what I can understand," Dawson says. His eyes are intent on mine, not wavering, daring me to look away, which of course I can't do.

"You *know*," I whisper. "You *saw* me. You saw Gracie. You'll never see anything else now."

"Am I treating you like a stripper?" He says the word casually, as if the truth of it doesn't rip a hole in me.

"No." I can barely whisper the answer.

"You think you're the first girl to strip her way through college? You're fucking amazing at it, Grey. You should own it. It doesn't have to define you."

"But it does."

"Then that's your problem. You're going to let it ruin your career before it even begins? Seriously? If it's that big of a deal, I won't tell anyone. And I'll talk to Armand and make sure he doesn't, either. Adam and Nate were wasted, and I doubt they'd be able to pick you out of a lineup. Just come to work tomorrow."

"Just…go. Please." I'm near tears, holding them back desperately.

Dawson shakes his head slowly, as if confused and irritated. "Damn it, Grey. Just let me—"

"Let you what? What are you going to do? Change reality?"

He sighs in exasperation. "Fuck, fine. Be that way." He turns to the door and put his hand on the knob, then stops as if remembering something. Pulling a set of keys from his pocket, he crosses the small room in two strides, takes my hand in his, and places the keys in my palm. "Here. You shouldn't be walking everywhere alone."

I look down and see a Land Rover emblem, the key folded into the fob, a silver oval on the black plastic with the signature green lettering. "What? I can't—I mean…what?"

"It's my Rover. It's in the lot out there. Those are the keys. I want you to drive it."

"But…no. I mean, you don't even know me. We've met twice. I can't drive your car."

"Yes, you can. And you will. You're my assistant for this project, which means you have to do what I tell you. Your job is to keep me happy. So drive my car."

"But…what if I crash it?"

He snorts. "Babe, I'm Dawson Kellor. I could buy a dozen of them with my debit card. I couldn't care less if you crash it, except for you getting hurt, that is."

"You have a debit card?" I ask. It seems so commonplace a thing for a celebrity of Dawson's caliber to have.

He seems puzzled. "I have a bank account, so therefore, yes, I have a debit card. I also have credit cards. And a driver's license." His tone shifts to teasing. "You know what else? I'm a guy. I pee and miss the toilet. I take shits. I eat cheeseburgers. I watch baseball and drink beer."

I glare at him. "That's not…I mean, I just—"

He laughs, and brushes a finger over the frown lines on my forehead. "Relax. I'm teasing you. My point is, I'm just a guy."

"You're not, though. You just said it yourself. You're Dawson Kellor."

"Does that intimidate you?" He's closing in, and his mouth is centimeters from mine, his breath on my cheek and his eyes boring holes in me.

He could snap his fingers, and any woman in the world would jump to do whatever he wanted. Yet here he is, in my dumpy little dorm room, acting like he likes me, like he sees something special in me beyond the fact I'm pretty enough. This isn't vanity but more about who I am. I'm not the kind of girl he's used to. I'm not an L.A. girl. I'm not an actress or someone sexy and confident and sure of who I am. I'm a mess. A confused, embarrassed, shameful mess.

And he's the god of Hollywood.

He's the face of Cain Riley, hero of the *Mark of Hell* trilogy, a series of paranormal action–adventure/romance books that outsold both *Harry Potter* and *Twilight*. Those movies made Dawson's career. His face is on the books now. There's a *Mark of Hell* ride at Universal Studios, with Dawson's face plastered all over it. There are toys with his likeness, fan clubs and cosplay costumes and parodies and *SNL* skits making fun of him.

His portrayal of Cain was darkly sexual, James Bond meets Batman. Women swooned over Cain Riley, fantasized about him. What makes Dawson even more famous is the fact that he seems to emulate in his own life the character he played in the movie. Women don't just swoon over Cain Riley the fictional character, but over Dawson Kellor, the very real and wild, sexy young debonair playboy with more money than God.

I see this dark and sexual Dawson Kellor in the way his eyes devour me. They are burning thunderhead gray right now, and I realize the color of his gaze is a mutable thing, changing with his emotions and his clothes. His hands settle on my waist, and I'm not breathing, unable to look away from his eyes. I feel his breath on my lips, feel the power of his hands on my skin, and I remember the taste of his kiss, the luring hypnotism of his mouth on mine. My lungs burn with held breath; my eyes waver and blur, and the heat of his body radiates against my skin and I want him. I want to kiss him again—I want to get lost in his touch like I did for that moment in the club. For that briefest instant of time, I was just a woman being kissed, a girl experiencing her first brush with passion; nothing mattered, nothing existed but Dawson and his mouth and his hands and his eyes and his heat and his broad, hard, muscular body.

I want the very same in this moment.

I have to stop this. I have to turn away. Kissing him would be wrong. If I have to work with him, I can't kiss him. I can't think about that night in the club, silk shirt against my bare skin and his hands on my backside, owning me.

Except I want him to own me. I want him to do whatever he wants. I want to give in to my own shaking need and trembling desire. I want him to show me what I've never known.

His lips are soft and wet against mine, and I'm breathing his breath, clutching his shirt desperately and holding on for dear life, letting him kiss me again. The kiss…God, the kiss. I scold myself for taking the Lord's name in vain, and then I remember that I don't care about that anymore, and then his tongue slips between the slight parting of my lips and scrapes my teeth, touches my tongue in a rapturous tang. I can't breathe, can't begin to think, can't do anything but grip his T-shirt in my fists and kiss him, move my mouth against his and touch his tongue with mine. And now I'll never return from this place, for I know the taste of temptation. I've sinned; I've fallen.

His lips pull away, and I'm left empty. I sag forward and rest my forehead against his chest, and then sobs overtake me, sending me into shuddering spasms, wracking, jerking, heaving sobs.

"Grey? Jesus, what's wrong?" His voice is plainly confused.

"Go. Just…go. Please go." I can barely speak.

"Why are you crying? Was it that bad of a kiss?" He's trying to joke but it falls flat. The wince on his face shows he knows it.

I can only shake my head. I stumble away from his hypnotic heat, away from his touch, his lips. "Go! God…please just leave me alone! I can't…I can't—I can't do this with you. You have to go." I climb my ladder to the top bunk, feeling like a child trying to hide from punishment.

I feel him standing there, watching me. I'm facing away from him, so all he can see is the curve of my waist and the wide bell of my hips and the taut expanse of my backside. My gray linen skirt is tangled beneath me, stretched tight across my hips, and I feel his gaze on my body. I want to shift and adjust the skirt, but I'm too conscious of his eyes on me to move. I hear a jangle of keys and then the sound of metal on wood as he sets them on my desk. I hear him shoving the empty carryout containers into the paper bag, and then the sound of the knob turning. Excited voices grow louder as the door opens. Greg growls an injunction to calm down.

"Grey, I—" For the first time since I met him, Dawson sounds unsure. I almost turn over to look at him, but don't.

Then the cocky voice is back. "Be there tomorrow. Drive the car."

He leaves then, and the clamor as he emerges from my room is deafening. There are screams and squeals. I hear one female voice tell Dawson that she wants to have his babies. Another asks him to marry her. A chorus of voices asks for autographs and pictures, and I hear Dawson saying that he'll sign autographs for ten minutes, and then he has to go. The noise quiets, and I can hear the murmur of Dawson's voice as he talks to the women he's signing for.

Eventually the noise dies away, and in the distance I hear the throaty purr of his car. Lizzie comes in after a few minutes.

"Holy shit, Grey!" She climbs up and hangs on the ladder. "Do you know who that was? Why was he here? Did you fuck him?"

I want to ignore her, but I can't, because she's too loud, too in my space and obnoxious.

I roll over, and I don't have to fake the tormented expression on my face. "He's my boss, Lizzie. He's my assignment for my internship. So yes, I know who he is. And no, we didn't—I mean, I—no."

"Omigod, why not?" She grabs my arm and shakes me. "He's the hottest piece of man-ass on the entire fucking planet! How could you not!"

I don't know what to say. I just shrug. "I work for him. I couldn't…I mean, my grade, my internship, my career, it's all riding on this." It's the bald truth and why I can't let anything happen. Why I have to resist the hypnotic pull.

"Jesus, Grey. He's Dawson *fucking* Kellor. He's Cain Riley, for god's sake! It's a crime against all straight women to not get a piece of that. And you can't tell me he's not interested. I saw the way he held you."

I snap, just a little. "God, Lizzie, do you hear yourself? He's not a slab of beef. He's not an object for me to 'get a piece of.' He's a man. A person. And I…he didn't hold me any kind of way. He carried me in because I fainted. That's it." I don't know why I'm lying to her. I know better.

Lizzie frowns at my outburst. "You're dumber than I thought. Send him my way, if you're not interested." She vanishes back out the door then, and I'm finally alone.

I try to fall asleep, and fail for the longest time. When I do fall asleep, I dream of Dawson. They're erotic dreams, torturous dreams, in which he touches me in places that make me sweat and squirm and pant. He kisses me in the dreams, and I let him, and I kiss him back, and it becomes more than a kiss. It becomes something that makes me ache between my legs.

I wake in a sweaty tangle of sheets and stare at the ceiling, unable to forget the dreams. I fall back asleep, and immediately the dreams begin again. Dawson's hands on my waist, sliding down my hips. Curving over to cup my backside. Grazing beneath my breasts. Delving down and down and down between my legs to touch me in the most sinful way.

I see his eyes, blue-shot gray, like lightning-laced storm clouds, and I hear his voice whispering to me: "You can't resist me, Grey. You are mine, Grey."

I wake again at dawn, hearing his dream-whispered words, and torn between wishing they were true and being terrified that they are.

CHAPTER NINE

I MAKE GREAT MONEY at the club, but financially, I'm still barely making it. My tips just cover tuition, room and board, and books. Barely. I have to scrimp to eat and buy new outfits for the internship. If I leave the campus at all, I walk as much as possible. Even bus fare is too expensive and I need every penny. I hate it though, because USC is in a bad neighborhood, and a girl on her own—even in broad daylight—isn't safe.

I stand in the parking lot outside my dorm room, staring at a brand-new Range Rover. It's white with black-tinted windows. The keys are in my hand, and I'm warring with myself. I have my driver's license, but I haven't driven since leaving Georgia. I Googled Range Rovers, and this model in front of me starts at $137,000. I simply cannot fathom that amount of money. And he just left it here in this university parking lot, on a whim, for me to drive. And then claimed he could buy a dozen of them if he wanted to. Reading about or hearing about twenty-million-dollar movie deals is one thing, but understanding the reality of a man actually having that kind of money, seeing the evidence of it, is another thing. This Range Rover, this $137,000 SUV, is pennies to him. Even the Bugatti, which probably cost somewhere near two million dollars, is nothing. Dawson made four million on the first *Mark of Hell* and sixteen more between the other two. He's done four other big-budget films since then, none of which were salaried at less than ten million dollars each.

It's unusually hot outside today, and I'm sweating just standing here, debating with myself. It would be prudent to drive the Rover. I click the "unlock" button and open the door. I slide into the driver's seat, gasping at the blistering heat of the tan leather under my legs and against my back. I start the engine, which hums to life with a low and powerful purr. Within seconds, the A/C is blasting cool air. I breathe in and then out, carefully. I'm terrified of this car. I'm terrified of what it means, that I'm actually doing what he told me to do. I'm going to finish the internship, and I'm going to spend the next few months working with Dawson professionally.

He's seen me naked. He's touched my bare skin. He's kissed me, twice. My body responds to him in a way I don't begin to understand.

Delaying the moment of actually having to drive this vehicle, I fiddle with the infotainment center until it turns on. Heavy metal blasts so loud the car shakes. I scramble to turn it down, then manage to turn it to the radio. I flip stations until I find 102.7 FM, the pop station. "Can't Hold Us" by Macklemore comes on, and I turn it up a little. Not anywhere near as loud as Dawson had it, but enough to give me confidence, dance in my seat. I take a deep breath and put the SUV into reverse, backing out of the spot slowly.

The drive to the office is horrifying. I'm a terrible driver. I'm either going too slow and being honked at, or I'm forgetting how powerful the Rover is and going twenty over the limit. When I change lanes, I cut several people off and then I nearly miss my turn, forcing me to cut across several lanes of traffic. I nearly cause two accidents. By the time I'm sitting in a parking spot outside the office building, my nerves are shot, leaving me trembling and near tears.

And now I have to go in and face Dawson. His Bugatti is parked parallel across three spots, way in the back of the lot. I let the engine idle as I attempt to collect myself. I'm nearly calm when the passenger door opens and Dawson slides in. He's wearing a faded orange Billabong shirt and khaki cargo shorts with black Old Navy flip-flops. A pair of Ray-Bans cover his eyes, and his hair is spiked with gel, looking prickly and stiff. His jaw is covered with scruff, thick and dark, almost a beard. I want to run my hands over his cheek, feel the stubble tickle my palms.

I clench my fists around the leather of the steering wheel and try to breathe through the need to touch him.

"You look tense." He leans against the car door, legs stretched out in front of him. He's calm and utterly composed. A small smile graces his beautiful, expressive mouth.

I lick my lips and grind my hands around the wheel. "I'm fine."

He snorts. "Babe, don't lie to me."

"Don't call me that. I'm not your babe. I'm not anyone's babe."

"See? Tense. It's just a word." He drags the seatbelt across his torso and clicks it in place. He points north. "We have errands. Drive."

"Drive where?" I glance at Dawson, who has his nose buried in his phone.

"First, back to my place. We gotta grab my script. I forgot it. Then we have a meeting with one of the secondary production firms…uh…Orbit something."

"Orbit Sky," I fill in.

"Yeah, them. And then back here. Jeremy wants to go over some things with me and Rose. Since you're my assistant for this project, you're with me."

"So we're going to the Orbit Sky offices?" I ask.

He shakes his head. "No, it's a dinner meeting. Spago."

Even I know what Spago is. "Am I dressed for that?" I give Dawson a once-over. "Are *you*?"

He shrugs. "Does it matter? You look great. We're stopping at my place, so I'll put on some jeans or something. It's not like they'll tell me I can't come in, you know."

"So where do you live?"

"Just head toward Beverly Hills," he says, not looking up from his phone. When I hesitate, he glances up at me. "What?"

"I've…I've never driven around here. Or…any-where, really, before today."

"You what?" Dawson frowns at me. "How have you never driven before? You have your license, right?"

I nod. "Yeah, I got my license, but I never drove. I never had to, or got to, depending on how you look at it. My mom or dad just drove me where I had to go. Here I take the bus, or I walk."

Dawson seems like he's fighting laughter. "And I gave you a Range Rover Autobiography?"

"A what?"

He does laugh then. His teeth are white, and the laughter transforms his face, makes what is already beautiful almost unbearably so. "This? This is a 2013 Range Rover Autobiography. It's…" He sighs and shakes his head. "You know what? It doesn't matter. It's just a car. Come on."

He reaches over me and yanks the keys out of the ignition. His forearm brushes my chest, and electricity zaps through me at the contact. He doesn't notice, just slides out of the car and strides toward his Bugatti. I researched his car this morning during class. It's a Bugatti Veyron 16.4 Grand Vitesse, and by all accounts it's the most expensive car in the world, especially since he ordered some kind of special features that make it one of a kind. There was a whole magazine article on the fact that Dawson bought one, and there was also an article on his other cars, since he apparently has several super-luxury sports cars, including an Aston Martin Vanquish, a Bentley, and a Maserati. I had to look up what each of those were.

I grab my purse and follow him to his car. He's waiting for me, holding the door. I slide onto the leather seat, and he closes the door after me. It's a gentlemanly gesture that confuses me. I buckle up and clutch my purse on my lap, refusing to watch Dawson as he folds his frame into the seat and brings the car to life. We're gone with a squeal of tires and a lurch of my stomach. He weaves the car through traffic, disregarding traffic laws left and right. He blows through at least one red light, carving the wheel to the right to narrowly avoid a cube van. I'm breathless, terrified.

I seem to spend a lot of time terrified around this man.

He squeezes the car between lanes, fitting into spaces I wouldn't have believed a car could go. Having just navigated the streets of L.A. myself, I realize the mastery he has over his vehicle. He makes it look effortless, as if hurtling through the congested traffic of Hollywood at sixty miles an hour is totally normal.

His phone chimes and he pulls it out, tosses it to me. "Can you see who that is?"

I hold the unfamiliar phone in my hand and stare at it. I don't have a cell phone, since I can't afford one and don't have anyone to call. I have an iPad that I use for the internship, though, and it's just like that. I slide the little green icon across the screen. "It's from…Ashley M." I start reading the text aloud. "She says, 'You should come over tonight. I have an eight-ball and some Blue Label.'"

His faces contorts. "Shit. I thought it was from Jeremy."

"Who's Ashley M?" A thought strikes me. "And why just the first letter of her last name? Do you know so many Ashleys that you have to differentiate between them?"

"Shit," he says again. "She's…a friend of mine."

"A friend." It's not really a question.

He grabs the phone without looking at me and shoves it between his thighs. "Yeah. A friend. And yeah, I know lots of Ashleys. And lots of Jens. Last names…aren't usually necessary."

"So should I answer her for you?" I know exactly what the message meant. Well, maybe I don't know what an eight-ball is, but Blue Label is high-end whiskey. I'm guessing an eight-ball is drugs of some kind, which means sex. Ashley M is probably glamorously beautiful and sophisticated and knows how to please him in ways I don't.

My heart clenches. I force myself to remember that he's my boss. I work for him. He can do drugs and drink and have sex with anyone he wants. This has nothing to do with me.

He shifts gears, and grabs the phone, spinning it idly between thumb and forefinger. Then he tosses it to me. "Yeah. Answer her for me."

I take the phone and bring up the message from Ashley M. "What do you want me to say?"

"Just tell her no, thanks, that I already have plans."

I type the message into his phone and send it, and within seconds, a response pops up in the gray bubble. "She says, 'Awww, are you sure?'" I choke a little and set the phone on his lap. "I'm not reading the rest."

My heart clenches, and my stomach flips. It's none of my business. I don't care. I don't care. But… as much as I tell myself not to care, I do. I shouldn't, and I don't have any place feeling possessive over Dawson, but I do. The rest of the message said, *If you come over, you can put it in my ass again.*

My eyes blur. Dawson pulls the car to a stop at a red light, and on impulse I throw off my seat belt, shove the door open, and get out. I'm wearing heels, so I can't run, but I slam the door behind me and start walking as fast as my precarious sense of balance will allow. I'm not looking where I'm going, and I don't know where I am. It doesn't matter. I hear Dawson's angry voice behind me, calling my name. I don't know what I'm feeling. Angry, sick to my stomach, jealous, confused. Lost. Loss, like some sense of possibility has been taken away. He likes anal sex. He has random women, whose last names he doesn't even care about or know, texting him for a night of meaningless sex, drugs, and booze.

He's a star. A celebrity. He lives a celebrity life, and I know nothing about that.

I hear honks and shouts from behind me, and I ignore it. I keep walking, fighting the stupid tears and losing. I don't even know why I'm so upset about this.

I'm lifted off the ground, spun in place, and pinned against the plate-glass window of a storefront. Dawson's arms are around me, under my backside. One of his hands is on my cheek, forcing my face to his. He's breathing hard, sweat dotting his forehead and upper lip. His eyes are blue-gray, the color of his anger.

"Damn it, Grey. It's not what you think."

I writhe in his grip. It's too much, like this. I'm wrapped up in him, held in place by him. I can't get away, can't move, can't breathe anything but his scent and his power. "Let me go."

"No."

"Why?"

"Because you don't understand."

"There's nothing to understand," I whisper. "You can do what you want, with who you want. And it's exactly what I think."

"She's—"

"She wanted you to come over for sex. It's simple." I suck in a deep breath, close my eyes to block him out. He sets me down and I shove him, hard. "I'm an intern. That's all. You don't owe me any explanations."

"But what if I want—"

"It doesn't matter!" I'm yelling, and I'm still crying through it, for some reason. I strive for calm, especially because a crowd is gathering. "Just…God, just stop, Dawson. Just stop."

"I can't. I'm sorry you read that, but…look, you're right, it doesn't matter. I'm done with her. I have been. She was a one-time thing. That's it."

I start walking again, and he catches up with me. We're being followed by clicking and flashing cameras. "I don't know what you're trying to convince me of. It doesn't matter."

"You keep saying that, but you're the one crying." His hand catches mine and his other goes around my waist, drawing me to him. Once again, with a mere touch, I feel as if I belong to him. It's wrong, and it's right, and it's confusing. "Stop running."

"I'm not."

He chuckles. "You're a shitty liar, Grey."

I push him away and struggle out of his hold. I'm struggling against myself as well, since I like how it feels to be held by him. I'm lost, disoriented. Why am I fighting this? He clearly wants me in some sense. But I don't know what he wants, and I don't know what to do with his desire, or how to feel, or what I feel. All I know is survival, work, and school. I don't know men.

I turn away and walk back the way we came, but I'm stopped dead in my tracks by the crowd of paparazzi. There's dozens of them, and they're photographing me.

"Miss Amundsen, are you and Dawson an item? How long have you been together? Did you catch him with another woman?" A middle-aged man with thick brown hair and square-framed glasses thrusts a voice recorder at me and shouts a train of questions.

How do they know my name? That scares me more than anything else.

A stick-thin woman with gaunt features and frizzy dishwater-blonde hair speaks over him. "Miss Amundsen, why did Dawson carry you to your dorm yesterday? Are you a USC student? Is it true you and Dawson walked in on your roommate having sex? What's Dawson like in bed?"

My mouth opens and closes. I feel compelled to answer their questions. I was raised to be polite, to speak when spoken to. I don't know what to say. I don't want to be news. "I—I—we're not, um…I don't—"

"Can you comment on your relationship with Dawson Kellor?"

"How old are you? Do you have a husband?"

"Grey, have you ever thought about modeling?"

"Look this way, Grey!"

"Grey, over here!"

"Grey, has Dawson ever asked you to do anything in bed you didn't want to?"

I'm looking from one voice to another, flapping my mouth open and closed, blinking at the flashes. I feel Dawson's arm go around my waist, pull me back, and then he's standing in front me, shielding me.

"Grey has no comment at this time, guys." He steps forward a bit, and I feel him shift, feel him become stiff and formal, as if he's putting on a suit of armor. "How about I take a few questions about the film?"

The man who asked the first question pushes forward, jostling for position. "Dawson, we've all heard that you're rumored to be in a remake of *Gone With the Wind*. Can you confirm this?"

Dawson shifts his attention to the man. "Hey, Bill, how are you? Yeah, I can confirm. I'm playing Rhett. We're about to begin filming next month. We're almost done with pre-production and development."

"Is Grey part of the project?" I can't see who asks this.

"She's an intern working for John Kazantzidis at Fourth Dimension."

"What were you arguing about? That didn't sound like a work-related argument to me. Are you two involved?"

Dawson's shoulders flex and tense. "I'm not going to comment on that, other than to say, no, we're not involved, and we never have been. She's an intern on the project. It was a business-related discussion."

The same voice speaks up, a young-sound-ing male voice. "It sure didn't sound like it to me,

Dawson, and we all know your history with interns and assistants. Come on, man, give us something."

Dawson's voice turns hard. "I *am* giving you something. Don't be a douchebag, Tom. Leave Grey out of it. I'll comment on the film, but that's it. Any more questions about Grey, and this is over."

All I can see is Dawson's broad back, the orange T-shirt stretching over his shoulders, and the back of his head, the hair curling around the base of his neck. He needs a trim around his neck. I want to run my hands over the expanse of his shoulders, but I don't.

"Why are you protecting her, if you're not involved?" The same voice, whom Dawson had called Tom.

"She's never dealt with you guys before. You guys are fucking barracudas."

Tom again. "Sure you won't comment on her? She's hot, Dawson. You guys look great together."

Dawson wraps his arm around my shoulders, pulls me close as we push through the crowd, ignoring the blinding camera flashes and barrage of questions. He doesn't speak, and all I can do is trot in my high heels to keep up with him. His arm is a platonic vise around my shoulder, a show for the journalists, paparazzi, whatever they are. My heart is pounding. They've already caught on to the fact that there's something going on. They know who I am. They're going to find out I'm a stripper. Kaz will find out, and he'll fire me. Everyone will know I'm a stripper, and it's all I'll be to anyone. A chick who's willing to take her clothes off.

We've gone three blocks and we're still not back to the intersection where I jumped out of Dawson's car. I had no idea that I had run so far. After another half a block, we see a crowd gathered around a policeman, and a flat-bed tow truck preparing to load Dawson's car. Dawson curses under his breath.

"Hey, you don't need to tow it."

The cop turns around, recognizes Dawson and then looks intimidated. "Sorry, Mr. Kellor. You can't leave your car parked in the middle of the street like that."

"No shit. But I'm here now, so it's fine."

"But—" The cop seems flustered.

Dawson steps closer to the policeman, who is an older man with a rounded belly and salt-and-pepper hair. "You have a daughter, Officer…O'Hare?"

"I…yeah, but—"

Dawson takes the officer's ticket pad from him, and pulls a thick black Sharpie from the cargo pocket of his shorts. "What's her name, Officer O'Hare?"

"Jill, but that won't—"

Dawson shoots the man a gentle, disarming smile, and writes horizontally across the pad. I read what he writes: *To Jill, because your Dad is a hero. Your friend, Dawson Kellor.* The name is written in a dramatic slanting scrawl, the inscription printed neatly. He hands the pad back to the policeman and re-pockets the marker, then claps the older man on the shoulder.

"Listen, Officer O'Hare. It was a bit of an emergency. It won't happen again. I'm sure you understand." Dawson is striding into the street, pulling me by the hand. The officer is drawn along as if by a magnet, spluttering and blustering.

"Mr. Kellor, I appreciate the autograph, because my daughter is a huge fan, but I can't just let you drive away."

Dawson opens the passenger door and hands me in, then crosses around to the driver's side, sliding in, pushing the keyless starter button so the engine roars to life. He guns the gas pedal so the motor revs. "Then write me a ticket. There's no point in trying to tow it, since I'm here now. Write me a ticket for whatever you want. Just make it quick, if you could. I have an important meeting with my producers in an hour."

Officer O'Hare is clearly befuddled. His eyes are flicking to the huge crowd, to Dawson, to me, to the car—which is worth more than he'll make in his whole life. He's hesitating, and Dawson is giving off an air of disarming impatience. He digs a card out of his wallet and hands it to the officer. "How about this? I really have to go. Here's my attorney's card.

You can send a ticket or a fine or whatever to him if you want." I'm shocked at his gall.

"I guess I could—I mean…" Officer O'Hare glances at the crowd, and then back to me for some reason.

I'm sitting quietly in passenger seat, buckled, waiting, trying to be invisible.

"Good. Glad we got that figured out." Dawson slams his door closed, reverses the Bugatti to within an inch of the police cruiser parked diagonally behind him, and then peels out into traffic around the tow truck, cutting off a white convertible Bentley. He blows through a yellow light and has the car doing fifty-five within seconds, zipping around slower-moving traffic, stomping on the brakes when he can't find a path around. At one point he even crosses the center double yellow lines and swerves around a semi into oncoming traffic. I'm breathless, clutching the armrest with white-knuckled fingers as Dawson floors it, pressing me back into the seat as the powerful car rockets to over a hundred miles per hour, and then I'm thrown to the left as Dawson cuts back into the proper lane, braking and doing something with the gears to make the car slow drastically.

The scene of the incident with the police officer is already several miles behind us, and we only left the curb minutes before. My heart is drumming in my chest, and not just from Dawson's skillfully insane driving. In between shifting the gears, his hand rests on my leg, his finger tracing idle patterns on my knee. I stare at his hand. It's huge and tan, strong, the pads of his fingers callused and rough on my skin.

"Do you always drive like this?" I manage to ask.

"Yes." He glances at me with a quick grin. "Why?"

"It's scary. What if we wreck?"

"We won't."

"But how do you know?"

"Because I know what I'm doing. I'm not just a rich dickhead with a fast car."

"Then what are you?" I ask.

"Um. A lot of things. Before I got serious about acting, I was a street racer. You ever see *Fast and Furious*? Kind of like that. Except we weren't gangs and street kids. We were rich and privileged brats with too much money and no one to tell us not to be stupid. We'd drag up and down Sunset at midnight, or in the poorer areas where cops don't like to go. We'd take our dads' Ferraris and Lamborghinis out into the desert and race. We'd go up and race the curves in the mountains. So driving was what I did anyway. And then I got the role of Anderson in *Redlight Gods*, and they wanted me to take, like, actual race-car driving lessons. Like, with government defensive and offensive-driving course instructors and NASCAR guys and shit. The funniest part was when they wanted to have me take this tutorial on street racing with some supposedly reformed racer who decided to become a Hollywood consultant or something. And it turns out it was a guy I'd raced—and beaten—half a dozen times over the years." He's talking as he drives, and I notice he's slowed down and is driving more sanely. For my sake? "So yeah, I know how to drive. You don't have to worry."

"Have you ever been in a wreck?"

Dawson laughs. "Of course. You don't street race and not crash. I totaled this NSX I had. I mean, *totaled*. It was the kind of wreck you don't expect anyone to live through, but I walked away without a scratch. I was dragging on the edges of South Central against this cat named Johnny Liu. I think his dad was Triad, actually, but I never knew for sure. It was like, three in the morning and we had pink slips riding on the race. It was a preset thing, a big four-mile circuit. I was in the lead, about to make this wide left. I had her drifting right in the groove, you know? Tires smoking, engine howling. Johnny was behind me and closing in fast. He had this killer fucking black and red '68 Charger with a fat-ass blown Hemi. It was so backward. Here I was driving this Acura NSX, which is a Japanese car, and this Asian kid is driving a classic American muscle car. So anyway, I was drifting through a left onto Washington. I don't even know what happened, except that suddenly my car was in the air, flipping. Like, I must've flipped thirty times. I think I got T-boned from the passenger side. God, that hurt so fucking bad. I rolled and rolled and rolled, and I guess I was lucky that I didn't hit a streetlight or a building or something. I was lucky any way you slice it, really. I have no clue how I didn't get hurt. I mean, the car was a crumpled ball of shit, and I just crawled out of it, bruised but unhurt."

"You said, before you got serious about acting. What's that mean?"

He checks his mirrors, and then, without warning, cuts across traffic and down a side street, zipping left and right, suddenly back to the crazy-fast and erratic driving. I'm clutching the armrest again and holding my breath as he barrels down side streets at fifty miles an hour, then out onto the main road again, carving across all lanes of traffic and onto the freeway. We're doing ninety on the shoulder, narrowly avoiding wreck after wreck, and then exiting at a more normal pace.

"What was that?" I breathe.

Dawson grins at me. "Had fuzz after me. Lost 'em."

"Fuzz?"

"Police? Traffic cop?"

I frown at him. "Who actually says fuzz?"

"Me, it would seem."

"So you just evaded a policeman?"

"Yep." He's glancing behind us as he drives, but seems confident he lost the cop. His eyes lock on me as we sit at a red light. "So. What did you think about your first encounter with the pop?"

"Pop?" I ask.

"Paparazzi."

"Oh," I say. "It was…scary. They're not afraid to ask anything, are they?"

He laughs. "No. And they're relentless. You realize, even though we didn't answer any of their questions about you, and that we said we aren't together, they're still gonna print whatever they think will sell copy. This is probably one of those 'don't look down' things, but I wouldn't recommend reading any gossip rags. You won't like it."

I'm not sure what to think or say. I probably will go and look my name up online now. I sit in silence for long minutes, avoiding his eyes, keeping my knees to the side so he can't touch me. His touch makes me lose my sense. I can't keep getting sucked into his orbit.

We pull into a Beverly Hills gated community, passing gargantuan estates worth tens of millions of dollars, rolling expanses of green grass and sculpted shrubs and wide curving driveways. As we roll at a surprisingly sedate pace through the neighborhood, I see a well-known actress getting her mail, and then a high-profile L.A. basketball player washing a sports car. Dawson glances at me as if to gauge my reaction to the neighborhood.

"You're driving like a normal person," I remark.

He shrugs. "This is my community. I know these people. They have kids." He waves toward L.A. at large. "Out there? It's a warzone. I was born and raised in L.A., and I know this city backward and forward. I know its traffic patterns, I know where the speed traps are, and where the really dangerous neighborhood are. In here? I live here. I'm not gonna drive like a jackass in here."

"You never answered my question. You said before you got serious about acting. How did you get into it?"

He doesn't answer. He pulls the Bugatti down a long driveway and under an archway into a courtyard. The house is a massive Spanish hacienda-style mansion, with balconies looking into the courtyard, in the center of which is a fountain spewing water. On one side of the courtyard is an expansive wall of garage doors, a few of which are open, showing the tails of various kinds of cars. The Bugatti is parked near the front door, behind a classic cherry-red convertible. I want to say it's a Ford Mustang, but I'm not sure.

Dawson sees me looking at it. "That's a 1969 Ford Mustang Boss 429." I must look baffled. "It's pretty rare, in terms of that year and that particular style."

"Did you build it?"

He nods. "Yeah. Well, *re*built is more accurate. I bought the chassis from a guy in Mendocino, and then found a Boss 429 engine and cleaned it up. It's got the original radio, leather bucket seats—the whole interior is in mint condition and almost entirely original." His expression lights up as he talks about the car, and I get out and follow him over to it. It's a pretty car, I think. More masculine. It fits Dawson perfectly. If I picture him driving, it would be in this car. The Bugatti is a status symbol, I think. He's got the hood open, and he's pointing at various parts of the engine, rattling off facts and figures and names, and I can't possibly keep up or understand anything he's talking about, but God, is it cute watching him get excited. He's a totally different Dawson, talking about his car. His eyes are greenish now, the luminous shade of lichen on stone.

And then I realize he still hasn't answered my question. It seems he's evading it. I let it go and watch him talk, listening and trying not to get pulled into the orbit again. It's a constant battle. His face is animated and boyish and, god, so *so* handsome. The lines and angles of his face are sculpted as if by an artist. I don't believe in God anymore, but if I did, Dawson would be proof of His handiwork.

Eventually Dawson realizes I'm not really following anything he's saying and stops mid-sentence, blushing. He rubs the back of his neck and grins sheepishly at me. "Shit, I just went all guy on you, didn't I?" He closes the hood, grabs me by the hand, and pulls me toward the front door. "Sorry. Cars are my thing, and I kind of nerd out when I talk about them."

I can't help grinning at him. "It was cute."

"Great. 'It was cute.' That's the kiss of death for a guy."

"What's that supposed to mean? It *was* cute. It's not a bad thing." I follow him through the front door and into an echoing foyer with an elaborate faux-candle chandelier.

"Grey, no guy ever likes to be called 'cute.' Cute is the diametric opposite of sexy."

I feel myself blush furiously, and he gives me that look again, the one that says he doesn't understand how I don't know what he's talking about. "You blush at the drop of a hat, you know that?" He touches my cheek with his fingertip, and my skin burns where he touches me. I want to pull away, but I can't. My clear discomfort amuses him even more. "Where did you grow up that you're so innocent?"

I sigh. "I grew up in Macon, Georgia." He gives me an …*and?* look. I turn away from him and busy myself with examining a suit of armor that stands between the two wings of the curved staircase. "I was sheltered, okay? Just…just leave it at that." I'm nowhere near ready to tell him about my upbringing.

"Sheltered, huh?" He moves to stand behind me, and even though I can't see him or even feel him, as he's not touching me, I can sense his presence like an inferno. "So how'd you go from a sheltered girl in Macon to a stripper in L.A.?"

I almost managed to forget, for a split second, how I earn my living. It's Thursday, the last of my three days off; I work Friday through Monday. On Tuesday, I'm relieved that I'm not working, that I can just be me and not have to perform. On Wednesday, the awful fact of what I do has receded just a bit, fading to the back of my mind as I focus on school and the internship. By Thursday I can almost forget. I can almost pretend I'm just Grey, a normal college student. And then Friday rolls around, and I'm forced back into reality: I'm a stripper. I take off my clothes for money, for men's sexual fantasy and desire.

Thursday is my golden day. It's my only day to be Grey, just Grey. And now Dawson has to go and remind me.

I'm filled with an unreasoning rage. I whirl and yell, "Desperation, okay?" shoving him backward, not to hurt him, but out of raw anger and frustration. "I didn't have a choice! It was the only job opening I could find, and I looked for months. Months! I didn't have any job experience in anything. I ain't got—I don't have anyone to ask for help. I got…I've got nowhere to go. I can't and won't go back to Georgia.

My scholarships ran out, and those covered everything from tuition to room and board and books. I hate it. I hate it. I hate…I hate it!" In my upset, the Georgia twang is seeping in.

I'm sobbing, and I can't stop. I turn away from him again, stumble, and sink to the cold marble floor. It all breaks out, all the emotions I've kept bottled up for months now. The loneliness, the homesickness, the shame and the guilt. It doesn't come out as words, but as raw and ragged sobs.

I feel him kneel beside me, feel his arms go around me. I push at him, but I've got no strength left and he's too strong and too warm and comforting.

"You're not alone anymore, Grey." It's the worst possible thing he can say to me. If I was sobbing before, it turns into a storm of tears, into whatever comes after sobbing.

He doesn't say anything else. He just holds me, there on the floor of his foyer, and lets me cry. I wish I could say this outburst is cathartic, but it's not. It's just necessary. A crisis of self-pity. It doesn't help. It doesn't change anything.

"Let me go," I say, struggling against him.

"No." His voice is gentle but firm, and his arms unrelentingly strong.

"Please. Just let me go. I'm fine."

"Bullshit."

"What do you want from me?" I give up struggling and go limp, but I'm tense.

"The truth about yourself?"

It's the one thing I can't give, won't give. I don't know what the truth is, and even if I did, Dawson isn't someone I could explain it to. He's Dawson Kellor, Hollywood movie star. I'm just Grey from Macon, Georgia.

His phone chirps in his pocket, and even though he doesn't move to answer it, it's a reminder of reality. His arms are around me, warm and comforting, and I want to stay here forever, just like this, because I can almost…*almost* forget about who I am and who he is and the reality that's waiting for me.

Almost.

His lips brush the shell of my ear, and I tremble, shocked by the tenderness and the intimacy of the moment.

But I can't afford to let myself think this means anything. That text message from Ashley M reminded me of an important fact: Dawson Kellor and I come from two drastically different worlds. I got sucked in and hypnotized by the intensity and charm and ruggedly masculine beauty that is Dawson. But then, I'm not alone in that, am I? He's paid millions of dollars to be that way. He graces the silver screen and gives Oscar-worthy performances because of that ability, that innate seductiveness. It's in him, a part of him.

He seduces without trying. He's an accidental incubus. His quicksilver eyes draw you in, one moment hazel, a muddy and serene gray-green-blue, and then he gets excited and they're greenish, or he's angry and they're blue. His body seduces, too, the angles of his shoulders and the line of his jaw, the exotic lift of his cheekbones, the power of his hands and the broad expanse of his shoulders and the tapered hardness of his waist. His lithe and lethal grace is hypnotic, too, in the way he moves like a leopard in the African grass, even if it's just striding down a sidewalk.

I got sucked into all this, but I can't afford to let it happen again. He doesn't know me, nor I him. We're not friends. We're not lovers. He kissed me, but that means nothing. To a man like Dawson, a kiss is no more than a handshake. He's used to a night of sex and then a quick goodbye. It's an exchange of pleasure for him. Nothing more.

For me, sex is a mystery. A fantasy. A dream. The future. It's always been the future. Someday I'll meet the right guy; that was my teenage philosophy. Now, I just want to graduate and get a job and be able to stop working at Exotic Nights. I want to stop stripping. I don't think of the future, except for a vague idea of hope that it'll get better. Dawson isn't the future. He's my present, and he's nothing to me. Nor I to him. I'm not an object of desire, except in that he's seen me naked and wants me for that one night of pleasure.

And I want more. I want a future.

I shake myself then breathe deeply. When I've established a sense of equilibrium, I stand up, and now Dawson lets me. I feel his eyes on me as I straighten my skirt and tighten my ponytail. "Thank you."

He stands up, and his hands go to my waist. I don't even think about it for several seconds, because it just feels so…right. But then I remember and step away.

"Are you okay?" he asks. His eyes are back to muted hazel, but his expression shows his concern.

I nod. "I'm fine."

"You're a woman. 'Fine' has a lot of meanings."

A clock tolls somewhere, marking the half-hour.

"I'm fine. I'm okay. I'm sorry I lost it like that," I say with forced professionalism. "Your meeting is in half an hour. You should change."

"Grey…" He reaches for me.

I tug at the hem of my shirt. "Where's your bathroom? I should clean up if we're going to Spago."

"I don't care about the meeting. Have a drink with me. Talk to me."

"Talk about what?" I meet his eyes briefly. "It's nothing for you to worry about."

"But I am worrying about it," he says and I can tell he's being sincere.

"Well…don't. It doesn't matter." I turn and move deeper into the house, figuring I'll find a bathroom on my own. I have to get away from him. It's too easy to believe he actually cares.

"Damn it, Grey. Just stop. I'm not stupid; it's obvious you're not okay." He's still standing in the foyer near the suit of armor.

I find a half-bathroom and stop in the doorway, look at him, and smile. It's fake, though, and he knows it. "Maybe not, but it's not your problem. I'm just the intern. My private life isn't part of the assignment."

"You're not just an assignment. I didn't meet you as Grey the intern. I met you as Gracie, the stripper. But that's not you, and you don't belong there." He moves toward me, bulky and intimidating, his eyes freezing me in place. "I knew it then, and I know it now. I can't…I can't even picture you there. You're so much more than that shitty club."

"But that's my reality. It's all there is. You…we barely know each other. Just—stop confusing me, okay? Please?" I'm shrinking away from him, backing into the bathroom. Whenever he's this near, just inches away with his eyes on me, dark and inscrutable, I can't think and can't remember why I'm supposed to stay away from him.

"Confusing you? How am I confusing you?"

"You just do. Everything about you. You talk to me and act like you know me. Like…we're something." My backside hits the sink, and he's right there and I have nowhere to go.

"Why does that confuse you?"

"Because it's not true?" I hate that it comes out as a question, like there's doubt.

"But what if it is? What if I do know you? What if we are something…or could be?" His hands rise to rest on my hips, and I feel myself being drawn back to him, closer and closer.

His mouth draws nearer, his eyes inches from mine. No, this can't happen again. I lose more of myself every time he kisses me. But that's not true. It's what I feel *should* be true. The reality is that I gain more of myself when he kisses me. As if layers of lies and confusion and shame fall away, and everything is just him and me and our mouths and the sensation of his kiss.

It happens.

His lips touch mine, and everything else falls away. I'm possessed by him. He kisses me with the same effortless mastery that he drives his car. He pulls a moan from me, draws my body against his and molds me to him and guides me into a place of acquiescence, with just his mouth and hands.

I'm not just letting him kiss me; I'm kissing him back. My mouth moves, my lips taste his, my hands settle on his chest between us and curl into his shirt, and I'm pressing in against him, crushing my curves against his angles. I'm taking part, I'm encouraging.

His hand slips from the upper bell of my hip down and around to cup my backside, and a spark is lit inside me. It's a forbidden touch, a familiar, possessive, erotic, provocative gesture. It's a step toward *more*.

A kiss is just a kiss, but his hand on my bottom, holding me and owning me like that…it's more.

I *like* it. Heat builds in my belly at his grip on my bottom. One hand, and then, when I don't stop him…two. Both hands on my backside. Just holding at first. Then exploring and caressing in slow, expanding circles. His fingers claw in, dig into the muscle, grip tightly, release, and grip again. Caress gently, circle and hold. He lifts me closer. I feel his desire.

I moan into his kiss. He lifts farther and I'm sitting on the edge of the sink. Of their own volition, my traitor legs curl around his waist. His hands hold me aloft, and his mouth is devouring mine. I'm losing myself. He sets me back on the counter and the sink's lip hits my tailbone, wakes me from my trance.

I break the kiss, push weakly at him. "No, stop. Stop. I can't…we can't."

He doesn't let go, and neither do I.

"Why?" he asks, his voice a harsh, ragged whisper.

"I can't. We can't." I don't know how to formulate a reason because I can't remember the reason.

I don't know what lies beyond the kissing. Intellectually, I *know* what lies beyond is sex. But that's a foreign land. A myth. An unreal idea. A scary notion of naked bodies and intrusion, vulnerability and pregnancy. Sin.

And I'm not ready for that, but I can't say that to Dawson.

I don't know how to formulate any of this into words.

"We're not…this isn't…" I grasp at anything to tell him, even cheap half-truths that aren't real reasons. "We're from different worlds. It won't work. And I'm your employee."

He backs away, and I see the knowledge of my lies on his face, in the hardness of his eyes. "Yeah. Okay. It's not you, it's me. We're too different." He spins on his heel. "Whatever."

And then he's gone and I'm partially on the sink, one heeled foot dangling over the marble floor, the knee of my other leg cocked across the counter. I turn and catch a glimpse of myself in the mirror; my makeup is smeared and running, my hair is rumpled, my clothes wrinkled and out of place. My eyes are sad, and my lips swollen.

I look lost.

Exactly how I feel.

I force myself to go through the motions of cleaning up, and then Dawson is outside the bathroom, dressed in a pair of pressed chinos and a white polo shirt. "Let's go, Miss Amundsen. Time to work. We're late." His tone is hard and formal.

I follow, having gotten what I asked for.

He doesn't say a word all the way to the restaurant.

CHAPTER TEN

I CAN'T BREATHE. I'm behind the curtain at Exotic Nights, waiting to go out for my first stage dance of Friday night. My heart is palpitating, beating so hard I swear I can see it thumping under my skin. My stomach is roiling with nausea, so hard I'm not sure I'll make it through this number without vomiting. I force a deep breath. I can do this. Nothing has changed. Nothing is different.

But that's a lie. Such a lie. Everything is different. I'm different.

The deep breath turns into a low whining moan in the back of my throat. Candy is finishing her dance, and now Timothy is introducing me. The crowd of men goes wild. I even hear a few female voices. I still find it odd that women visit strip clubs like this.

"…Please help me welcome…Gracie!" Timothy shouts into the mic.

My cue. I run my palms over my stomach as if that will settle it, and then down my hips. I have to force my feet to move, force myself out onto the stage. The whistles and cheers and lewd shouts increase to a crescendo. Stage lights blind me. I have to blink several times, and I peer into the sea of faces. I see no one I know, thank god.

I close my eyes, do my best to empty myself of my nerves, and then begin my routine. I open my eyes and stare into the middle distance, not looking at any one face. As usual, by the end, I have over a hundred dollars in ones, fives, and a few tens. Tears mingle with the sweat on my face.

I rush back to the dressing room and the tiny bathroom, dropping the fistful of bills on the vanity as I pass. I close the toilet lid and sit down, letting the tears go.

Dawson's face emerges in my mind's eye.

You don't belong here. You're so much more than that shitty club.

All I can see, though, is the closed-off hardness of his eyes as we sat through the business dinner. I took notes, chimed in with a few ideas, and pretended that I didn't see the hurt lingering behind Dawson's shuttered expression. He had Greg take me home and walk me to my door.

Before he left, Greg handed me a business card. "You need anything, call me." He wiped at his forehead with a knuckle. "This is from me, not him."

When I got up the next morning, the Rover was back in the parking lot, and the keys were in my mailbox with a note.

It had two words: *Be safe*. It was signed with a casually dramatic letter "D" and nothing else. I still walked to classes but drove to work, grateful for his thoughtfulness even in the face of our awkward situation.

A fist pounds on the dressing room door. "Come on, Grey," Timothy shouts. "Time to work the floor. It's a busy Friday—we don't have time for your emotional bullshit."

I splash water on my face, touch up my makeup, and work the floor. I hate this part as much as dancing on stage. I'm face to face with raw lust.

I make a killing, which is good since tuition is due soon. The end of my shift nears, and the club begins to empty. I do two more stage numbers, and I cry after each one.

I leave the stage after my last dance, cry, retouch my makeup, and hit the floor for a few last table and lap dances. It's almost three in the morning, and the club is mostly empty, except for a few scattered guys by themselves or in small knots. I'm about to clock out when a man gestures to me. He's young and good-looking, dressed in what was a fancy suit, except now his jacket is off, and his dress shirt is unbuttoned and the tie removed. His torso is bare between the edges of his expensive shirt, tan and hard-looking and rippling with muscle. His eyes are glazed and unfocused, he's sweating and his hand holding his beer shakes slightly. He eyes me hungrily, gaze lingering on my chest and hips. I unconsciously re-tie the knot in my shirt to make sure my breasts stay in place; his gaze narrows at the gesture.

I stop a few feet away from him. "Five bucks for a table dance, ten for a lap dance."

He pulls out a twenty, folded into fourths, and extends it between his index and middle finger. "Jus' dance for me. Bring it over here." His words are slurred, but his gaze is sharp and dangerous-looking.

A chill runs up my spine as I force myself closer to him. I suck in oxygen and make myself shimmy a little. He watches, lifting his beer bottle to his lips at frequent intervals. I make it sexier, swaying my hips, bending at the waist to give a glimpse down my cleavage. I force myself closer, and he smiles.

"Turn aroun'," he slurs.

I turn around and shake my backside at him in time to the beat of the pop song on the house speakers. I arch my back and lean forward, pushing my bottom at his face. I feel his hands touch me, and I shift away from him. "Ah-ah. No touching."

He doesn't answer, just smiles with a leering curl of his lip. "Take off th' shirt, babe."

I smile back at him. "That's only for stage dances. This is what you get on the floor. You want that, I can bring Candy or Monica over for you."

He digs in his hip pocket and brings out a wad of hundred dollar bills and counts out ten. He rolls them up, and tucks them into the back pocket of my shorts, shoving the wad back into his pants pocket. "I said…*take it off*." He hisses the last part clearly and lucidly, and my skin crawls at the threat of violence in the sound of his voice, in the anger of his gaze.

I withdraw the roll of money and hand it back to him. "I'm sorry, sir, but that's not what I do."

He sneers at me, then pulls out the wad of cash again. He shoves it all at me. "You're greedy, huh, bitch? 'S almost four grand there. Now. Show me your tits."

I back away from him. "I don't think so." I let my voice harden and glance around for Hank, the bouncer. He's watching from the chair by the entrance and stands up when I wiggle my fingers at him.

The customer watches Hank rise to his feet, all six-foot-six of him, and then back to me. "What kinda fuckin' stripper are you, bitch? Won't even take off your shirt for a lap dance? Shit. It's not like I asked you to blow me or some shit. I come to a strip bar expecting to see some tits. You're gonna turn down four grand to do what you do anyway? Stupid bitch." He climbs unsteadily to his feet, drains his beer. He fumbles with the wad of money, then curses under his breath and tosses it on the table. "Fuck it. Fuck it, and fuck you." He stumbles toward the door, with Hank trailing behind him. He stops in the doorway, wavering, turns back and stares at me, and something in his gaze makes me afraid. Hank gives him a gentle nudge out the door, and then he's gone.

I gather the wad of money off the table and count it; there's $3,900 in hundreds and fifties. I glance at Candy, Monica, and Iris, who are counting their own tips at the bar while drinking margaritas. Candy is still naked except for her thong, her huge breasts brushed with glitter of some kind. Monica and Iris are in dressing gowns open to their navels. I'm the only one of the girls who works at the club who stays clothed…except for when I'm dancing on stage. Not that the shirt counts as clothed, necessarily, since my breasts are basically bared.

All three women pretend not to watch me. Candy is working to keep a roof over her and her teenaged son's heads, Monica has a severely autistic son with special medical needs, and Iris is like me, working her way through school. All of them are as desperate for cash as I am.

I recount the money, adding a hundred from my tips, dividing it evenly four ways, then deposit the stacks of a thousand dollars in front of each of the other girls. "I didn't really do anything to earn this," I say. "It's only fair that I spread it around."

Candy shoots me a grateful glance. "You didn't have to do that, honey. It was your table."

I shrug. "It's fine. He didn't really mean to leave it, he was just too hammered to get it back into his pocket."

The girls laugh, as we've all seen men leave too drunk to even know their own names. Usually, though, they don't leave thousands of dollars lying around. The girls all hug me as thanks, finish their drinks, and cut their tips. I sit at the bar, but Brad brings me a Sprite; he knows I don't drink. With the extra grand, I've pulled in more than $1,500 tonight, which means I'll have enough to pay the university and still buy the new pair of heels I've been needing for the internship. Tim had left around midnight, leaving Brad and Hank to close up. The girls leave before me, so Brad's Explorer, Hank's F-350, and my borrowed Rover are the only cars in the lot.

I dress in yoga pants, flip-flops, and a loose pink T-shirt that slips off the round of one shoulder. I'm grateful to have a bra on again, as spending so many hours without one is uncomfortable, given the size and weight of my breasts. Hank walks me out because

I'm parked near the back of the lot. He realized half-way across the lot that he'd forgotten his keys and headed back in. The parking lot is empty and I'm only twenty feet from where I parked so I don't wait. A street lamp sheds sickly orange light on the edge of the lot, casting long, deep shadows. I've done this dozens of time but for some reason, my skin crawls. I stop in the center of the lot, considering going back in and waiting for Hank to walk me to my car, but my car is right there. I click the "unlock" button on the Rover key fob and the lights blink and turn on. As I move closer, the hair on the back of my neck prickles. My heart is suddenly hammering. I peer into the shadows, clutching the keys until my knuckles turn white. I tell myself there's nothing to be afraid of.

Then, as I reach for the handle of the car door, I realize there is something to be afraid of. A cold, clammy hand closes on my wrist and jerks me back-ward into a hard male chest. Hot breath on my ear smells of beer. Cruel fingers dig into my ribs, clutch upward, grasp my left breast hard enough to steal my breath.

"Now…now you'll take it off." His voice is an evil murmur in my ear.

He grasps the neck of my shirt where it hangs over my shoulder and tugs it down, almost gently at first, then with increasing force until it begins to rip and pull at my neck. He lets go of my wrist to clap a hand over my mouth. His other hand darts down my shirtfront. His fingers dig into my breast, pinching and mashing. I whimper, and then find my resolve. I lift my foot and smash down on his instep. He doesn't release me but hops on one foot, cursing. I don't have time to kick him again before his hand leaves my mouth and curls around my throat with brutal strength. My air supply is cut off, and I can't scream. He shoves me forward against the cool car door, hand around my throat. His other hand yanks down my yoga pants, shoving them down on one side, then the other. My panties go with them. I kick and thrash, but I'm backwards and can't breathe. His grip on my throat tightens.

I hear the *zzzzzrrrhhriiip* of his zipper going down, and then something hard yet soft and warm nudges against my thigh. I can't get air. My vision is blurring. I feel the thing touching my leg. I try to scream, and thrash even harder, panic welling in me. His grip on my throat unrelenting. I'm seeing spots, darkness dancing in my eyes.

"You want this." He whispers it in my ear, his breath hot and foul. "I know you want it."

A lucid thought strikes me: I'm being raped.

Another thought: I'm going to die.

His hand rips at my shirt, and it's gone. He rips at my bra, freeing my breasts. He's clutching at my boobs, crushing them, and the hard, thick thing on my skin prods and pokes, and I'm trying to scream, trying to fight, but I'm dizzy and can't breathe. My pants are around my knees, and a thigh wedges between mine, forcing my knees apart.

No.

No.

No.

I can't stop it from happening.

And then he's gone, just suddenly gone, and I'm off balance, sucking in cool sweet air, stumbling. I fall, tripping on my tangled pants. I hit my head on the car door so hard I see stars. I hear sounds behind me. Thumps. Wet thwacks, groans. Pained growls. Flesh on flesh.

I can only writhe in agony and try to breathe, seeing stars, head throbbing.

A voice above me: "Fuck. *Fuck!* Grey?" It's Dawson.

I can't even moan. I'm gasping, my throat raw and throbbing. I cough, suck at the oxygen.

I feel Dawson's gentle hands touch me. He tugs at my pants, pulling them up. Even though it's him, I shrink away from his touch.

"Ssshh. It's okay. It's me. It's Dawson. I'm here. You're okay." He puts a hand under the small of my back and lifts me slightly off the ground, tugging my pants in place. "I've got you. I'm gonna put my shirt on you, okay?"

He does something, and the remnants of my bra, which I realize got ripped somehow, fall away. I sob again, a shuddering indrawn breath, and Dawson's palm smooths down my cheek, wiping at the tears I realize are pouring down. "It's okay, Grey. You're okay."

My head throbs, and there's something wet and sticky on the back of my head. "Head…" I moan. "Think 'm…bleeding."

Dawson curses, and I hear fabric rustling, and then something soft that smells of Dawson is eased over my head. He takes my hand in his and gently guides my arm through the hole, like I'm a child, does the same thing to the other side. I'm dressed, now, covered, and it eases the pounding terror in my gut. Dawson saved me.

I sob then, and Dawson's hand touches my fore-head, brushes away tears. Fingers curl tenderly under my neck and help me sit up, and I hear a whispered "fuck" from Dawson as he sees the blood. I watch him grab the ripped shred of my pink T-shirt and press it to the back of my head, and then his arm goes beneath my legs and he lifts me easily. The door of his Mustang is open, the engine idling with a noisy animal rumble. He sets me in the passenger seat, leans over me to click off the radio, which is playing the heavy metal I've come to associate with Dawson. I'm dizzy, seeing double, and I'm tired. I glance out into the parking lot, and I see a lump on the asphalt, dark pants, and a white shirt stained red. A pool of dark liquid glints around one end of the form. It's him, the rapist.

He's not moving.

Dawson has his phone to his ear and he's murmuring into it. "…Piece of shit…yeah, he's pretty fucked up….I don't know, maybe? Just take care of it, okay? Got it. 'Bye."

He shoves the phone into his pocket and stalks back to the Mustang, folding his tall frame into the driver's seat. A glance at his face scares me. He's lost in a murderous rage, his eyes all pupil, jaw clenching and teeth grinding, all angles and anger. His eyes catch mine and go soft. He glances out his window, catches sight of my attacker, and slams the shifter into reverse, guns the engine, and we spin around in a backward circle. Another violent jerk of the shifter, and we're rocketing forward out of the parking lot and onto the deserted street.

I wonder if I'm the reason for his anger. He had to save me at three in the morning, when I rejected him.

He's driving with mad precision, hitting over ninety and a hundred miles per hour on the straight stretches of road, blowing through red lights and taking turns in wide, drifting, squealing arcs. Red and blue lights flash behind us, but Dawson drives on unheeding. He jerks us through a dizzying series of lefts and rights in a random subdivision, squeals to a stop, and reverses suddenly into a narrow alley-way, shutting off his headlights. The police car flies by, siren howling. I can only clench the armrest in white-knuckled fingers and try to breathe. Dawson is still seething, his breathing coming in long, deep gasps, as if he's trying to contain himself and barely succeeding.

"Dawson, I'm sorry." I can't quite look at him. "You can just take me home now. I'm fine." I press the shirt to the back of my head, and the pressure hurts, but when I pull the cotton away, it's only lightly blotted with blood. I press again, and it comes away clean.

He glances at me in utter confusion. "Sorry? What?" He stares at me for a long moment before understanding. "Oh, Jesus. You think I'm mad at *you*?"

I shrug. "I guess. I mean…I don't know. You're scaring me, though."

He reaches out and places his palm on my knee. "Babe, I'm mad *for* you, not *at* you."

"I don't…I don't understand."

He frowns, and then sighs. "I'm taking you home. *My* home. We'll talk there."

"But…I'm okay. I'd rather go to my dorm."

"Too bad." He pulls the Mustang out of the alley and onto the main road, and from there to the highway. Once we're on the freeway, he puts the muscle car through her paces, accelerating steadily but evenly until the needle is buried. Going a hundred or more in a Bugatti is like being on a jet—the sense of speed is contained and dampened by the expensive hand-crafted shocks and whatever else. Going a hundred and twenty in a classic 1960s muscle car is terrifying. You feel every bit of the speed. You feel closer to the road, as if you're strapped to a rocket that could wobble off-course at any second.

"Can you slow down a little, please?" I ask.

He shoots me a split-second glance, perhaps seeing that my hands are frantically clutching at the armrest and the dashboard. I feel him back off the accelerator immediately. "Sorry."

I can sense the questions in him. I have plenty of my own.

I want my bed. I want the familiar surroundings of my dorm. It's not much, but it's all I have.

He's not taking me there, though. We're pulling up to the gate and Dawson's waving at a middle-aged uniformed guard in the guardhouse, and then we're under the arch and softly jerking to a stop in front of his doors. I barely have time to register that we've stopped before the car is off and Dawson beside me unbuckling me and lifting me from the car. I should protest but I'm dizzy, and my neck won't support my head. I'm so tired. I lay my head on his shoulder and let my eyes close.

Dawson glances at me, and then his voice rouses me. "Grey, no. You gotta stay awake for me, okay? You might have a concussion. You can't sleep yet, okay?" He sets me down briefly, and I sway against him as he unlocks his front door and shoves it open, then lifts me again through the entry and kicks the door closed. I never got beyond the hallway with the half-bath the last time I was here. His footsteps echo on the marble of the foyer, and I see through cracked eyelids that we're passing through an open-plan kitchen and into a huge but comfortable-look-ing living room. He sets me down gently on a deep leather couch.

I can't help staring at him as he hovers over me. His jaw is brushed with dark stubble, making him look a little older and a little harder. I notice that he has dots of crimson crusted on his forehead and cheekbones, and on his shirt. I reach up without thinking and scrape at the blood on his cheek with my thumbnail.

Dawson jerks away, scrubbing at his face and star-ing at his hand, at the flakes of dried blood. "Shit. I've got his blood on me."

"Is he—"

Dawson interrupts me. "He's none of your concern." He moves into the kitchen and comes back with a bottle of peroxide, a wad of paper towel, and a bag of ice. He examines my head with something resembling professional tenderness, dabbing at the cut with a peroxide-dampened paper towel. I wince at the sting, but it only lasts a moment.

"What's Greg going to do with him?"

Dawson shrugs. "That's not a question I want to know the answer to. I hired Greg because he scares the fuck out of me. He used to be president of a biker gang that made the Hell's Angels look like a bunch of tea-sipping pussies. Except Greg also has a degree in business from Brown. So yeah, don't piss him off."

I have to ask. "Do you think he's dead? The guy who tried to—who attacked me?"

"Do you care?"

I shrug. "I don't know. I just—"

"Listen, babe. He tried to rape you. He would have killed you. He nearly did, and you've got the bruises on your throat to prove it. Don't think about that piece of shit anymore, okay? He's gone, and he won't hurt you or anyone else ever again. That's all that matters. His blood is on me, and Greg. Not you."

"But you can't just—"

"Grey." Dawson moves to sit next to me, and I want to curl into him. Let him hold me. I stay still and try to keep my turbulent feelings in check. "Stop worrying about that fucking pile of scum. Okay? Please? He doesn't deserve your pity. If he's dead, it's too good for him. He deserves to suffer." The vehemence in his voice and in his eyes makes me shiver.

I look away and focus on breathing, in and out. Dawson is a huge, hot, confusing presence beside me, and I'm filled with sensory memories of his arms around me and his lips on me…and then the memory shifts abruptly, and I feel again a hand clamping over my mouth and hear the hiss of *his* voice, and I gag.

Dawson pulls me into his lap as I start to shake and sob, his arms curling around me. I tense initially, sure that the feeling of male arms holding me will trigger the horror again, but it doesn't. I feel safe with Dawson. He protected me.

"It's okay, Grey. You're safe." His mouth is beside my ear, whispering.

Then, something odd happens: Dawson presses a soft kiss to my temple. It's…tender. It's a kiss designed to soothe, to comfort. Not to ignite desire or passion. It confuses me, and it makes me feel…loved. Cared for.

And that is something I can't handle.

My instinct is to flee, but I can't move. I simply cannot make myself leave the protective cocoon of Dawson's embrace, and I don't want to. My confusion and fear aren't strong enough to push me out of his arms. It's a bad dream, a nightmare, and it's fading quickly.

I stop crying after a while, and I let myself be safe in Dawson's arms. His mouth brushes my temple again, and then the curve of my ear. He settles a blanket around me, and his hands skate up and down my arms and across my back and shoulders, keeping me soothed and warm.

I yawn, and Dawson shifts beneath me, cradles his arms under my knees and around my shoulders, stands up with me. I'm sleepy, emotionally, mentally, and physically exhausted. Dawson's shirt is soft cotton and smells of him. He's warm, and his muscles shift under my hands as I cling to him, like stones beneath silk. I let my head settle against his chest and absorb the feeling of comfort, of being cared for. It's so unfamiliar. Ever since Mama died, I've felt alone. Unloved, unnoticed.

He carries me up the stairs, down a long hallway and up three more stairs, through a pair of open French doors and into a cavernous master bedroom. The bed is the only furniture besides a huge flat-screen TV on the wall opposite and a pair of nightstands on either side of the bed. He carries me to the bed, leans against it, and sets me down.

My heart stops, and my breath catches in my throat. I'm tense all over.

And now here's Dawson, this god, this iconic movie star, this all-too-real man, and he's paying attention to *me*. As if I mean something to him. As if he wants something from me that I don't know how to give. I don't even know what he wants, honestly.

Well, that's not true. I do. He wants sex. I know this. I see it and sense it. It's in the way he touches me, in the way he kisses me. I know it, because that's what men want from me. It's what he wants from me. And I don't know how to give it. But I get the feeling he also might want something else from me. Something more. But that's not his style. Nothing I've ever heard about him has said he wants anything from a woman he's involved with but sex.

All this runs through my head as he grabs at the pile of throw pillows neatly arranged on the bed and tosses them to the floor two at a time. Then he reaches under the pillows and tugs the blanket down until it's stopped by my body. "Slide under," he says.

I tuck my legs beneath the blanket and lie back into the pillows, watching Dawson like a hawk. Is this where it happens? Now? In his room? My heart is pounding, but I'm still barely breathing. My fingers clutch at the edge of the blanket. Dawson moves across the room toward a pair of closed French doors, which he opens to reveal a closet larger than two of the dorm rooms at USC put together. There's an island in the center with a marble countertop, and an actual sitting area complete with a deep leather chair. Dawson peels his shirt off and tosses it into a nearby hamper, and then his shorts. He's in nothing but a pair of tight black boxer-briefs. My throat closes, and my fingers curl into fists at the sight of him. He's… nothing short of glorious. The muscles in his back are clearly defined, rippling as he moves. His shoulders are like slabs of granite, and his arms thick and bulging with muscle. I simply cannot take my eyes off him as he opens a drawer, pulls out a pair of gym shorts, and turns toward me as he shoves one foot through and then the other. He tugs the shorts up, but not before I catch a glimpse of the front of him. Of the bulge in his underwear. My eyes are drawn there, almost instinctively.

I blush and look away quickly, but he saw me staring. The corner of his mouth tilts and tightens into a small quirk of a smile, quickly gone. He moves toward me, and I'm tense once more, staring at the ridged field of his abs and the narrow column of his waist, the inward cut of muscle where his hips guide inward to his groin. My mouth is dry as he approaches. I'm not breathing, not moving, not thinking. I'm totally panicked.

He sees it in my face, and raises his hands. "Relax, Grey." His voice is a low, soothing rumble. "You need to sleep. I'm just going to hold you. If you'd rather not, I can sleep in one of the empty bedrooms."

Just going to hold me. I've never slept in a bed with a man before. Not ever, in my whole life. My dad used to tuck me in as a little girl, but that stopped around nine or ten. I don't know what to say, what to think, what to even want. I'm scared, exhausted, and nervous.

"I don't want to be alone," I murmur. It's the only true thing I know right now.

He carefully slides into the bed beside me, then curses when he realizes the overhead light is on. He gets up and turns it off, and the room is enveloped in sudden shadows. A slim sliver of lesser darkness carves across the room from the doorway, but all else is pitch black. I'm not afraid of the dark; I'm afraid of my confused welter of emotions regarding this man.

The bed dips, and I feel the warmth of his nearness. I hear him breathing. His hand touches mine, and our fingers tangle.

"Are you okay?" he asks. "For real?"

I don't answer right away. It's a serious question. "I don't know. I don't know how to feel. It was… terrifying, and so sudden. He was in the club. He was the last customer there, and he asked for me. He was…so drunk. Maybe on drugs. I don't know. He was creepy. He wanted a dance, and he got all mad when I wouldn't take my shirt off. I—I don't usually do that, you know. If I'm on the floor, I'm wearing the shirt. I only take it off when I do stage dances.

It's basically nothing, that shirt, so it kinda makes the customers act crazy. Like, they can see, but not totally, and it's different." I'm not sure why I'm telling him this, but the words are pouring out, and I can't stop them. "I couldn't do it, being totally topless all night. I hate it enough as it is, but…the whole shift? Ugh. I couldn't. I just couldn't. The customers like the mystery, so Timothy lets me wear it. It's my thing, and I enforce it. I only take my clothes off on the stage or in the VIP rooms. Not that it makes me being a stripper any better, but…it helps, I guess."

It makes it easier that I can't see him, that he can't see how hard this is for me to talk about, although I'm sure he can hear it my voice.

"So you hate it? Being a stripper?"

"God, yes. So much. Every—every single time I do it, I hate it." I shudder, and his fingers tighten around mine. "I—I throw up, pretty much after every stage dance."

"Did you throw up after I left, that first time we met?"

I shake my head, then realize he can't see the gesture. "No. You…that was different somehow. I don't know why."

He doesn't say anything for a long time. "So he got mad that you wouldn't take your clothes off for him, and then left and waited outside for you?"

"I guess so. Hank made him leave when he got too upset. I thought he was gone. I went to my car… your car, I mean." I shudder again, remembering. "I should've…I should've listened to my gut. I had this bad feeling, but I ignored it. I didn't want to seem silly."

"Listen to your gut," Dawson tells me. "Always listen to those feelings."

An awkward silence follows. I don't want to talk about what happened anymore; I just want to forget.

"Why were you there?" I ask. "I mean, how did you happen to be there, right then?"

Once again, Dawson pauses before answering. "I wanted to talk to you. I figured I could catch you after your shift."

"What did you want to talk about?"

I realize now, perhaps belatedly, that the brief pause before answering is a Dawson thing. He thinks before replying, puts together his thoughts and how he'll say them. "You confuse me."

This isn't what I expected him to say. "I…what? What do you mean, I confuse you?"

"You're a contradiction, Grey. I can't figure you out." He rolls toward me, and my eyes have adjusted enough to the darkness that I can just barely make out his features and the glittering hints of his eyes.

His fingers trace my hand, my wrist, gentle caresses and slow exploration. I barely notice as his touch slides carefully up my arm, barely notice as he shifts closer to me with every breath.

"I'm not that tough to understand," I whisper.

He chuckles. "To yourself, maybe. You're you. You know everything about you. But to me, you're a complete contradiction. You mess me up." He's grazing my upper bicep, and now my shoulder over the T-shirt, rubbing my back. I like this. Too much. I couldn't stop it if I tried. "You seem…innocent somehow. You mentioned growing up sheltered, but you closed down when I asked about it. You exude this effortless sensuality, but it's—I don't know, it's not sexual, somehow. Like, it *should* be, considering what you do, but it's not. It's sensual, this weird mix of innocence and raw beauty. I just…I'm not explaining it right. But then, you're a stripper, and you hate it. I could see it. You don't belong in that dirty club. And…you and me. That's the most confusing part. I don't know how to handle you. I want you, that's no secret at this point, I think. I want you so bad I can taste it. I can taste your skin. I've seen you, and I've gotten these little teases of touching you. But…I want all of you. Yet as soon as we get close to things happening, you bolt."

His hand is kneading the muscles of my back, around my spine, down to my waist. My heart begins to thump and pound madly as his touch nears the small of my back and continues downward.

"You're such a mystery," he says, inching his body closer to mine. I can smell him; I can feel his breath on me, intimate. "I think you want me, but I can't tell for sure. And if you do want me, I get the feeling you don't *want* to want me. And, not to sound arrogant or whatever, but there are probably millions of women who would love to get even five minutes with me, yet you consistently run away. I don't know what you want, and I don't know how to find out what you want because you're closed off and touchy and don't answer questions." He says all this gently, as if I might take offense.

And honestly, it's hard not to.

"I'm not trying to be difficult, I just—"

"Tell me one true thing."

"I want you, and you're right that I don't want to want you. You scare me."

"Why?"

"Because you're…so *much*. You're Dawson Kellor. You're…you're Cain Riley. You're the man every woman in America wants. You're the man every man in America wishes he was." I'm so glad for the darkness. I can speak truth in this darkness. "I want you, and it scares me, because I don't know what to do with it. How to handle it. I don't know how to be around you."

"Just be you."

"It's not that easy. I don't—I don't know who I am. I don't know what I am." My voice catches, and I swallow hard. I've cried too much, and I won't do it again. I refuse.

Dawson doesn't answer, but this isn't a pause—this is the silence of a man who knows nothing he says will make it okay, so he doesn't say anything. It's perfect.

After a long moment, he tugs me closer and murmurs, "Let me hold you."

I'm still, totally tensed now. "Hold me?"

"Yeah. Just hold you. No pressure. It's not going anywhere. Just be in the moment with me."

"Okay…" I don't know what he means. I've never been held, except when he's comforted me while I cry. Which, it seems, is the majority of our relationship thus far.

I feel him smile, somehow I sense his amusement at my hesitancy. He slides his arm underneath me, pulls me closer, and now I'm cradled against his bare, warm chest. My head is pillowed in the hollow where arm becomes chest, and I can vaguely hear his heart beating, and his hand is skating over my shoulder blades and down to the gap where his oversized T-shirt has rucked up to bare the skin of my back. I'm pressed all along the length of his body. I find myself tracing the grooves of his abdominal muscles with one finger, and I'm just breathing. I'm not thinking, not trying not to cry, not worrying about bills, not doing homework, not stripping my clothes off. I'm just…here.

It's absolute heaven. My eyes prick and my chest contracts, but I breathe through it.

"This is okay, right?" he mutters into my hair.

I nod. I can't get words out, so I don't bother trying. I'm overwhelmed by the peace I feel. He holds me, and doesn't try to kiss me or touch me.

Sleep takes me, and it's the best I've slept since my mother died.

CHAPTER ELEVEN

THE SMELL OF COFFEE wakes me up. Sunlight is bright on my closed eyelids, and I'm warm. At peace. I drowse in the comfort. There is no worry. I'm no one, just a content blot of warmth floating in nothingness.

Suspended in time where nothing matters.

And then coffee-scent wafts over me, and I drift upward to awareness. At length I open my eyes and see the white space of Dawson's bedroom, the black screen of his trillion-inch TV, a long sliding glass door with opened blinds letting in a gloriously brilliant day and a breath-stopping view of Los Angeles.

And then the most glorious view of all: Dawson in nothing but a pair of gym shorts. His calves are tanned with a scar running diagonally across his left calf, a puckered line of lighter skin. The scar humanizes him somehow. He's not polished and gemstone perfect. God, I got a glimpse of his body last night, but now he's moving with feline grace through his bedroom with a huge mug of coffee in his hand, and his body ripples with each motion. There's a slight dusting of dark hair on his chest, and a thicker trail of black hair leading from his navel to under his shorts. The sight of his nearly naked body sends shivers running through me, sends quavering spears of heat into my belly. It makes me feel…hot, inside. It makes me feel entirely feminine.

Dawson sits on the bed near my knee and smiles. He has a plate in his other hand, a toasted plain bagel with a generous slathering of cream cheese. I sit up, and my stomach rumbles as I smell the bagel.

He's brought me breakfast. In bed. And he's done it shirtless.

Women of America, be jealous.

I snatch half of the bagel off the plate and inhale it, washing it down with swallows of coffee. I burn my tongue, but it doesn't register. I burn my tongue on my coffee every day.

Dawson is watching with a slightly stunned and bemused expression. "In a hurry?"

I set the bagel down slowly, wipe the corner of my lip with my thumb, and then lick the cream cheese off my thumb. I catch Dawson staring at my mouth, and I blush.

"No," I say, fighting embarrassment. "I'm just…
I've always eaten like that, I guess. Especially in the
morning."

"It's cute. You act like the bagel is going to run
away from you." He laughs at my further embarrassment. "Don't slow down on my account. Just relax."

"Relax?" It's an alien concept.

"Yeah." He takes the mug from me and sips some
coffee, then hands it back. "Just…chill. Take today
and spend it with me. Doing whatever. Just hang."

I'm disoriented. "What day is it?"

"It's Saturday. It's a little past eleven. We both
slept in. Usually I'm up by six, but I slept in today."

I gasp. "Eleven?" I haven't slept past seven in years.
"It can't be eleven. I have a paper to finish before
work tonight."

His eyes darken and harden. They've been the
soft, muted hazel of his at-ease mood, and they
instantly shift to the stormy almost-blue of building
anger. "When's the paper due?"

"Tuesday. But I have another paper due
Wednesday, and a test Monday, and I work all weekend, so I have to get it done—"

He silences me by shoving the other half of the
bagel in my mouth.

"Yeah, no. You're done working there." His voice
holds a note of command that has me bristling.

"What? What do you mean, I'm done working there?" I'm talking through a mouthful of bagel, and I swallow it and set aside the rest. "I don't like it, but I don't have a choice in the matter. That's my job. It's how I survive. If this internship works out, Kaz will hire me full-time, but I can't quit until then. I have tuition due…Wednesday, actually, along with room and board for my dorm and food plan. I can't…I can't just quit."

"Yes, you can. How about we make it a condition of the internship? Would that make it easier?"

"No!" I scramble off the bed, away from him, putting the massive California-king bed between us. I'm a mess of emotions that I can't begin to sort out, not with him right there, watching me, calm, quiet, determined, beautiful, and all man. He distracts me from my own anger. "You can't just demand that I quit my job. It doesn't work that way. What, you'll pay my bills until the end of the internship, and then what? What if things at Fourth Dimension don't work out? I'm supposed to just—just depend on you? I don't think so, Dawson. No."

"Don't you want to quit?" He's maddeningly calm.

"Yes. More than you could ever possibly comprehend. But I can't." It comes out "cain't."

"Sure you can. You can make the choice to trust me. Let someone help you."

"I'm not a charity case. I can take care of myself."

He stands up and paces away. Even his back is sexy and seductive and hypnotic. "I *know* that, Grey. Goddammit. I'm just trying to—"

"To what? Tie me to you? Make me one of your booty calls?"

He whirls, and before I can blink he's across the room, around the bed, and has me pinned to the wall with his body. His eyes are blue, angry, hot. His body is hard and huge and he's breathing heavily, and his hands are on my arms and his mouth is inches away. "I'm trying to be *kind*." He hisses the words. "It's called generosity. You hate what you do, and I hate you having to do it. I can take away your problems, Grey. You just have to let me."

"I can't." I have to look away from him. I can't bear to meet his eyes, can't take the intensity.

Except I look at his mouth, his lips, the pink tip of his tongue running over his bottom lip, and I know what those lips feel like, taste like, and I… I want that again. Even in the midst of my weltering boil of emotions, I can't help the confused desire I feel for him.

"You can. You just won't. Big difference, babe."

"Don't…don't call me 'babe,'" I say. "I'm not your babe."

"You could be." He drops this bomb calmly.

"I…what?" My eyes flick to his, stunned.

"I said: 'You could be.'"

"What does that mean?" I wish I had the fortitude to move away from him, out of his embrace, away from his touch.

I don't.

He stares down at me, into me. "Do I have to spell it out?"

"Yes."

"Be mine. Be with me." He's whispering. His hands are rock steady, but his eyes flick back and forth, the only sign of nerves.

"Have sex with you, you mean. Be a one-night stand, you mean."

He growls. "No. Fuck. No, Grey. I mean, yes, I want to be with you. But…in every way. *With* you." He runs his hands down my arms, to my waist, to my hips, and he lifts me up. My legs instinctively go around his waist and his hands are on my backside, and I feel him all around me, so, so close. "I want to kiss you whenever I feel like it. I want to tell you when you're being ridiculous. I want to make love to you. I want to fuck you. I want to hold you. I want to be yours. I don't know you, like, at *all*, but I want all this. It's total craziness. I feel like I should be admitted for saying this to you. Fuck, I should have my man-card revoked for being all emotional and girly and telling you my *feelings*. But…I'm nothing if not honest. So there it is."

I can't breathe. I'm not hyperventilating; I'm whatever the opposite of that is. My lungs are burning because I'm literally not breathing. I'm staring into his eyes and hearing his words and completely at a loss. I can't believe it.

"Say something, Grey. Jesus. I just put my goddamn heart out on a wire for you, and you're not saying anything." His voice is a harsh whisper.

"You want that?" I swallow. "With me? But… you don't know things about me. You don't…you don't do that. You don't have girlfriends."

He frowns. "No, I have—rather, I've *had*—a shitload of girlfriends. Girlfriends are a dime a dozen. I could snap my fingers and have six girlfriends, one for every day of the week and Sunday off. I don't want that. I've had that. It's boring. I want you." His eyes are going thundercloud gray, dark, threatening. "I don't know anything about you. But that's the point: I want to know."

All I can do is kiss him. It's necessary, more than breathing. He kisses me back tentatively, as if not quite sure I'm really doing this. But I am. I'm kissing him because it's the only answer I have. My legs tighten around his waist, and my hands feather through his hair and cup the back of his head and pull him to me, and I'm beyond desperate.

This man wants *me*.

He spins in place, and suddenly I'm on the bed with Dawson above me. It's so right like this. He's delicious. He tastes like coffee and bagel and the faint trace of toothpaste. His tongue slips between my lips and my teeth and touches my tongue. I'm holding on to him for dear life and kissing him with everything I have, letting him capture my mouth with his, letting him possess my tongue. He pulls away gently, and I'm lost briefly, spiraling with need to have his kiss, and then his teeth take my lower lip, nibble, bite, and then my lip is in his mouth and he's shifting his weight. His hand brushes my hair away from my face, and his eyes are a thousand shades of gray and blue and green and brown, indefinable, indescribable and he's gazing at me as if I hold the answer to every question in his mind. His palm brushes down my neck, and his thumb skates over my jaw, and then down my arm to my waist. His shirt is bunched under my breasts, baring most of my belly; he touches my hip, his palm hot and strong and callused against my soft, white skin. I suck in a breath as he dares upward, touching my ribs. His knuckles brush the underside of my right breast, and I let my eyes fall closed, but he doesn't take my breast in his hand. He just pushes the shirt up a little, and stares down at me. My eyes are closed, but I feel his stare. I let him look. It's not like on stage, though; his gaze is tender. It's too much, and I have to kiss him again, before I completely lose myself in him.

He kisses me, and then pulls away and lowers his mouth to plant a kiss between my breasts. I'm terrified, my heart hammering. His mouth is hot and wet on my skin, and now he's moving his slow kiss down the slope of one breast and my heart beats wildly against my ribs—surely he can feel it pounding?—but he shows no sign of noticing my terror, he just slowly and carefully continues his small, slow kisses all over the round weight of my right breast, until he's ringing my nipple with kisses. My nipple is erect, hard, almost as if begging him to plant a kiss there.

And then he does, and the moan that erupts from me is loud, breathy, and erotic. I feel myself blush at the moan, but I have no time or thought-space for anything else as he sucks my nipple hard, flattening it. I moan again, gasping, writhing underneath him. I've never, ever felt anything like this. It's overwhelming, earth-shattering. I clutch the back of his head as he releases my nipple with a *pop* and then flicks it with his tongue, grazes it with his teeth. Heat and pressure build inside me, centered low in my belly, in my core. It's a desperate pressure, a volcanic need, and I don't know what to do.

While his mouth is busy with my right nipple, his left hand is doing similar things to my left breast, and I'm gasping and breathless, making all sorts of embarrassing noises. I know, deep inside me, that I shouldn't be doing this. My pastor's daughter guilt is kicking in, telling me I'm sinning with this man. I do my best to ignore that little voice, that leftover seed of shame.

He moves his mouth to my left nipple, and his right hand carves over my ribs, over my belly, to my hip, and his fingers slip under the waistband of my yoga pants, and then stops, eyes on mine. I take over for him, pushing my pants down, rolling them away.

I'm helpless. I have no will left, no capacity to resist his touch, no ability to stop this. I know I should, but I can't. I'm so weak. So weak. He's all over me, kissing my mouth, kissing my throat, tweaking my nipples in his fingers, keeping me breathless and restless and writhing, and the pressure is mounting inside me, in my core. I'm damp down there, slick. I press my thighs together in a vain attempt to relieve the pressure, but it does nothing.

My tight black yoga pants are rolled down far enough that the top of my underwear is showing, a strip of red cotton. My eyes are closing and opening, taking in Dawson's face, his eyes as he glances at me, his mouth as he sucks at my nipple and stretches it, making me moan and squirm and gasp as the heat and pressure build to an unbearable level. And then his fingers graze the elastic line of my underwear and pause. I'm completely at his mercy. I *know* that I shouldn't let this happen, that I'm crossing some line I shouldn't cross, but I won't stop it. He's touching me; he owns me. He knows exactly what I need, what I want, even if I don't.

And now, oh, god. His fingers, just his middle and ring fingers are slipping under the elastic to touch the waxed-smooth skin, and I'm trembling all over. I want this. I want him to touch me.

I've never even touched myself there. Never. It was an unspoken sin, shameful and disgusting. And then, as an adult, I had no reason or time. I've never known desire, never known the need to touch myself like he's touching me.

His eyes are greenish now, a color I've never seen in him before. He's watching me as he moves his touch—oh, so gradually, so carefully—downward. My thighs are pressed tight together, but loosen to welcome his touch, as if my body wants this even though my mind, heart and soul are at war. My body responds. His long middle finger is nearing the top of my opening, and then the tip of his finger is slipping inside me. I whimper, a noise of need and fear.

"Tell me to stop," he murmurs. His eyes are on me, and I know he's reading my emotions.

I open my mouth, but no words come out. I just meet his eyes, and then my back lifts and my hips rise, and again my body makes my decision for me. His middle finger sinks deeper inside me, and now a word finally escapes my lips.

His name. "Dawson…" It's a whispered plea, but I don't know if I'm asking for more or begging him to stop.

I'm trembling all over. My knees shake, my hands shake. My lips shiver, and my eyes can't focus. I feel his finger between my lips, a foreign feeling, a fullness, and then he's delving deeper. His hand curls, and his finger moves deeper yet.

And then his finger touches me in a certain way, and lightning hits. A moan rips from my throat as raw pleasure rifles through me. He's watching me, and I watch him watch me. He's lying partially on his side, and my shirt is rucked up over my breasts, which are heavy and falling to either side of my body, and my hip bones are visible as I arch off the bed under his touch. I can't help the whimpering moan as he touches me just right again, and the heat and pressure deep within me build and build and build into something unsustainable, something violent and on the knife edge of detonation. Something has to break.

"Oh, god, Dawson!" I hear the words leave my lips, and I've never, ever sounded so needy, so erotically breathy and womanly.

"Grey…god, Grey. You're so gorgeous. You're perfect." His voice is a murmur in my ear.

And then his touch becomes motion, a gentle circling around that spot, and I'm lifting my hips to the rhythm of his touch, and I'm blushing hot at the way my body is responding, but I can't help it. Nothing has ever felt this way, and I can't stop it and I don't want to, even if it's wrong.

His mouth descends to suck my left nipple into his mouth and the ratcheting pleasure bursts open, becomes a scattering pulsating series of explosions in my chest and my core, and my heart is a wild tribal drum in my chest, and my breathing is all moans and gasps, and his whispered name.

His fingers are moving swiftly now, and the detonations inside me are building, and I don't know what to do. I'm going to come apart, I'm going to lose myself to this, I'm going to be lost in the hurricane of sensation, but he doesn't relent. He bites my nipple and I hear myself make a noise that's almost a scream, and then his fingers inside me find that perfect spot and his mouth sucks my other nipple between his lips and worry at it and now I'm gone…

Everything inside me comes apart. I'm screaming, actually shrieking as white-hot lances of raw ecstasy spear through me. I'm shattered, convulsing, completely unable to stop the way my hips lift clear off the bed, seeking his touch, needing more, and he gives me more, so much more. He kisses me on my mouth as I shatter under his touch, and his tongue is inside my mouth and his lips possess mine. I'm grabbing at him, clawing at him as my muscles clench and release. My head spins and my breathing goes erratic.

I hear my own long moans of pure sensuality and erotic desperation.

His hand withdraws and his mouth presses against my cheek, and he holds me against him as I tremble uncontrollably.

When I'm capable of speech, I lift my head to meet his eyes. "What…what did you do to me?"

He doesn't realize I'm serious. "I gave you a taste, babe."

It's not lost on either of us that I don't protest at the term.

"A taste of what?" I wonder if I should tell him I've never done anything even remotely like that before. If his fingers had gone any deeper inside me, he'd have felt the evidence of my innocence.

"A taste of us."

I don't know what to say. Part of me expects him to ask me to do something for him, because as inexperienced as I am, I know something of the way things work. But he doesn't. He just holds me until the trembles subside. It's then that the sense of shame and guilt overtakes me.

Technically, I'm still a virgin but I gave him more of me than anyone has ever had. And I still don't know what this is or where it's going. I know what he said, that he wants me, but…wouldn't he have said that to the others? There have been dozens before me. Dozens of women, and they knew what to give him, how to touch him, how to please him, and they knew what to expect. Did he whisper the same words he did for me?

I know only one thing for sure: I want more. What he just did to me…I need more. I see what the big deal is now, and that was just a taste. I'll never be able to get enough but I can't have any more. I can't. Because I need more from him. I know my feelings for him are going out of control. I know where they're leading.

And I cannot afford to fall in love with him. How can I let that happen? How can I trust him? How can I give myself to him when I've only known him for a matter of days, and if I fall in love, what then? I move in with him? Would he marry me?

Do I want to get married? Does he? Is that where this is going?

Not for him, surely. And what about his movies? They have sex in them. Meaning he has sex, with actresses, on screen for millions of people to see. And yet he'd come home to me and I'd kiss him and touch him and have to know that another woman just did all that, even if it was for a movie and not real emotion? Even without emotion, it would be real kisses, real sex.

I'm hyperventilating as these thoughts pound through me a mile a minute.

I let him touch me. I let him give me an orgasm. His fingers were inside me. His mouth was on my nipples. I basically had sex with him, and I barely know him. He can get me fired and make sure I never work in Hollywood again. He can do anything he wants and get away with it.

He touched me. He kissed me. He made me feel so much, so much.

Tears leak down, tears of raw confusion and desperation and fear.

He sees them. "Grey? What…what's wrong?"

"I…I'm sorry. I don't… I can't…" I scramble away from him, off the bed and into the bathroom.

My stomach heaves, the welter of emotions turning to nausea, as it always does. I don't throw up, though. I taste bile, fight it down. Dawson is on the other side of the closed door; I feel him there. I know I have to face him. I open the door and there he is, huge and gorgeous and clearly upset.

"Grey, what's wrong? I thought we'd—"

I shake my head. "Dawson, I'm…God, I'm messed up." I want his arms around me, because even when he's the one who upsets me, he comforts me. I can't let that happen because I'll get lost in his touch all over again. "I'm so confused, and I don't know what this is, what we are…I don't know anything."

"Don't—don't you want to be with me?"

"I don't know! You make it so hard to think! You touch me, and I can't make sense of anything. You could have anyone, or several people, and I can't compete with that. And you're a movie star. You're going to be in *Gone With the Wind*, and you'll kiss Rose. Or, knowing how Jeremy directs, you'll have a love scene with her. And then what about us? Am I supposed to be okay with that? Where is this going? And what we just did…it was…amazing, but I couldn't stop it. It was so much, so fast, I didn't know it could—"

"Are you saying you felt like I was forcing you?" There's a razor-sharp edge to his voice.

"No! I'm saying it was me…I wanted it, but I shouldn't have…It wasn't…" I don't want to admit that I'm a virgin. I don't know how he'll react or what he'll say or do. What it would mean for us, or whatever this is between Dawson and me. I push past him, adjusting my clothes. "Just…I need to go home. I need to think. This is all happening so fast, and I'm so mixed up—"

"You're running away again." He's equal parts angry and resigned and sad.

"No!"

"Then what would you call it?" His eyes are blue-gray, and he's pacing away from me.

"I don't know. I'm just saying I need some time."

"Time for what? Either you want me or you don't."

"It's not that simple, Dawson—"

"Then explain it to me." He turns back to me and stands over me and stares down into me, into my soul. "Tell me one true thing."

"I want you so much it terrifies me." I can't look at him.

"Why does it scare you so much?"

"Because it's so much, and I don't know how to handle it. I don't know what this is between us."

"It's a romantic relationship, Grey. It's not that complicated. I like you, you like me, we spend time together. We make love. We tell each other true things about ourselves."

"Then you tell me one true thing about you."

He rubs his hand over his face, and then through his hair. "Okay, fine. You've still not told me anything real, anything deep. I know you're afraid, that's no secret. But I'll show you what I mean when I say 'one true thing.' I'm the son of Jimmy Kellor. My mother is Amy Lipmann. You're in film, so you have to know those names."

I knew this. Of course I did. Dawson being Jimmy's son was public knowledge. But somehow I never thought of the effect that would have on Dawson. Jimmy Kellor was—and still is—one of the best-loved directors of all time. He was notoriously difficult to work with, demanding and exacting and quirky, but he was brilliant. He's mostly retired now, and is famously reclusive. No one knows where he lives, but he'll sometimes consult on a film from his home, via email and phone. Amy Lipmann was a romance actress from the seventies and eighties. She had a reputation as a wild child, and her relationship with Jimmy Kellor was a huge scandal at the time, since he was over forty and married with kids. Amy was barely twenty-one. Jimmy left his wife and kids for Amy, and the two stayed together for almost twenty tumultuous years. Tabloids recorded every accusation of cheating on Jimmy's part and every visit Amy took to rehab. Eventually Amy overdosed on cocaine in the mid-nineties. Jimmy's last film was the year Amy died, and he hasn't directed since.

Dawson sighs. "So yeah. I grew up around Hollywood. I was an extra in Dad's movies starting at the age of four. He got me my first real acting role when I was six. *Mountain on the Moon*. After that, I got my own roles. Mom and Dad managed me." His eyes go dark, brown with remembered pain. "You want another true thing? I found Mom. When she OD'd, I mean. She was in her bathroom. She was naked in her tub. The tub was empty, not filled with water. She was just sprawled in it, covered in puke. I was just a kid. It was in ninety-six, so I was like…eight, I guess. The puke was all bloody. I didn't speak for six months after that. I was in the middle of filming my second feature film and when I shut down, they had to recast and reshoot."

I put my hand over my mouth, trying to imagine what that must have been like for a little boy. I can't.

"My mom died of cancer. When I was a senior in high school." I'm barely whispering. "She was my best friend. My everything. She was the only one who understood me or supported me. My dad…I've never gotten along with him. We'll just leave it at that. Then she died, and I watched it happen. Day after day I watched her fight and fight, but she lost, and she died and…she—she left me! She died, and left me alone, and God didn't stop it."

Dawson wraps his arms around me, and I sink into him, absorb his scent, the feel of his skin against my cheek. I'm losing myself in him, bit by bit.

I push away. "I need to go home," I say, wiping tears from my eyes. "I can't deal with all this."

"Grey—"

"I'm not running from you, Dawson. I just…I'm overwhelmed." I am running, though, and he knows it.

"Okay. Fine. Whatever." Dawson rubs at his jaw with his knuckles. "Greg brought the Rover back for you. It's in the driveway. In fact, hold on."

He disappears, and I sit on the bed and sip at the now lukewarm coffee. He comes back after a few minutes with a piece of paper, a pen, and my purse.

"What's that?" I ask.

"Do you have any cash?" he asks, apropos of nothing.

"Um, yeah. Why?" I reach for my purse and dig out a roll of bills.

"Give me a five." I hand him a $5 bill, and he turns the piece of paper around to face me. It's the title to the Range Rover. "Sign here, and date it." He points at a line.

"Dawson—"

"Just do it. Please." He's not looking at me.

I sigh. "I'm not taking your car. It's worth, like, $140,000."

"Grey, money means nothing to me. It never has. You want the Bugatti? I'll give you the Bugatti. Fuck it. I can buy another one."

"I don't want any of your cars. I don't want your charity."

He throws the pen and title on the bed next to me. "Goddamn it, Grey. It's not fucking *charity*."

"You don't have to swear at me."

He slumps, rubbing the back of his neck. "I'm sorry, I just…God, Grey. Just sign the title. Take the car. Do it for me." I stare at him, and then I cave. I sign the title where he pointed, date it. "Thank you. Take it to the DMV on Monday. I'll add you to my insurance policy."

"Dawson, you're not adding—"

"Have you won any of these arguments yet?" He looks at me with a quirked eyebrow. I shake my head and sigh, then fold the title and put it in my purse and start to leave the bedroom. I feel Dawson's hand close around my wrist. "I don't want you to go."

"I'm just going home for a little bit. I need a shower. I need clothes. I have to do homework."

"But you're not going to work." This is not a request, judging by his tone of voice.

"I have to."

"No. You. Don't."

"I have tuition due. I have—"

"How much would you have made this weekend? Tonight and Sunday night? On average."

"You're not gonna try—"

He glares at me, speaking over me. "How... *much?*"

"A thousand, maybe?"

Dawson whirls in place, stalks to his closet, and opens a safe built into the wall. He pulls out an envelope and counts out some bills, returns the envelope, and closes the safe. His expression is grim and hard. "Here. Five thousand dollars. Take the week off."

"You can't buy me off, Dawson." I'm both touched and insulted.

"Fuck, you're stubborn," he growls. "I'm not buying you off. I'm giving you a chance to have some time off."

"If I take time off, I'll never go back."

"Good."

"No! Not good! You can't be my sugar daddy, Dawson. I'm a stripper, not a whore."

"And I don't want you to be either! I'm not asking you to *do* anything for the money, goddamn it!" He's shouting, and I cringe away. He winces at my obvious fear and immediately quiets. "I'm sorry. God, I'm sorry. You're just making me so crazy. I'm not…I get how you would think that. I do. But…it's a *gift*. The Rover is a *gift*. You won't be with me, and that's okay. Or no, it's not. It fucking sucks. But at least let me help you. It's not much, but it'll make me feel better."

"Feel better? About what?"

"You don't get it? Really? You don't see how I'm feeling? What you're doing to me? How hard this is for me?" I don't answer, and he tosses the sheaf of $100 bills on the bed beside me. He stands over me, staring into the middle distance. "Just go, then. Take it, don't take it. What the fuck ever." He moves past me, around the bed, and shoves open the door to his balcony.

I watch him stand with his hands on the ornate stone railing, staring out over Los Angeles. His posture reflects conflict, defeat, coiled anger. His shoulders are slumped, his head hanging low, his breathing slow and even. He looks like he's trying to crush the railing into stone dust by sheer brute force. He looks capable of it.

I want to say something, to comfort him, but I can't. I have no answers for myself, let alone him. I stand slowly, and then stop and stare at the thick pile of money, and I consider. In the end, I can't take it. I want to. I want to not have to work, to not have to take my clothes off. But I can't take anything else from Dawson. It makes me even more his, and I'm already losing myself in him, losing track of who I was and who I am and where that stops and he begins.

I get home, and I shower and put on clean clothes. I fumble my way through an essay on the use of lighting in *Schindler's List*. It's a poor essay, as my thoughts are scattered at best. Finally, I give up and close the cheap, refurbished laptop. I should have taken the money. I'm honestly terrified of going back to the club now. I'll jump at every shadow, see a rapist in every customer. The horror of what I experienced was drowned and buried by the raw intensity that is Dawson, but now that I'm alone, it's rushing back.

I put on a movie and try to watch it, try to distract myself, but even stupidly brilliant comedy like *Black Sheep* can't keep my thoughts away from the hiss of that awful voice, the cruel steel of hands stripping me, crushing the air from my lungs. Panic becomes hysteria, which in turn becomes hyperventilation. I duck my head between my knees and try to focus on long, deep breaths. I'm on the floor, sweating, shaking and sobbing.

Lizzie finds me like this. "You okay, Grey?"

As questions go, it's kind of stupid. I mean, I'm clearly not okay. But this is Lizzie, and she's not the sharpest knife in the drawer.

But her presence forces a layer of calm over my panic, and I'm able to work my way back up onto the couch, wiping at my face and sniffling. "Yeah. I'm fine."

She frowns briefly, then notices the movie playing on the TV, the medium-sized flat-screen Lizzie got for Christmas last year. "Oh, cool. I love this movie. Chris Farley is hysterical." She plops down next to me, oblivious.

We watch the rest of the movie in awkward silence. Well, awkward for me. Lizzie spends most of it watching while texting. I should be getting ready for work right now. But yet, I'm not. I've never been late, never missed a day, never called in sick, even when I had the flu. When the movie is over, Lizzie half-heartedly works on some kind of science homework, and I finish my essay. Lizzie doesn't notice that I'm not going to work. I feel like Timothy is going to burst through my door any moment and demand to know where I am. Or someone from the university is going to knock on my door and demand that I go back to Georgia.

Nighttime slowly rolls around, and I'm a mess. I'm jumpy, hungry, confused. I miss Dawson. I'm worried I've alienated him forever. I'm worried he'll never give up on me and something will happen that I won't be able to undo.

Eventually, I go to bed earlier than I have ever before in my teen and adult life. I lie in bed, dressed in a long USC T-shirt and underwear, and fail to sleep. I fail, because I think of Dawson. I don't think of his anguished eyes when I refused his help, or his angry pose on the balcony. I don't think of his rage-fueled driving. I don't think of his nearly naked form as he changed into a pair of shorts.

I think of his hands, roaming my body. I think of his fingers inside me, creating pleasure I didn't even know existed. Under the cover of my thin blanket, I slide my own hand down between my thighs, under my underwear, and I touch myself. For the first time in my life, I touch myself to find pleasure.

But my touch is cold and lifeless, compared to the memory of his hot, strong hands on me, and in me. I give up and try to remember how it felt.

I dream of Dawson when I finally fall asleep. The dreams take me to places that make me sweat in my sleep. I wake up throbbing between my thighs and panting, with an image of a totally naked Dawson crawling across a bed toward me.

Shadows obscure the parts of him I've never seen, but in the dream, in the waking memory, I can all too well imagine his lips on my breast and his hands on my hips.

However wrong, the dream leaves me desperately wanting it to be real.

CHAPTER TWELVE

"What?" My voice is more than a little hysterical. Several students in the Office of Financial Services waiting room lift their heads from their phones and notebooks to stare at me in curiosity. "What do you mean, it's been paid?"

The woman on the other side of the counter stares at me like I might be a little slow. "I mean… your balance has been paid." She taps at her keyboard, then looks back at me. "In fact, tuition as well as room and board have been paid. You have a zero balance. An escrow account has been established as well, it looks like." She's a small woman in her mid-thirties, pretty in a frizzy, harried kind of way.

"A what?"

She frowns at me. "An escrow account. It means there is money available, ear-marked and arranged for auto-debit, for the remainder of your degree. For dorm costs and your food plan as well, it looks like. I didn't know you could do such a thing, honestly." She gives me a tiny, tight smile. "Someone likes you, Miss Amundsen."

"I don't…I don't understand."

"It's very simple, really. Someone has paid for the rest of your education."

"I'm sorry if I'm coming across as stupid, I just—I don't understand who would—who could—" I cut myself off, because I do know. I close my eyes slowly and try not to either cry or explode. "Thank you." I whisper the words and turn on my heel to leave the office. Once out, I just sit in the Rover.

The leather is cool under my legs, and cold air blasts my face. It's hot as anything outside, but the Rover gets icy in moments. The Rover has satellite radio, and I'm addicted to it. Musically, I've come to like everything, even hip-hop and pop, but my southern roots come through in my love for country music. "More than Miles" by Brantley Gilbert starts to play. This song, god, it's tones from home, my home as it once was. I have a memory of riding in the front seat of Mom's BMW, windows down and the wind tangling our hair as Tim McGraw blasts from the speakers. Mom loved Tim. Dad didn't approve, since it wasn't, like, Steve Green or Michael W. Smith or Steven Curtis Chapman, but it was always our secret, on the way home from dance class or during errands around town.

The song ends, and a female DJ comes on, chatters momentarily, and then breaks my heart. "Goin' way back for this one, y'all. This is the ever-delicious Tim McGraw with 'Don't Take the Girl.'"

Mom's favorite song. I bawl uncontrollably, and I let myself miss her, really miss her, for the first time in months.

When I'm done crying, I have to do something, or I'll fall apart.

If I still have a job after being a no-call no-show Saturday and yesterday, my shift will start in about twenty minutes. If I don't go, Dawson has won. He's paid off my tuition, room, and food plan, basically leaving me with no reason to work.

I never said I wasn't stubborn.

I don't stop to think about it. I just point the expensive SUV toward Exotic Nights, and I marvel at how quickly I've come to feel comfortable in this vehicle. When I pull into the parking lot, however, I can't believe my eyes. There are no cars in the parking lot. Sure on a Monday afternoon there aren't many people, just Timothy and few of the diehard regulars, but there's usually *someone*. The lot is empty. I park the Rover and go to the front door, and my heart stops.

There's a piece of printer paper taped to the inside of the door, with a short and simple message printed on it in a huge font.

CLOSED   PERMANENTLY.   FUTURE HOME OF BOB'S BOOZE CAVE.

Is this a joke?

I pull at the door handle, but it just rattles, locked. I go around to the side, to the door that leads to the backstage area and the dressing rooms. It's locked, too, but that's not surprising, as it's always locked from the outside.

The club has been sold? What? I stand in the parking lot, baking in the late afternoon heat, sweat trickling down between my shoulder blades, my head spinning. How could it have been sold to a liquor store? It may not have been a thriving franchise like Deja Vu, or an upscale place like Skin or Spearmint Rhino, but it still turned a pretty profit. We served crappy booze to down-on-their-luck middle- and lower-class working men. But…a liquor store? Bob's Booze Cave? Really?

My head is about to explode.

Then…the penny drops.

No.

No.

Hell, no.

He did not.

I spin on my heel and storm back to the car. I sink into the leather seat of the Rover…what I've actually begun thinking of as *my* Rover…and try to decide if I'm going to scream, cry, laugh, or all three.

He did it. I know he's behind this. He has money to burn, and he said himself that money means nothing to him. But would he drop—I don't even know how much…several million dollars?—just to make sure I don't go back to stripping?

He just might.

In fact…I know he would.

I race the Rover through the streets of L.A. toward Beverly Hills at a speed and recklessness that would have made Dawson proud. In thirty minutes I'm at the gate of his neighborhood, and the guard just waves me through. How does he know me? Does he know this car? Did Dawson tell all the guards who I am? I resist the urge to squeal the tires down the wide street to his house. It's a neighborhood after all. I pull into his driveway at a sedate pace and park under the arch. His Bugatti is backed into the only open garage bay. A battered red pickup truck sits in the driveway, a massive beast of a machine with fat, knobby black tires and lifted spring-things making the mammoth truck even taller. Dirt coats the truck, and I hear the engine popping as I make my way past it. It doesn't seem like Dawson, this absurdly masculine truck, but then again, it does. I pound on the front door with my fist, clutching my purse strap at my shoulder with my other hand. I'm shaking all over, even after a half-hour drive to calm me down.

Dawson answers the door wrapped in a too-small white towel, his hair wet and plastered to his head, drops of water running down his sculpted chest. He has a toothbrush in his mouth and a dab of foamy toothpaste on his chin. He pushes the door open and holds it, and I move in past him. He smells delicious, like something citrus layered over shampoo and deodorant.

My hand moves of its own accord, reaching up to wipe away the toothpaste from his chin with my thumb. I'm standing close to him, and I feel the heat billowing off him.

I've momentarily forgotten why I'm angry at him.

He's got the toothbrush clamped between his molars on the right side of his mouth, and he's leaning against the door. His towel looks dangerously close to falling off, but he grabs it with one hand, pulling the toothbrush from his mouth with the other. "I was wondering if I'd get a visit from you." His voice is cool and amused, but his eyes are stormy and overcast-gray, the color of pensive tumult and boiling emotion.

"You…you…" I can't get words out.

He's as naked as a man can get without being actually nude, and it's awfully distracting, because I have visions running through my head of licking the drops of water from his chest. I physically stop myself from actually doing it by grabbing the doorframe.

"I was in the shower," he finishes for me. "And you look sweaty enough that you could use one yourself." He leans over me and sniffs. "But you smell good. You'd smell even better if that was my sweat smeared on your skin." His voice buzzes in my ear, intimate and suggestive.

What devilish new game is this? What is he doing to me? I'm trapped in place. He's letting the towel slip, just slightly. I can see the V of his groin muscles, and now a shadow of black hairs closely trimmed. He's going to let it go, right here in his foyer. He's trying to distract me from being angry at him. It's definitely working.

I turn around and put my face to the door. "Damn it, Dawson—"

"Did you just swear? I wasn't sure you ever swore." His voice is at my ear, so close.

Why can't he just leave me alone? And why don't I really want him to?

"You paid off my tuition."

"And your room and board. Don't forget that."

"And the club?" I whisper. Another tendency of mine when I'm dealing with Dawson.

"Oh, that?" He sounds pleased with himself. I don't dare look to see his matching smug expression. I can imagine it well enough. "My buddy Avi was in the market for a new property, so I made that slimy fucking worm Tim an offer he couldn't refuse." He says this last part in a passable Marlon Brando impression, but I'm so shocked and angry that even his *Godfather* quote doesn't impress me.

"Tim? Timothy van Dutton?"

"Yeah, that little cocksucker. He didn't want to sell, but everybody's got a price. Turns out your buddy Tim's price was two million." He says this casually.

I can't help wondering what Candy and the others are going to do, now that the club is gone.

"You spent two million dollars to close down the club, just so I wouldn't work there anymore?" I steal a glance at Dawson, which is a mistake, because he's loosely holding the towel around his waist, teasing me with glimpses of what lies beneath.

He just shrugs. "Yep. It was a filthy shithole anyway, and Tim was an oily cockroach. You can't honestly say you're mad about this, can you?"

I pace away from him, struggling for breath and for words. "You…but—my tuition and all that. It had to have been—"

"Not even fifty grand." He makes a dismissive gesture. "Chump change. But it's not about the money. It's about you."

Fifty grand. Chump change. My head spins. "I don't get—"

He stops me with a hand on my arm and gently pulls my back against his chest. He's wet still, and my shirt sticks to his chest. "It's simple, Grey. I'm a spoiled brat. I've always gotten what I want. Always. And I want you all to myself. I don't want you working there anymore, and I knew you'd fight me on it, so I took the fight away from you. I don't care how much it costs, I have to have you all to myself."

"That's cheating."

"Where's the rulebook for this? What's that saying? 'All's fair in love and war'?"

"Which is this? Love? Or war?"

"Both. Neither. It's whichever you make it, babe." His voice rumbles in his chest, vibrating against my spine. His hand is around my arm, the other wedged between us, keeping his towel in place.

Oh, god. Oh, lord, help me. I can feel him, *all* of him, pressed up against my backside.

"Dawson, why are you doing this?"

"Why are you fighting it?"

"Because—it's all so much. You're…you overwhelm me."

"I'm just a guy."

I shake my head. My hair clings to the beads of water on his chest. I'm hyperaware of how my breasts sway. He makes me aware of myself, of my body. "No, you're more. You're so much more. You're…this—this *experience*. I'm getting…I get swept away in you, when I'm around you. I lose myself when I'm with you."

This gets him. I feel him tense at my words. "Do you have any idea the effect you have on me?" He laughs gently. "You turn me inside out. I've never…I've never cared before. Not this much. Not about anyone. After Mom died, I just kind of shut down, and I never really recovered. Dad was always weird and quirky and reclusive, but when she died, he just—vanished. I basically raised myself…well, Vickers the butler was there for me a lot. And Betty, the housekeeper."

I can't help laughing. "You had a butler named Vickers?"

"Shut up." He laughs. "I didn't name the guy. And 'butler' is just a catch-all kind of word. Think Alfred from Batman. He did everything for Bruce, you know? That's how Vickers was. Ran the house, kept track of everything. Made sure I went to school and shit. He wasn't a 'hugs and tuck me in at night' guy, but he bailed me out of a few scrapes over the years."

He pauses, breathes in, his chest swelling against my back, and exhales deeply. He's pushing away memories. I know a little about that.

"Anyway. You, and me. What you do to me. You can't distract me from this. You need to know." He leans closer and his nearness makes my skin prickle, and my nipples harden. Traitors. I feel that now familiar hot throb down deep. "You make me feel things. And you have to know what a big deal this is for me. I started acting—really acting, you know? Taking it seriously and doing roles I chose—because I wanted to *feel*. I had to act it out onscreen, because I couldn't feel anything when I was just Dawson. Nothing, except this vague sort of loneliness. I was used to it, because I grew up alone. Vickers was all stoic and British, and Betty was just this frumpy lady with her own kids to worry about. So I stopped feeling things because it was easier. Being in Hollywood, you grow up around the life, you grow up in it like I did. Drugs and booze are just normal. I did my first line of coke when I was…twelve? I learned to party early. It filled the holes, kind of. Then, when I hit puberty, girls were part of it. I always had swag, you know? Always. It was just easy. And girls? They filled the spaces in me, too. But…all of it was fleeting. It was my life. Girls, drugs, booze, parties, shooting films all over world. Being a star. It was great—it was the life everyone dreams of. But it was always just me. Alone, after party ended and the girls went home. Meaningless. None of those girls meant anything. A whole messy train of clingy bitches I used for distraction. They couldn't do shit for me when it mattered."

I try to turn in his arms, but he won't let me. He's speaking into the hair at the top of my head, his breath warm on my scalp. I stay still and let him talk, taking in these revelations. Each word makes Dawson more and more real, and that much more all-encompassing, absorbing, intense.

"I was working on the last Cain Riley flick. We were shooting in…Prague? Yeah, Prague. Last couple weeks of shooting. I'd been partying like a fucking rock star for days, going to shoots wasted. But I'd nail the scenes. Cain was this dark and brooding kind of character, all hard edges, a badass. So the half-wasted slur and the 'I don't give a fuck' glaze to my eyes in the whole movie was real. I *didn't* give a fuck, but it worked for the character. I was so strung out. And then one day I woke up in the back of a club in the nasty back end of Prague. I'd passed out, and they'd shut the place down, just for me, so I could pass out. Like I would've known or cared had the club party gone on while I was out. But whatever. I woke up, and I had blood on my face, under my nose and chin. There was puke everywhere. They'd just…left me there. Let me puke. It had become so commonplace for me to pass out that they didn't bother checking on me, because I was always fine. Take a few shots, do a line, drink some coffee. Go shoot the next scene."

Dawson tips his head back, drifting away into memory.

"And I realized, you know, they didn't care. As long I shot good scenes, they didn't care. And I was gonna end up like my mom. It was pure luck that I hadn't died that night in the club, that I didn't just OD like Mom. So then I tried to sober up on my own and push through the rest of the scenes, trying not to end up like her. So…I finished shooting *Veiled Threats* and went into rehab. That was when I disappeared. Rehab was more to get myself away, you know? I mean, shit, yeah, I had a problem, but it wasn't addiction to the drugs. It was addiction to the *feelings*. I felt things when I was acting, when I was strung out. Numb, good things. But empty things. You know? Maybe you don't. Maybe you feel too much, feel it all so much that you can't make any sense of it. That's what I think your problem is. You feel too much."

I'm a captive audience as he rests his chin on my head and continues to speak, one arm wrapped around me, holding me in place. "I don't feel enough. Never did. So then I met you. In that stupid titty-club. And you were this…this glorious creature. You were like an angel, trapped in hell. You couldn't have been more out of place if you tried. I watched you out on the floor, you know. And that dance on stage. You… captured them. All those poor, sweaty, greasy, miserable assholes. You were so different from the other blank-eyed, apathetic strippers you see in clubs like that. Where the smiles don't reach their eyes. Where the affected sexuality is just…plastic. Fake. Put on. You? You…*ooze* sensuality, and you don't even know it, and it's like a drug for guys like me. I may have more money and sophistication than those other guys, but I'm just like them. Looking for a cheap thrill, a quick escape. And you? You're a high we could never get anywhere else. Watching you dance? The way you move? The way you wait until the very fucking last second to take the clothes off? It's maddening. You don't even know. You can't. There's something inside you, beyond that innocence. I see it. It's…fuck. It's bright as the fucking sun, but it's hidden, because you're miserable."

I'm squirming, tearing up, sweating from his heat and from the way he's talking about me, but I can't escape his hold, and I have to hear his words. I have to keep listening. He's ripping this straight out of his soul and giving it to me. It's a priceless gift, and I'm hoarding it in my heart.

"And I met you," he continues. "And you made me feel something. I wasn't drunk. I can drink, you know. I'm not and never was an alcoholic. It was just…a Band-Aid on the wound. Anyway, I saw you, and then you came in to the VIP room and you were…so bright. But so scared. And you made something in me just…implode. Like I'd had an epiphany, you know? Like I knew, I had to know you, had to hold you and touch you and tell you everything. But you keep running. And you kiss me and you get me rock fucking hard, but then you run and you leave me aching and alone and worked up. You know I've put on, like, fifteen pounds of muscle since I met you? Because you get me worked up and then I can't get off on my own, because it feels wrong, and I need to let it out, so I work out. You turn me on, just breathing. You make me feel like I'm someone, and not because I'm Dawson Fucking Kellor, either."

He backs away from me, and I wrap my arms around his broad shoulders, palms sticking to his hot, damp skin. He stills, and looks down at me as he continues.

"But that doesn't matter to you. You run any-way, maybe *because* of that. And I can't figure you out. You confuse me, and that's a feeling. I know women, okay? I do. I thought I knew how women think, but you? I can't figure you out. You never react how I think you will. One second, it's like you can't get enough of me and I'm going to make you explode, and then the next you're about to hyperventilate and having a nervous breakdown because you can't han-dle me, or us, or something."

He's going a mile a minute, and I've never heard him say so much, never heard anyone say this much all at once. It's just pouring from him.

"You make me want you. Not just…want to fuck you. That feels cheap, even saying it. You're not the kind of woman who *fucks*. You're more than that. But fucking is all I know, and you're worth more. And that's an odd feeling for me. I've always been entitled, you know? I'm that horribly obnoxious kind of person who's always had everything and owns the fucking world, okay? But I'm not entitled to you. I have to earn you. And I can't even earn the truth of where you come from or why you're the way you are, or anything. You don't give me a damned thing, and that's maddening. But that's a feeling, too. Wanting you, needing you, being confused, being mad, frustrated, needing a release I can't find, wanting to even hold your hand like some fucking sappy teenager… it's all feelings. And that…it makes me feel alive in a way I've never known before."

He finally stops the flood of words. He turns me in his arms, and his hands go to my face. I hold his towel in place with my hands as he brushes my hair out of my face, wipes a strand of blonde hair from my mouth with an index finger. His eyes are all colors, no color, that perfect hazel that's its own shade of Dawson.

And then he speaks again, in a voice that's pure magic. And his words…they floor me.

"You make me feel alive, Grey. And…I love that feeling."

"You feel all that? From me?" He just nods. "I don't…I'm not…I mean—I'm just Grey. I'm a pastor's daughter from Georgia. My mom died, I told you that. She was all I had, really, and my dream was to be here, so I came here. I had to earn money when my scholarship ran out, and I couldn't find a job, so I took the only job I could find."

"There's so much more to you than that, Grey."

"Like what?" I honestly don't know. I feel like that's all there is.

"Grace. Fluidity. Beauty. Intelligence. Talent. Potential. Tenderness. Innate sensuality." He touches me under my chin, and I can't look away from him. "Tell me one true thing."

"I'm a dancer." I don't hesitate. "Not…not like on stage, not like that. But real dancing. Jazz, and modern, and ballet."

"Dance for me?"

"What, like now?"

He nods, kisses my cheekbone, and turns away from me, leaving the towel in my hands. I'm stunned, and it's impossible to look away from his backside as he runs up the stairs, naked as a jaybird. I want him to turn around, but I'm also glad he doesn't. He comes back down in a pair of shorts, and takes my hand. Leads me through his cavernous, palatial house that he lives in alone, to a huge gym. There are all sorts of weight machines in one corner, a punching bag hanging from the ceiling, one of those big, heavy ones you kick and punch, and then an area of open space.

He gestures at the open area. "I do tai chi. It's badass, and it's calming. It gives me a center, somewhere I can be just…nothing but motion."

I go into the center of the open space, a lightly padded floor beneath my feet. I spring gently, and I realize how long it's been since I danced for me.

"Can you put on some music?" I set my purse to one side and unbutton my shirt, toss it by my purse.

I'm wearing a button-down blouse over a tank top, and a pair of capris. Good enough for dancing. I'm excited at the idea, but nervous. Dawson pulls his phone from his pocket and fiddles with it, then plugs it into some dock built into one of the walls. Music swells through the space, and it's such perfect music to dance to. I've never heard it before, but it's all Dawson. It's symphonic, orchestral, but with heavy gothic overtones to it, and guitars and drums layered through it, giving it a hard edge. The lyrics are pensive and dark and vaguely religious. I can't help but move.

There's no technique to this; it's just pure movement. My body flows, stretches, twists, and becomes an extension of the music. I leap, and bend, *jeté* and roll into pirouettes, and there's nothing but the music and my body moving. Such purity of expression forces things inside me to give way.

I'd forgotten about dancing. I'd let it go in the face of work and school. I'd lost it. Lost that part of myself, and now…Dawson has given it back to me. I dance, and I dance. Another song by the same band comes on, and I keep dancing. I feel him watching, and I don't care.

No, that's not true. I do care. So much. I feel his gaze, and I dance harder for it. I want him to see me as I am. He's asked me several times to tell him one true thing, and so now I do. I tell him one true thing, not with words, but with something more tangible, something that comes from deeper within me. Words can lie. Words can deceive and delude and conceal and avoid. But the things you do, how you move, how you touch, those things cannot lie.

When the music ends, I'm left panting, heaving, sweating. Dawson is standing with his arms crossed, an expression on his face that I can't decipher. I catch my breath and wait. He comes toward me, his eyes are hot green-gray, the color of desire. He reaches for me, smearing sweat on my arms, brushing the hair from my face, infinitely gentle, touching me with pent-up desire.

He hesitates a beat, and then kisses me.

And now I'm lost all over again. God, his kiss devours me. Sucks me under with the riptide force of his heat and power and sexuality and dominance. Even the light taste of toothpaste on his lips is sensual. I inhale the scent of shampoo in his hair and the citrus aftershave or lotion or whatever it is. His hands touch me and caress me and hold me and incite need inside me. He kisses me, kisses me, kisses me.

And I kiss him back.

I'm free. I give in completely.

CHAPTER THIRTEEN

HE'S ALL THERE IS. All there will ever be. I'm falling through eternity, and his touch is the fabric of that forever. His kiss is the substance of infinity. These thoughts make no sense even to my own mind, but they remain true in some strange way.

His arms are like prison bars, but it's a cell I have no desire of escaping. He's all contradictions, hard yet soft, sweet and salty, perfect and flawed.

My hands are curled against his bare chest, my nails scraping his skin as our mouths merge. My nipples are pebbled against his chest, stiff through the material of my bra and the thin cotton tank top. His shorts are a barely-there layer of slippery rayon, and I feel the stiff, thick, hot intrusion of his manhood against my belly, physical evidence of how I make him feel. That presence, that thickness against my stomach, it scares me. It's huge and hard as rock, and…I want to see it. I want to touch it. I want to feel it…and to taste it. I feel sinful and wrong just thinking that, but so help me, it's true. I want to taste all of him. I want to feel all of him.

I want to give him all of me.

But he needs to know he'd be the first, the only one. I try to make the words come out, but I kiss him instead.

I'm lifted, cradled in his arms, and our kiss doesn't break as he carries me through his house. My hands clutch his shoulders and his neck, and I gasp for air into his mouth, panting, eyes closed, fighting for clarity and lucidity and unable to be anything but swept away by need.

We're in his room. I'm on my back on his bed. I pull his lips down to my greedy mouth. Strong and insistent fingers strip away my shirt and toss it aside. My bra is black and basic, clasped in the back by three hooks and eyelets. I arch my back, and he makes short, efficient work of unlatching it, pulling it from me and setting it aside.

I cross my arms over my chest, and he lets me. He lounges on his side next to me and stares into my eyes. "Let me see you, babe."

I squeeze my eyes shut and shake my head.

He laughs, and traces an idle pattern on my belly with his forefinger, lazy, roaming circles leading downward to my khaki capris. His eyes are on me, and I force my lids open, force my gaze to his, and lie stone still as he pinches the edges of my waistband together and releases the clasp. I don't move as he slowly unzips, baring a sliver of black lace to match my bra. I continue my still acquiescence to his stripping of me as he takes the waistband of my pants in his hands and works them down over my generous hips. I don't help, but I don't hinder, and soon I'm naked but for my underwear.

A familiar state of undress, but I've never felt more vulnerable.

His eyes burn green-brown-gray, hints of blue at the edges. Unmitigated desire and fire scorching me from his gaze. One hand on my belly, then a single finger dipping under the black elastic, beneath the *Victoria's Secret* printed in pink script. I blink, twice, and swallow the pulsating knot of fear. That finger, his right index finger, slides around the circumference of the elastic, from hip to hip, and then again, gently tugging down. I do not lift my hips; I keep my eyes on him and let him strip me.

He's already stripped me bare. Now he's merely completing the task. He's seen everything else, and now he'll see me completely nude.

But he stops when the underwear are just barely covering the top of my cleft. "You take them off. If you want this, take them off."

This is my last chance; I see that. If I deny this now, he'll know I'm too afraid.

Am I?

I'm not nauseous, not hyperventilating, not doing any of the things that usually accompany my strongest emotions. I'm terrified, because I feel the three words of truth bubbling on my lips.

Well, there are two truths vying for utterance, and both come in three-word sentences.

I go for the easier one. "I'm a virgin."

He doesn't respond at all. He just stares at me for a long, silent moment. Neither of us even breathes.

Then he quirks one eyebrow. "That explains a lot." He licks his lips, and in that tiny motion, his nerves are revealed. "How, though? I mean, how can you be a virgin and a stripper? That doesn't…it doesn't make any fucking sense."

I swallow hard and try not to feel the distance rising between us. "It just happened. I told you my dad was a pastor. I grew up in a very strictly con-servative home. Until you, I'd only even kissed one other boy, but that was him kissing me when I wasn't ready and didn't want it, and it didn't even last half a second, so it doesn't even really count. No one… no one has ever touched me like you, looked at me like you, held me or kissed me or anything. No one has ever wanted me, and…and, more importantly, I've never *wanted* anyone before you. I don't…I don't know what I'm doing. I'm scared. Of this, of you. Of everything."

My crossed arms are covering my chest, and I tighten my hold on myself. I've bared all, told the truth and I fear letting myself dive into him. "I want this. I do. I want you. But…all I have left of my family, of my dad, of what I used to believe, is that this has to mean something. It has to be real. It has to be…maybe not forever, but…it has to be more than just right now. I've waited too long. I've been lonely and scared and desperate too long for this to be a just-once thing."

Dawson opens his mouth to speak, to protest, but I kiss him to quiet him—only I pull away, almost violently, before I get lost in it.

And then I continue, "You have this hold on me, Dawson. I *need* this. I *need* you. You're…stripping away all the ideas of who I used to be and who I am, and I'm…I'm yours. I don't know how that happened, but it did. But…if this isn't—if it isn't *everything* to you, then I'll be totally lost. Does that make any sense? If I give you this last piece of who I am, I won't have anything left, and if you stop wanting me, if you don't…" I trail off, unwilling to use the four-letter word hanging so thickly between us.

He touches my mouth with his fingers, but I was already done talking. "Babe. Baby. Grey. I won't stop. I want to tell you what this means to me, but I'm afraid if I do, you'll just think I'm saying it to get what I want." He closes his eyes briefly, then opens them. "I can't believe you're a virgin. But then again, I can."

The room is cold, and I'm mostly naked. I shiver, and Dawson sees it. He reaches down and unfolds the patchwork quilt folded lengthwise along the edge of the bed, and drapes it over me.

"Tell me how I'm stripping away all the ideas of who you think you are. Explain that."

"I thought you were going to tell me—"

"It has to be my timing. And I need to understand this. Because I want you to be you. I don't want to strip away who you are."

"It's not like that. Or maybe it is. It's hard to explain." I clutch the blanket under my chin and roll into him. He snags a pillow and tucks it under our heads, nooks me into his arm, and I let it spill out. "I was a pastor's daughter. For so long, for my whole life. That was my identity. I was a mama's girl. That was another part. But then Mama died, and I ran away to USC to go into film school, and my father disowned me for it. I haven't spoken to him—phone, text, letter, email, nothing—since I left Macon more than two years ago. I never will, I don't think. I chose my way. I chose sin. So he's done. So that left me without being a pastor's daughter, without a mother, alone in L.A. Alone at USC. I never really made any friends. I was…too busy with school, and then the scholarship ran out and I had to find work to stay here, because I've got nowhere else to go, nothing else to do with my life, so failure's not an option. And then I was too ashamed of what I do—"

"*Did*," Dawson interjects, forcefully.

"What I did," I agree. "And I just…I've never made friends easily. I had one real friend back in Macon, Devin, a dancer at the studio where I took lessons. But I came here and she went to Auburn, and we lost contact. We still email every now and then, but…it's not the same. I can't…I can't tell her things. So…I never made any friends. All I was, all I am, is school. And stripping. But now stripping is gone, and school isn't…it isn't enough. And so there's you. I was just going from day to day, surviving, basically. I wasn't dancing, and that was as close to an identity as I had. You gave that back to me just now. And when I'm with you, I feel like I'm—like I'm a person again, not just this point of sentience floating from class to class, essay to essay, test to test, stage dance to lap dance to VIP room. And this, being here with you, this feels like…like…*home*." I whisper the word, and it's a single, broken syllable.

Dawson is breathing hard, like he just lifted a thousand pounds. He's trembling all over. I crane my neck on his shoulder to look at him, and his eyes are closed, as if trying to summon something from deep within. Or fighting back emotion.

"Home." He utters the word much like I did, almost a curse, shaping a syllable that has no meaning on its own.

His eyes open, and he meets my gaze. A tear shimmers in the corner of my eye, and he leans in, kisses it away.

"So—so…" I struggle for the courage to say this next part. "So if this, if me and you, if this isn't real, then don't—don't play games with me, Dawson. If it's not real for you, then tell me and I'll go—"

"I love you, Grey." He speaks over me, cuts into me with three razor-sharp words.

I thought I would cry when I finally heard those words spoken to me again, but I don't. I bury my nose in the hollow of his throat and breathe in his scent, and feel my tension bleed away. I hold the nape of his neck and just breathe him. And he lets me. He doesn't demand anything from me. He just holds me, breathes deep breaths of my hair and strokes my back over the quilt.

"My mom made this quilt," he says, apropos of nothing. "In rehab. It's really all I have of her. You know, she never told me she loved me. Neither did

Dad. The closest I ever got to hearing those words was from Vickers, once. He'd just bailed me out of jail for speeding and reckless endangerment—drag racing Dad's Ferrari—and he just looked at me, Vickers, I mean, and he goes, in his perfect, arch, British accent, 'Lord love you, dear boy. This wild hair of yours will get you killed yet.'"

"No one? Ever?"

He shakes his head, then shrugs in a strange rolling motion. "Well, I mean, I've *heard* it before. But not from anyone who's really meant it. In the heat of the moment things from a one-night stand don't count."

I grew up knowing I was loved. Mama loved me. Completely. Daddy did, too, in his own way, just not unconditionally. Not enough. But I knew, down to my atoms that Mama loved me inside and out. If she were alive, she'd still love me, stripper and all. And Dawson…he's never had that. Not ever.

I summon all my courage, and I roll over so I'm mostly on top of him. My breasts squish against his chest, and the quilt—which I understand to be the only evidence Dawson has of his mother's maternal affection—slips down around my hips. I wriggle and writhe against him, shifting until I'm pressed entirely into him, every inch of me against every inch of him. My leg is thrown over his hips, and I feel something thickening and growing against my thigh.

I know this is true, so I say it, because he needs, more desperately than me, I think, to hear it: "I love you." I don't garnish it with his name, or anything else. I just let it float out, let it hang. And I hold my breath for his reaction.

His eyes are closed tight. His hands are curled into vises on my hips, holding me against him. "Say—say it again. Please."

I've never heard such vulnerability in a man. In anyone. He's just completely open, bare to me. I see the nerve endings of his heart, the pinkness of his inner need, the thick, tough skin peeled away to show the tenderness not meant to be seen.

I writhe closer, pressing against him, cradling myself to him. I brush my lips over his jaw, then nip his earlobe as I utter the words again, a whisper so quiet it barely counts as speech but I know he hears it like a bullhorn shout. He flinches at every pho- neme, every breathed letter.

"I love you."

Dawson shudders beneath me, shaking, and I know he's as pierced and speared as I am by this moment. All the world is silent and still. The sun hasn't moved in its arc across the sky. Motes of dust hang in the sunlight, frozen like beads of amber. There is only him, his heart beating against mine, the slow tangling of him into me, and me into him.

His eyes flick open, and they're all-colored and fusion-hot. He doesn't have to ask me to do it. I reach down of my own will and push away the quilt, roll to my back, and strip away my underwear. I'm naked but no longer vulnerable. I'm nestled in the cocoon of Dawson, of his love, his need. His eyes rake me, take me. Cover me. Face, cheekbones and lips and eyes and nose; the delicate curve and hollow of my throat. He takes in the heavy swell of my breasts, the erect nipples, my ribs and taut belly; hips, belled and generous; my strong thighs, the sliver of a gap between them, knees and calves and feet; then back up, to my core waxed smooth, tight and touched only by his hand. And mine, once, briefly. My hair is a tangled mess spread across the pure white duvet. My skin a natural tan in contrast to the white sheets.

And then there's him. Male perfection. Evidence of God's handiwork. I believe in Him when I'm looking at *him*. Dark hair that's not brown nor black nor dirty blond. It's a color like his eyes, nearly black when wet, but now it's drying and lightening in color, muting into a kind of auburn. Messy hair, uncombed, gel-free, un-styled and perfectly imperfect. Trimmed close to the scalp at the back and around his ears, but long enough on top to style artfully mussed or swept to one side in a classical, sophisticated part. The changeable beauty of his eyes, technically hazel but brownish when he's feeling kind and soft, almost blue when he's angry, faded moss-green when he's raw with lust, always somewhere in between, never one shade. High cheekbones, a jaw like chipped granite, lips that can curl into a smile or a leer and still make women swoon. His chest is massive muscle with deep-cut washboard abs that ripple down to a trim waist. Strong muscular arms encircle me. His almost swarthy dark skin, a thin dusting of hair at the center of his chest, a thicker trail of hair on his belly.

I need to see. I lick my lips and run my hands over his chest, and he tenses, flexes. My palms flatten against his stomach, and then my fingers turn to face his toes. I slip my palms down to his hipbones, sharp knobs under my hands. I don't dare take my gaze from his as I swallow my nerves and fear and summon the boiling ocean of desire. The shorts are loose at his waist, an untied drawstring hanging over the elastic waistband. I slowly and too gently peel his shorts down, down. His breath catches, and my eyes are now inexorably drawn to his erect manhood as I bare it, inch by inch.

A broad pink head, a groove running around underneath that where he was circumcised. Veins and tightly drawn skin, tan and thin-looking, stretched over so much manhood. I'm not breathing. My lip hurts and I realize I'm chewing on it, and I release it. But I don't stop my hands as they draw his shorts off;

he frees one leg, then the other, and now we're both naked. I'm in bed, naked, with a man.

But I love him, and he loves me.

So this is okay.

Right?

I can't and won't stop, even if it's not.

He rolls with me, places his hands on either side of my face, kneeling next to me, but not straddling me. His lips lower to mine, and now I don't just lose myself in his kiss, but actively throw myself into it. I dive deep, drown myself. I suck his lip in between my teeth and lick it with my tongue, and I hold his face in both hands, then caress his neck and shoulders with one hand while searching the hard ridge of his jaw with the other. Then my hands explore more. Oh, lord, oh, god. There's so much to explore, so much man to get to know. He kisses me unhurriedly and lets me learn him.

My palms follow his chest, his ribs under his arms, over his back and down his spine. I hesitate, and then my palms move closer, clutch his backside in both hands. Cool and hard, firm. I explore the fullness of his backside and then down his thighs. I curve my hands over his quadriceps and to his hips, and then he's collapsing to one side and onto his back.

Now it's my turn to hover over him, weight planted on one hand near his shoulder. My breasts are heavy pendulums swinging freely, and then they're caught in his hands, and I gasp at the heat and strength of his touch. His thumbs graze over my sensitive nipples, and they turn hard as diamonds.

It's time.

I watch my hand as it travels to hover near his erection. Dawson is holding his breath, eyes narrowed, watching my hand as well. My fingers curl into a fist around him, grasp him gingerly. He expels his breath in a long, slow, steadying sigh. I just hold him at first, marveling at the way my small hand looks wrapped around his manhood. I love the feel of him in my hand. It's nothing like I thought it would be. It's hard and hot, but it's also soft and springy, cushion layered over iron. I try to breathe, partially succeed, and then I slide my hand down, feeling the ridges and veins against my palm, and I cradle his…I'm at a loss for what word to even use to think of that part of him…but they're even softer than his erection, pulled tight, prickling with trimmed hair. I cup him there, hold him, touch him, and then my hand resumes its curling grasp of his shaft and slides upward. The tip fascinates me. There's a tiny hole at the very top, and immediately beneath that he's spread out into a mushroom wideness. It looks soft and springy, and it is, when I rub that area with my thumb.

Dawson is tensed all over, shoulders turned into boulders, and his hands are loose on my breasts. I glance at him, at the narrow-eyed look of concentration. I cannot fathom his thoughts.

"Am I…is this okay?" I ask. "I just…I want to see you, feel you."

He smiles at me, and his expression is tender. "Of course, babe. Anything, everything. As slow as you want."

But he's struggling, it seems. With what, against what, I can't know.

I stroke him with my one hand and then move so I'm kneeling next to him, out of his reach. He crosses his hands under his head and watches me as I touch him. Not just his erection but his chest and stomach and thighs as well.

I still want to taste him. I know this is something women do to men, because men at the club have asked me if I'll do it, sometimes offering exorbitant amounts of money if I will. I never thought I would actually do it, though. Today I am. I hold him in one hand, then both, hand over hand, spanning most of his length. His tip and a sliver of the shaft rise above my top hand, and I bend over him, lower my mouth to him. I kiss the tip first. An actual kiss, but that doesn't seem quite right. So I extend my tongue and taste the groove. He's salty and soft. I put my lips around him, and I taste something smoky and salty on my tongue, and then I move my upper hand away and lower my mouth slightly.

Dawson groans and his back tightens, arches. I take in more of him, thinking this is what I'm supposed to do. And, in truth, I do like the way he feels, the way he tastes. My lips are stretched and my jaw is forced wider as I take his full width into my mouth, and now the tip of him is brushing the roof of my mouth and pushing at the back of my throat, so I pull my lips away, so slowly.

"Grey…Jesus, Grey." He takes my face in his hands. "You have to stop that now. I'm not ready for that, and I *really* don't think you are."

"Ready for what?" But then, yes, I do know the mechanics of how sex works, of course, and I realize what will happen if I keep touching him, keep my mouth on him.

And no, I'm not ready for that. Someday I'll experience that, but he's right. Not now. "Yeah, you're right," I say, and lie down over him, settle my boobs on his chest and my mouth on his mouth, and his erection is hard between us, against my hip.

He must see the question in me, because he answers before I can form the words. "The things you do to me, Grey. God. It's all I can do to hold back right now. You are so perfect. The way you touch me…" He buries his fingers in my hair, tight against my scalp, and interrupts me with a fiery kiss. "You make me feel…so good. It's never felt like this before."

And then I'm on my back suddenly, and he's above me, and this is home as I've never experienced home before. I wrap my arms around his neck and pull him down for a kiss, and we're lost for a timeless moment. But it doesn't last, because he's pulling away. I tangle my fingers in his hair as he kisses my throat, the hollow of my neck. The rising slope of my right breast, around the areola, the puckered flesh, and then my nipple is in his mouth and there's a sharp tug between my thighs, a burning pressure. His hand smooths over my belly, over my thighs. I willingly part my legs for his touch, sinfully and wantonly spread my thighs wide as his fingers delve deep. Then his touch is slicking into my cleft and the tug is a hot jerking inside me, ropes of nerves being twisted and pulled and braided by the rhythmic, searching sweep of his fingers inside me. My hips lift high off the bed as he brings me to the cusp of explosion and then slows his touch and lets me agonizingly back down, but the pressure doesn't relent, only builds into a weight that I cannot bear. He doesn't offer me relief and I don't know the language to ask him for it, because all speech has been stolen away.

I have an identity in this moment, in this time: his touch. My climaxing eruption is who I am. His mouth on my breasts and his fingers inside me are who I am.

And then, and then…his kisses move down my breastbone and down farther, over my belly, then a tongue over my slick-smooth mound. I'm shaking my head no, no, but of course I don't mean actually no, I just mean to ask if he's really going to do that… and he does. His lips touch my cleft, and I shudder. It's a kiss of hesitant questing. I lift my hips in a silent encouragement. I'm lost to this experience, and I want everything he can give me.

He looks up at me, the question in his eyes. He doesn't want me to feel rushed.

I have no shame left. "Please…please yes." My words are inaudible and gasped, but he hears them.

He takes my ankles and drapes my knees over his shoulders, lifts me by the bottom and, with no warning whatsoever, spears his tongue into me. I clutch the bedding with a noise somewhere between a whimper and a cry and a shriek and a moan. Instead of the bedding, I decide to clutch him. My hands tangle in his hair and tug, curl into his dark locks and hold on as he uses his thumbs to spread my lips apart and he kisses me deep inside. It is a kiss, too. His lips move over my slick inner parts, and his tongue explores me, just like the way he kisses my mouth.

There has never in life been pleasure this intense before. Not ever. I alone know the meaning of true heavenly bliss.

I don't try to hide or muffle the embarrassing sounds coming from me. In fact, as his lips suckle me, I begin to find my own noises arousing. I'm totally abandoned to this. I have no reason for control any longer, and I'm completely at his mercy. I let myself moan as loud as my voice will go, and for as much as I moan, Dawson redoubles the intensity of his oral attention. The more erotic my moans, the more wildly his tongue spears into me; the more I allow myself to cry out his name, the more swiftly he suckles and circles with his tongue, and now I'm all noise and thrashing hips.

I lock my legs around his head and keep him coiled against me, and now his fingers are slipping into me, too, two fingers into my cleft, delving in and sliding out, and that move from empty to full to empty makes me whine high in my throat, so he does it again, but more fully, and I throw my head back and arch my spine and I shatter beneath him, scream and gasp for breath and then scream again as wave after wave of orgasm hits me. I have no ability to stop the way I move against his mouth and buck my hips into his spearing tongue, and indeed his hands urge me onward and upward, not relenting when the orgasm hits, but pushing me beyond it into helpless breathless frozen ecstasy of fire released.

And then I'm coming back down and dizzy, and I moan in desperation as he moves away from me, off me, and I hear something crinkle. I crack my eyes open to watch him roll something thin and clear onto his erection. I know what's next, a moment of fear, but then I have no time for it take hold because Dawson is back with me, kissing me.

I taste myself on his mouth and tongue, vaguely salty tangy and decidedly feminine musk, the smell of me as a taste. His kiss is desperate, and I know he's preparing himself for me to freak out. It's there inside me, the panic, but I deny it. I kiss him and revel in the weight of his body against me, and the strength of his arms around me, and I know I want this. I kiss him with everything I have, and I curl one hand around the back of his neck.

"Grey, you don't…we don't have to, if you're not ready."

"I'll never be ready. But I've never wanted anything more." But I owe him all the truth inside me. "But I'm going to freak out at some point. I know I am. I'm lost in you, lost in this, in us, but I'm going to flip out. You should know that. But you also have to know that I *do* want this. So much. Please, do this with me."

His belly is hard and warm against my stomach, and I feel the tip of him at the inside of my thigh, huge and hard. His arms are strong and now-familiar bars at either side of my face. His eyes search me.

I put my lips to his, and I let him taste the words as I say them: "I love you, Dawson." I feel him swell, see his eyes fill with emotion, feel his chest expand, and even his erection grows harder and thicker against me.

"Grey…I love you. God, I love you."

I have to ask him. I have to say the words. "Make love to me, Dawson. Please, make love to me."

"With all my heart, yes." But he doesn't push into me.

Instead, he reaches down between us and finds my sweet spot with his fingers, finds my breast with his mouth and he patiently, slowly brings me to writhing, breathless arousal. When I reach the cusp of orgasm, he kisses me, and I open my eyes to stare into his every-colored eyes. He doesn't slow his fingers on my pleasure-center; he nudges at my vagina with the tip of his erection. It's just a slight pressure at first, just the very smallest part of him inside me, and I let my legs fall apart because otherwise I'll clamp them shut. I am panicking a little. My heart is pounding with as much fear as pleasure, and he knows it, because he lets me fall away from the edge of orgasm, and he slides in a little farther, letting me feel the stretch of him filling me, and I gasp and tears start at the corners of my eyes, because he's so *huge* inside me, filling me past my ability to take it.

But I do take it and he stills, and I begin to need the fullness, begin to understand how much I'm going love this, but there's pain in the way, so I don't yet love it, but I *will*. And then he speeds his fingers inside me and nips sharply at my breast with his teeth and brings me to the furious edge of orgasm, and this time he keeps going, sliding a little deeper with each circle of his fingers, and then I'm bursting apart and gasping and moaning, and Dawson's eyes lock onto me, silently pleading with me to watch his eyes, hold the gaze, so I do, and he thrusts once, hard, and there's an instant of blinding pain, but it's buried under a tsunami of starbursts, pleasure laced with pain. He stays buried deep, fingers and mouth giving me pleasure as the throbbing pain subsides. And then I'm completely filled by him. He's in me. Hips to hips, mouth to mouth. Our fingers entangle, rest by my face. Our tongues taste tongue and lips and teeth, and he's *huge* inside me, stretching me to pinching pain that bleeds into pleasure.

And then…he moves. He slowly slides out of me, and I'm empty and lost without that fullness. I bury my face into the column of his neck, feeling his pulse on my eyelashes. He glides back into me in infinitesimally slow motion, and I clutch and scrabble at his backside, because the bliss that suffuses me is heaven, beyond heaven, it's pure wonder, everything that's good in the universe exploding inside me. It's the presence of love welling up inside me.

I'm crying, but I'm smiling, and he sees that, and he kisses the tears, kisses my cheekbones and my eyelids and my chin and my mouth and my neck, and all the while he's drawing out, and pushing in. But slowly. So slowly. So gently. Lovingly. A sinuous, gentle glide in, breaking every notion of fullness with every in-stroke. And then out, and I'm whimpering at that loss, but it makes the flush of his erection back into me so much better.

I'm arched, spine bowed, and then I lift my backside and my hips to meet his, and I untangle one hand to claw my fingernails down his back and clutch his backside as he slides in, and I'm making a sound that has no one single word. It's a screaming gasping breathing erotic moan of his name.

"*Dawson…*"

I repeat it with every swell of his shaft into me. I want to have the words to tell him how this feels, how much I love this, how perfect this is, but I don't have them. All I can do is try to communicate it with my whimpers and groans, with my whispered utter-ances of his name.

He continues his glacially slow pace, but he lifts up on one elbow and brushes the tangles of hair from my eyes. "Ride me," he says.

"What?" I can barely speak even that one-sylla-ble word clearly.

"I want you on top. Ride me. Take your pleasure. Let go."

I open my mouth to speak, because I'd like a moment to think about it. I like him being in control. I like being able to delve into him and not think or do or anything but feel. But he rolls with me, buried deep inside me, and now I'm straddling him, clinging to his chest, face against his neck, clutching him fearfully as if afraid of falling from a great height. He stills, and I'm full of him, but I need the slide, the motion. I meet his gaze.

"Find where you are in this," he says. "I took you past the scary part, right? And now I want you to take, rather than give."

He brushes my hair away, buries his fingers into the roots of my hair just behind my left ear, the other hand resting on my hip. I sit up gradually, slowly, until my legs are bent at the knee, doubled so my calves are nearly parallel to my thighs. I find my balance, sway and steady myself with my palms on his chest. Our eyes are locked, and his hands caress the line of my ribs, a thumb under my breast and then across my nipples, back down to grasp my hips, then he begins a circuit all over again.

At first I try a simple rocking motion with my hips. I gasp and close my eyes, then do it again. And again, and my gasp turns to an open-mouthed moan. Dawson doesn't move, just holds my hips and watches me. I lean forward and lift with my hips and core, drawing him almost all the way out, pause with him poised tip in the folds of my cleft, and then bury him deep in a long, fast stroke. I groan loudly, eyes clenching closed and mouth falling open, gasping for breath, and then I draw him out again, nearly out, pause, and impale myself onto him.

And then I try something else. I want to feel everything. I lift with my core and hips so he slips partway out, and then sink down just a little, and draw out a little, shallow thrusts so he's never fully in or fully out. This kind of stroke makes me crazy. Each time I whimper and moan and refuse to let myself sink him deep, and he begins to groan with me. I'm not seeking orgasm, I'm just finding him, finding me, finding us. I'm exploring this thing, this act called sex.

It's so far beyond amazing that I can't comprehend it. I press my open, quivering mouth to his sweating chest and continue shallow strokes for a few moments, and then I feel Dawson tense beneath me. His pectorals go hard as rock, his arms coil into stone, and his face freezes, his jaw clenched.

"Dawson? What's wrong?" I ask.

"I'm—holding back."

I realize he's at that edge, about to orgasm. "Let go, then."

"No. I want to come with you." He leans up and kisses me, intending it to be a quick kiss before falling back, but I follow him down and devour his mouth with mine.

"Then come with me," I say.

He groans as I slide him all the way in, and I love, almost more than anything else, hearing him make involuntary noises. I draw him out, and then impale him into me quickly. Our groans merge as our bodies join. I start a rhythm of deep strokes, holding on to his neck, moving only my hips. He lifts me up and takes a nipple into my mouth, and I whimper louder than ever, and I feel the crest of orgasm approaching. He's rock hard all over, every muscle tensed, and then as my motions become more erratic and my wordless moans of pleasure become his name groaned over and over again, he starts to move with me, and I have no control at all, no rhythm. I'm just desperately plunging onto him, filling myself with him.

"Oh, oh, god," I say as I feel him lose control as well.

"Swear," he grunts. He sees the momentary confusion on my face, and he elaborates. "Let go, baby. I want to hear you swear. Come for me, Grey. Come hard, and don't hold back."

I am holding back. I snake my arms around his neck and lie flat, all my weight on him, and grind my hips against his and let myself go. Screams are muffled by his flesh, and now I erupt, and his name is the only sound on my lips, chanted over and over again as heaven thunders open within me. I'm crashing, hips madly plunging and hands clawing into his skin.

"Dawson," I gasp, and then I remember what he said, and I crack the last shell of control, and all I can do is cling to him as the words tumble free. "Oh, *fuck*, Dawson! God, oh, god, oh, fuck…come with me, come now…"

The world ends in that moment. Lights flash and my entire existence shifts, and then I'm moving. He's above me, thank god, and he's wild, uncontrolled, plunging into me, and I love every touch, every slap, every slam, and I hear him groaning, and I expect to hear him swear like I did, but he surprises me.

"Grey." It's a whisper, a crazy contrast to his wild thrusting. "Oh, Grey, sweet Grey…my Grey…" And he comes at last. I feel it happen, a tensing followed by heat and he's gone, wordless, just his breath on my skin and our bodies as close as can be, and I feel his soul next to mine, in mine, around mine, woven together.

We both still and go quiet, breathing, and his weight is on me. He goes to move, but I stop him. "Stay. I like your weight on me. I like feeling this."

"Grey?"

"Hmm?"

"I love you." His voice is as soft as silk, a verbal caress. Nothing can ever be as sweet as his voice in that moment.

I move slightly, and he moves with me, and now his face is cradled on my chest, between my breasts, my hands in his hair and tracing the shell of his ear and the small place where his jaw meets his ear. "I love you, too." I breathe it, and he smiles against my skin.

We fall asleep like that, in that time where afternoon bleeds into evening.

I wake to his mouth on my breast and his fingers at the apex of my thighs, and before my eyes are open I'm spreading my legs for his touch and breathing sharply in happiness and ecstasy, and I've come again within minutes.

But I want something, I want to feel something. I got a taste of it when we made love, but I want it more fully. I push him to his back and take him in my hands and caress the length and thickness of him. I move my face across his chest and belly, press a kiss to the tip.

"Grey?" It's a hesitant question.

"I want this. I want to try it."

He brushes my hair away in that familiar gesture, and I take him into my mouth. Just a little at first. He moans immediately, and I know he likes this. That moan is what I want. A part of it, at least. I move my fist around him and set his hips to moving with my rhythm, and he groans, so I accompany that rhythm with my mouth on him.

And then I remember a customer at the club asking me to suck him off, and I think about that phrasing. So I suck, taking him deeper and sucking as hard as I can, and he lifts his hips off the bed and groans loudly, his hands tangling in my hair as if struggling not to pull me against him, and his hips flutter as if trying not to thrust.

I take him out of my mouth, and he groans in desperation. "Let go," I tell him.

He lifts up and glances at me, and I bend closer to him, brush him with my breasts, and he flops back but then lifts his head to watch again as I wrap my lips around him and suck him deeper into my mouth, close to my throat. And now I suckle him to the rhythm of my fist on his length, and his hips match that rhythm, unfettered thrusting. I match his motion so he doesn't gag me, and I suck harder, backing away and taking him deep with each thrust and each suck, and now he's groaning nonstop.

"Grey, Grey, oh, god…" His fingers tighten in my hair, and he's pulling me down gently.

I don't mind, and I follow his urging, going deeper. I don't go so deep as to feel gagged, but nearly, and now he's arching his back and lifting his hips, but I don't hurry, don't rush.

"Oh, fuck, Grey…I'm coming…" It's a warning, but I don't have time to think about what I'm going to do, because he's erupting in my mouth.

I taste it, thick and hot and salty and nothing like I expected. I swallow it and keep going, because he's still groaning and thrusting, so I match his frenetic pace with my fist and my mouth, and he spurts again, and again, and I'm swamped. His groaning is uncontrolled and spasmodic, and his eyes are fluttering in his head and he's mad with pleasure, and *that* is what I wanted, to give him such pleasure that he lost control like he made me do.

When I'm sure he's done coming, I take my mouth off him, but he's still sort of hard, and I love the feel of his erection in my hand, so I hold on to him and keep stroking him gently. He shudders with each touch, as if hypersensitive. My cheek is on his belly, and I'm afforded a close-up look at him, at his manhood. It's a beautiful thing. I've overheard girls, including my roommate Lizzie, talk about how—despite how good they feel—men's privates are ugly. Although they used the word "cock," which makes me cringe just thinking it, but I'm not sure what other word to use. I don't agree with those girls. Dawson is beautiful all over, every bit of him.

Eventually he draws me up to his chest, into the nook of his shoulder, and we sleep again.

The next time I wake up, it's slowly, gradually. It's either late or early, somewhere in the dark hours of the night or morning. There's a touch of gray on the horizon, making me think it's early. I've never slept naked with a man before, obviously. His arm is draped over my hip, his face buried against my back, his breathing deep and even. We're both still naked, covered now by the blanket and sheet. I love this feeling. I'm protected, safe, sheltered. He loves me, he's holding me close, even in sleep.

And then I become aware of something: His manhood…his cock…is nestled against me. It's hard, fully erect and thick. He got up at some point after we made love the first time to discard the condom, and now, in the dim light of predawn, I see another square on the bedside table near me.

I feel his…I think the word more easily, but still with a guilty cringe…his cock between the cheeks of my bottom, and I'm greedy for it. I want to be filled by him again. I need it. I'm…so desperate for it that I can't think of anything else.

I reach for the condom, and it crinkles noisily in the silent room. I examine it, a gray plastic square, *Trojan* written in white lettering. I rip it open and pull out what's inside. It's a circle of slippery rubber, or latex, actually, a thicker ridge surrounding trans-parent latex so thin as to be nearly invisible. Which is the point, I suppose. I unroll it a little, and then I realize Dawson's breathing has shifted.

He's awake.

I roll in place, and meet his sleepy gaze. He just smiles at me, lifts a heavy hand, and brushes his thumb across my cheekbone. I glance down between us and fit the condom over the tip of him, then clutch him near the base and hold him still, unrolling the latex over him slowly with one hand at first, then both, hand over hand until the ridged rim is flush against his pelvis. Dawson reaches down and pinches the tip a little, leaving a gap near the tip. He reaches for me, starts to move, but I just shake my head. I turn in place again, and press my back to his front. I spoon myself to him, and wriggle my hips until his thickness is buried where it was originally. Dawson cups my hip in his hand and presses a tender kiss to my shoulder blade. I wait until the desperation inside me cannot be denied, and then I reach down between us and guide the thick head of him inside me. I'm wet down there, damp and hot and slick. He slides deep into my core. He's in me, there. Buried home. Neither of us moves for a long moment, and then he rolls his hips and I moan, and he groans in tandem with me.

And then, oh, god, his fingers delve to the apex of my cleft and slip in, and I press my hips outward to allow him access, and he's pressing with his long middle finger, and we're moving together. I shift my hips away, and he pulls his erection out, and then we push ourselves together. It's clumsy at first, but then we find a rhythm, and his fingers…oh, god, the way he touches me makes me come apart before

I've even stroked a dozen times against him, and I'm shuddering and gasping with my mouth open wide in a silent scream, and then a few moments later it happens again, and I'm breathless and he's desperate against me, moving as if he can't find enough purchase to let go.

Dawson shifts, and I'm lying on my back on top of him. Oh…whoa. One hand is at my cleft, giving me orgasm after orgasm, and the other is on my breast. He takes my hand in his, and we work my nipples together, and he's crushing up and into me, and he's so, so, *so* deep that I nearly can't take it, but I do I take it and I love it and I need it.

And then he challenges me again. He moves my hand, tangled in his, to my clitoris, and we stimulate me together, and that's the most erotic thing I can imagine, until he takes his hand away and watches me. Both of his hands are tweaking and pinching my nipples, and I'm moaning, and now I—oh…oh—I touch myself and with him buried deep, I can touch myself in a way that even he can't. I feel a rhythm inside me, matched to some nebulous pattern inside me, a slow-to-fast rhythm all its own that has me too breathless to scream, hoarsely moaning and arching forward, and I feel Dawson watching me touch myself, and I know it makes him crazy, so I touch myself all the more vigorously.

I don't recognize myself.

I'm on top of a man I've only known for a matter of weeks, and I'm in love with him, and he's in love with me, and his cock is buried to the hilt inside me, and I'm touching myself as he rolls my thick pink nipples between his thumb and forefinger. I'm chanting his name and he's murmuring mine, and we're lost to each other.

It's heaven…

…but I don't recognize myself.

He explodes. Dawson calls my name, shouts my name, and I cry his, and he comes. And I come again. His hands clutch my breasts, and then one hand is on my hip, crushing me against him with every desperate thrust, and our voices are a song together, our bodies are moving in a dance, synchronized beauty, perfectly matched motion.

Who is this woman doing this? Making love with such wild and desperate sensuality?

I can almost see us, see myself as if from above. My breasts bounce and jiggle with each thrust of the man beneath me. His hands paw and claw at me, and I shove my chest into his touch, because I love his touch. And me…my own hand is between my thighs, touching my privates. My other hand is up behind me, grasping at Dawson's face and neck. His eyes watch me, watch my moving hand, watch my bouncing breasts.

"God, I love you," he whispers as he comes.

Who am I? Who am I, that this man loves me?

I'm not a film student, I'm not a stripper, I'm not a dancer, I'm not anyone. I'm just Grey Amundsen. But this glorious man, this near-deity…he loves me.

Why?

What am I, that he feels so strongly about me? What do I offer?

I don't know the answer to that, but I know he does.

So why don't I ask?

Because my throat closes and sticks. He might see the panic on my face, but he's behind me, rolling to one side, still buried deep, still thick, still pulsating with the aftershocks. I'm still quaking, too, still shuddering and shivering uncontrollably in wave after wave of post-orgasm earthquakes. Some of the shudders are from panic, though. He doesn't see. He slips out of me, out of bed and into the bathroom. I hear him wash his hands, and then he comes back and sidles up behind me and presses against me. His manhood is still slightly turgid, and he buries it between the globes of my backside. Even in my panic, I love that feeling.

And loving that sets off more panic. I just sinned. I had sex with a man. Three times, I had sex with him. Well, twice. I'm not sure if making him orgasm with my mouth counts as sex, but it definitely counts as sin. And letting him do the same, more times than

I can count? He made me orgasm so many times. I never even bothered counting.

Does that multiply my sin?

I'm not married to him. Not even engaged. I'm not even positive of his middle name. I don't know where he went to high school.

In the darkness of predawn, it's easy to feel the condemnation. I haven't thought of my father, really thought of him, in months. But now I remember him telling me I'd fall into a life of sin. And I have. Look at the life I've been living. He was right. Oh. Oh, god. God, forgive me. He was right. I hear and feel Dawson fall back asleep, and so he misses the single sob that escapes me. I shudder, and his arm tightens on me, tucked just beneath my breasts. I can't breathe. Can't…breathe.

What have I done? What have I let happen?

Exactly what I knew would happen, right from the first moment I saw him. I knew I would fall and lose myself in him, and I have. I fell in love, fell into sin.

I try to rationalize my way out of it: It's not sin. I love him. He loves me. And I don't even really believe in any of that anymore, do I? No. I don't. I didn't just have sex; I certainly didn't fuck. I made love, mutual love, to a good man. A wonderful man who's never done anything but try to take care of me and protect me and give to me. I'm not a pastor's daughter anymore. I don't go to church. I don't believe in God. So I haven't sinned.

Have I? Or doesn't it matter whether I believe?

I once heard Daddy—my father—telling a man in his congregation who was caught in adultery that it doesn't matter whether you believe in God or sin; He believes in you, and will judge you regardless of whether you choose to believe or not.

My head is spinning crazily, whirling, throbbing.

Other parts of me throb, too.

I worm my way out of Dawson's grip, leaving him in the bed, clutching a now-empty space. He's so peaceful, so beautiful. I can't help but just stare at him, and for the briefest moment, my worries vanish under the weight of the sheer rugged masculine beauty of the man and the tumultuous, tempestuous storm of emotions he incites in me.

Then they are back with a vengeance.

I walk to the bathroom, although hobble is a more appropriate word. My privates throb, ache, and twinge. My thighs tremble and hurt. Everything down there aches, but the memory of how that ache came about is sugar-sweet. Even through my guilt, I can't regret doing it. I regret my guilt, regret my upbringing that I can't just enjoy the love of Dawson.

God, I'm so confused. I'm overwhelmed to the point of breathless pain by the guilt and shame of what I just did, but at the same time a part of me is contented and self-satisfied and smug and in total bliss. The guilt, the Baptist shame, tells me the smug satisfaction is the seed of sin.

After using the toilet, wash my hands, and find my clothes in the darkness. I dress quietly, facing away from Dawson. Even my bra chafing my nipples now feels sensual, arousing, because it reminds me of Dawson's fingers and lips there. And my underwear, too, brings Dawson to mind, the way his tongue speared into my folds...I almost fall in and drown in that rapturous memory, but Dawson stirs and I'm shaken into moving.

I'm creeping out, watching Dawson return to sleep, and then stealing down the stairs, out the front door with my purse over my shoulder and the keys to the Rover in my hand. I don't know where I'm going, except away. I'm too confused, and I can't think around Dawson because I'll just want him all over again, and I already do want him. Even sore and aching, each step making my core throb, I want him. I want more.

I leave the neighborhood, carefully navigating away from the overstated grandeur of Beverly Hills. I find myself in the long-term parking lot of LAX, at the Delta counter. I don't even know where the ticket I just bought will take me, and I don't care. Nothing sticks in my awareness. I'm on autopilot, struggling against the current of guilt, against the thunderstorm of warring thoughts, needs, fears, guilt, desires.

I shouldn't love him.

But I do. And why not?

It was sin.

It was the greatest pleasure I've ever known, and I'll spend every moment of the rest of my life wanting and needing more.

He loves me.

But he barely knows me, and what if he finds someone else? Someone prettier? Someone more experienced? What if he has to do a love scene and I can't handle it? There's no if there; I couldn't take that. It would ruin me.

But I'm already ruined. No longer a virgin.

That's not ruin, that's beauty. The ache between my thighs is a reminder of love. Of the fervor of his desire.

My internal struggle runs on a continuous loop and it makes me dizzy. I make my disoriented way to a gate somewhere in the depths of LAX. I'm not really hearing anything or seeing anything. I hear announcements, boarding notices, warnings. And then people in the waiting area around my gate stand up and start gathering around the counter that funnels into the boarding tube. I think I see Dawson's dark hair and broad shoulders, but it's not him. He's home—his home—sleeping. He doesn't even know I've left.

I find my absent way to a seat by a window in the very back of the airplane. I hate flying, and I should be terrified, but I have no room for anything but the vortex of guilt and shame and love.

I ran away from Dawson again. He probably won't come after me this time.

I've lost him.

I should never have had him.

After a while, the jet taxis, and the pilot's voice comes on over the PA. Something he's saying breaks through the fog: "…third in line to take off, so things should be moving along shortly. We've got some good tailwind, so we should have you landing in Atlanta in just a few hours from now. Thanks."

Atlanta? I bought a ticket back to Georgia?

Oh, God. Oh, God. God help me, what am I doing? Why am I going back to Georgia?

A possible answer strikes me as we lift off: I'm going back to Macon to find myself. I lost who I am in L.A. Or maybe I never knew who I was, and L.A. only muddled that further.

It's too late to get off now.

CHAPTER FOURTEEN

I LAND IN ATLANTA AT 10:40 in the morning after a stopover in Houston. My stomach flops as the wheels touch down with a soft bounce, and after a long taxi, we pull up to a jetway. People around me gather their carry-ons and purses and laptops; I have nothing but my purse.

I stink of sex and sweat. My hair is in a messy bun, which I did in the airplane bathroom an hour before landing, having realized I looked exactly like I was running from someone, with my mussed and unbrushed hair.

I stink of Dawson. I reek of his musk, his essence, his touch.

I sense him all around me, in me. Which is nonsense, but I can't shake the feeling. I shuffle along the aisle to the jetway along with the other travelers, and I hate myself with every step. Dawson loved me, and I ran from him. I left him in the gray hours of dawn, and I'm running back to the one place I swore I'd never return. I can just imagine his heartbroken expression when he wakes up, about now, maybe, reaching for me, hunting for me in that palatial monstrosity of a house, and not finding me.

I didn't even leave a note.

I follow the crowd out into the airport, and the noise of chatter and bustle washes over me. I take a few steps away from the gate, heart aching with guilt, a lovesick soul cut into a thousand broken pieces. I had sex out of wedlock with a man I barely know and I left him without so much as a note of goodbye. I don't have a cell phone. I didn't bring my laptop or Fourth Dimension–issued iPad. He has no way of knowing where I am, even if he is inclined to chase me.

I stumble unevenly away from the gate, hearing the familiar twang of Georgia accents. I feel my own accent coming back and I haven't said a word.

I've had four and a half hours to stew and think, and I'm no closer to knowing what's right or why I'm back in Georgia. All I know is I want to go home—go to my dad's house, and take a shower and sleep forever.

And then…I feel the too-familiar tingling of my skin and the prickle of my senses and the lurch in my belly. Hot, strong, unrelenting hands close around my hips and pull me backward. I feel his chest at my back. I don't turn and acknowledge him; I slump back against him and muffle my sobs with my hands.

"You can't run from me, Grey." His voice is soft and powerful and intimate.

"How…how did you know?"

He laughs. "I felt you get up. Heard you crying. I knew you were panicking, and I knew you had to do it. I let you go, and I followed you. I was right behind you every step of the way. I sat in first class, and you never saw me. But I watched you cry, all alone. I watched you agonize."

"Dawson, I…I'm sorry." My accent, which I worked so hard to eradicate, is back in full force, as strong as when I was a clueless, mostly happy fifteen-year-old. I sniffle back a deprecating laugh. "God, listen to me. I sound like a redneck all over again, and I've only been back for five minutes."

"I love your accent. Let it out. Just be you. Be Grey Amundsen."

We haven't moved, and people swirl around us like muddy river water eddying around a rock.

"I don't know who that is," I say, letting my head rest against his firm chest.

He tucks a stray wisp of honey-blonde hair back behind my ear. "Yes, you do. You're you. You're Grey. A mixed-up film student. A pastor's daughter from

Macon, Georgia. You're the most beautiful woman I've ever met, and you're the most dangerously sensual woman I've ever met. You're hopelessly innocent, a little naïve, a lot stubborn, and absurdly cute when you're mad. You make my cock rock hard with a single look, and you have no idea you do it. You gave me the best day of my entire life, and then you ran away from it, which I knew you'd would." He's whispering this in my ear; I'm not breathing as he speaks. "You love me. And I love you. It's not a sin. Or if it is, I don't care.

"And you miss your dad. That's why you came back."

"I—what?"

He takes my hand and leads me away. "We're going to go see your dad. You miss him, and you want him back in your life. And you're going to introduce him to your boyfriend, the famous movie star."

"I do? I am?" I'm trotting beside him as he takes long, purposeful strides.

"Yep."

"Oh." I consider everything he's said as he goes through the process of renting a car.

He's adroitly ignoring the stares and whispers of people who recognize him, and I'm trying to do the same.

We find our rental car, a one-year-old convertible red Corvette. He slides into the driver's seat and turns to me. "Address?"

I spit it out without thought. "16543 Maple Grove Avenue." I blink through my confusion. "Wait. We're actually going back to my father's house?"

He backs out and pulls out of the parking garage before answering, punching the address I gave him into his phone, a GPS app, most likely. When we're heading toward my parents'—my father's—neighborhood, he just smiles at me. "Grey, just breathe. I love you. Unless you can tell me, without lying, that you don't love me back, then everything's going to be okay."

"I do love you. I do." I whisper it, and the words are lost in the roaring wind, as Dawson has the top down.

He hears anyway, or he reads my lips, or he just knows the truth. "Good. Then it's going to be okay. You love me. I love you. We'll work out the rest." He gives me a sharp look. "Do you regret what we did? What we have?"

I shake my head vehemently. "No! I don't—I don't regret it. It was…it was earth-shattering. I'm just all…all mixed up. I don't know what to believe."

"Believe in me. Believe in the fact that I love you." He grins at me. "And believe in the fact that, once we get things a little more settled, I'm going to make you come so many times you won't be able to walk for days afterward."

"I can already barely walk," I admit. "I'm sore."

He just grins. "That was just a warm-up, babe. I haven't begun to shatter your world. You can believe in *that*."

I shiver at the hot, hungry gleam in his eyes, and I do believe him. I'm still mixed up, though, but Dawson is here, beside me, loving me even though I ran.

I try to breathe, and I try to imagine what to say to Daddy. I don't even know where to start.

After a nerve-wracking hour and a half drive from Atlanta to Macon, we pull up to the two-story red-brick colonial in which I grew up. There's a "For Sale" sign in the front lawn, with a "Sold" marker in red across the top bar. My stomach lurches. The garage door is closed, no cars in the driveway. Daddy always parked in the driveway so members of his congregation would always know he was home and approachable. I get out of the Corvette, with Dawson behind me, and pull at the front door. It's locked. I fumble my key ring out of my purse, so long unused, and try the house key I never got rid of. It doesn't work; the locks have been changed.

"He…moved." I'm stunned.

"Shit. Now what? Do you know his number? Or somewhere you can find him?" Dawson is beside me, and my hand is in his. I don't remember twining my fingers in his, but it calms me enough so I can breathe.

I back away from the door, stumble down the three steps to the sidewalk, stopped from falling by Dawson, and he helps me into the car. I sit in the ivory leather seat and suck hot Georgia air into my lungs. "The church. He'll be at the church. Go back out to the main road and turn right."

Twenty minutes later, we're in the mostly empty parking lot of Macon Contemporary Baptist Church. It's a huge, sprawling edifice, with a towering, traditional steeple over the main sanctuary, all white stone blocks and dark wood pillars around the sides. There's an older-model red Ford Taurus in the lot near the office's entrance. The car belongs to Louise, Daddy's secretary. Beside the Taurus is an ancient F-150 that used to be green, but is now all rust and red mud and dirt splatter, which belongs to Jim, the janitor. There's another car belonging to Doug, the assistant pastor, and a few others I don't immediately recognize. A few spots away from these cars is Daddy's silver three-year-old BMW. He's here. Of course he's here.

I can't breathe all over again. I'm suddenly twelve and waiting for Daddy to come out. Sunday evening, after second service and the staff prayer meeting. I would sit in the parking lot, in the back seat of the car, reading a book, waiting for Mama and Daddy to take me home.

"It's all right, Grey. I'm here." Dawson's voice is a low rumble, breaking through my distorted memory.

I shake my head, breathe deep, and ground myself in the present. Dawson is here. He's…my boyfriend. He's mine. I'm his. He'll help me face Daddy. I shouldn't need help, but I do. I wipe my sweaty, clammy hands on my thighs and then step up out of the car, hiking my purse on my shoulder. Dawson slams his car door behind him and draws up next to me, taking my hand. I hesitate outside the glass door to the office wing of the church.

The black metal handle is hot under my hand, and through the glass I can see Louise walking away from the door, down the main hallway, a box in her pudgy arms. I pull open the door, and she hears it open, turns, and sees me. Her face goes momentarily blank. And then her southern hospitality kicks in, and she brightens. Louise sets the box down on the floor and bustles toward me, arms extended to hug me. Dawson lets me go and stands with his hands in his pockets as I embrace Louise. She's the same as ever, medium height, carrying most of her extra weight in her hips, graying black hair coiffed into a thick helmet of hair-sprayed perfection.

I'm suddenly aware of how I must look, how I must smell. I'm sure Louise can smell the sex on me, see it in the rat's nest of my hair. I wish I'd had time to shower, but there's nothing to be done now.

"Grey, how are you sweetheart? Why, I haven't seen you in an age! I thought y'all would never come back to see us! Don't you look just beautiful, and my, oh my, who is this tall drink of water?" Louise chatters nonstop, her accent thick as sludge and twanging like a plucked guitar string. Then she really sees Dawson, and she recognizes him. "Oh. Oh. Oh my… but you're—oh."

She flaps her face with a hand, and her generous bosom heaves, eyes wide. She glances at me, and then her eyes widen even more, to saucers, as Dawson makes a show of wrapping his arm around my waist, low, nearly on my backside. I lean into him, rest my head against his chest, and it's not a show. I need his proximity—I need to draw strength from him.

Louise has recovered a bit of her equilibrium. "Is this really who I think it is?"

I nod. "Louise Eldritch, this is Dawson Kellor. My boyfriend." I've never introduced anyone using those two words before. I go a little giddy.

Louise laughs nervously as she shakes Dawson's outstretched hand. "My lands, Grey! However did you meet him? He's even more handsome in person than in his movies!"

I frown. "Why, Louise, do you mean to tell me you've seen his movies? I wouldn't have pegged you for those types of films."

Louise blushes scarlet and waves her hand dismissively. "Well, you see, I…my Iris wanted to go see those movies that were so popular, you know the ones, about the magic and what-have-you. So of course I had to see them to make sure they were suitable for my daughter. I didn't let her go see them, mind you. They were just too filled with needless violence and sexuality, and—well, no offense, Mr. Kellor, but we don't hold stock in that kind of behavior."

Dawson smiles evenly. "No offense taken, Mrs. Eldritch. I know some of my films aren't for everyone. If I had a daughter, I certainly wouldn't let her see much of my work until she was old enough to understand and be discerning."

Louise nods seriously, and then turns to me. "So, Grey. What brings you back to town? I was under the impression that you'd relocated to Los Angeles more or less permanently."

Which was Louise's way of saying that she knew about my falling out with Daddy, and wanted the inside scoop.

"Is Daddy in his office? I'd like to see him."

"He is, you know he is. He's just…well, I'll let him tell you." The affable, genteel exterior fades, and I'm afforded a glimpse of the sharply intelligent, protective, and rather judgmental woman beneath. "Things haven't been the same since you left, Grey. I must say. And your father…well…he's changed. Your poor mama's passing changed him, and not for the better. And when you left…. He hasn't been well, you know. But I've said too much. It's his story to tell. Come on, sweetheart. I'll take you to him."

She leads Dawson and me through the maze of hallways and interconnected offices to Daddy's expansive corner office. His door is closed, and Louise knocks once, perfunctorily, and then opens it. She pushes through, and I follow behind. What I see shocks me.

Daddy is sitting on the floor of his office, stacks of reference books piled around him between empty boxes. The built-in shelves are empty, and a carefully arranged pile of boxes sits in one corner, taped closed and labeled in Daddy's neat script. He's got four or five thick books on his lap, and he's flipping through another, which he then sets aside on a smaller pile, picks up one from his lap, checks the spine, flips through it, and sets it in a different pile. He doesn't hear us knock or enter. Music plays loudly from a small Bose iPod dock: "Hibernia" by Michael W. Smith. The distinctive and beautiful piano chorus with the orchestral backing washes over me, sinks into me. This was one of the few songs by him I actually liked, mainly because there weren't any words.

I watch Daddy flip through another thick reference book. He has changed. He's thinner, much thinner. His hair is more silver than blond, and it's thinning, and the bald circle at the top of his head has expanded significantly. He looks…old. And frail.

Louise bends over near him and whispers in his ear. His head snaps up, and his eyes lock on me.

I swallow hard at the welter of emotions I see in his gaze. I should have called. I should have checked on him. There's so much between us, and I have no idea what he'll say, how he's going to react to my unexpected return.

He struggles to his knees, and then to his feet. Louise catches his elbow and helps him, and I see something in the way they look at each other briefly, in the way she helps him to his feet. Louise is a widower, too, her husband having passed of a heart attack about three years before Mama died. I'm frozen in place as I put two and two together. Daddy brushes his hands down the front of his pressed Dockers, smoothing the creases, and then takes three hesitant steps toward me. He moves slowly, as if stiff.

"Grey?" His voice is unchanged, still deep and powerful and stentorian. "You came back?"

I glance at Dawson, who just smiles encouragingly at me. I look back to Daddy, and take a single step in his direction. We're separated by a few feet still, but I can see his features working, his eyes taking me in, searching me. "I...I just, I wanted to—I mean—" I have no idea what to say. I hadn't meant to come back.

Daddy's face crumples, and he rushes to me, wraps his arms around me, and holds me. He's crying loudly. "I'm so sorry, Grey. I'm so sorry. I was so stubborn. I should have…I should have loved you. I never thought I'd see you again. I'm so sorry, Grey." He takes a step back and wipes his face with a hand. "Forgive me, Grey."

I never, ever expected this from him. "I—of course, Daddy."

He closes his eyes and slumps, stumbling into Louise's side. She holds him up and pats his shoulder. "I never…I thought I'd lost you forever. I've missed you so much."

I look past him at the stacks of books, the boxes, the desk cleared of papers and pens and the computer. "What's going on? Why are you packing up the office? And—the house. You sold it?"

Daddy straightens, and then moves around behind the desk, visibly strengthening and reassuming some of his old authority. He clicks off the Bose stereo, cutting off "Hibernia" as it begins a second play-through, and then he roots in a drawer, finds a key ring with a circular tag and one key. "Yes, I'm—I've retired. Doug is taking over as full-time executive pastor. I'll still do a few sermons here and there, but…yes. As for the house…I moved out a few months ago, into a condo a few minutes from here. The house was…it was too hard to live there. It was too big, too empty." He looks down and rubs at the desk surface with a thumb. "There were too many memories. I saved all your things, though. Your belongings, along with what I didn't bring to the condo, are in a storage unit a couple miles from the condo. This is the key." He hands the key to me, and I take it.

Louise is still in the room, hovering in the door. "Are you okay, Erik?"

He nods, and smiles tenderly at Louise. "Yes, I'm fine, d—don't worry." It sounded to me like he was going to say "dear." He must see my questioning expression as I look from Daddy to Louise and back, wondering. He winces. "Louise and I…we're—what I mean to say is, we—"

I interrupt. "Daddy, that's your business."

"I just don't want you to think I've—"

"I'm not ready for that conversation. I'm just not."

He nods. "Yes. I see. Perhaps you're right." He glances past me to Dawson, who is leaning against the door with his phone in his hand, idly checking emails or something. "Who is this young man?"

Dawson steps forward immediately, shoving the phone into his pocket and extending his hand. I see Daddy scrutinizing Dawson, and I see when recognition hits, seconds before Dawson introduces himself.

"Dawson Kellor, sir."

"Erik Amundsen." Daddy takes Dawson's hand, and the two men shake. "How do you know my daughter?"

"We're working on a film together." My heart skips as Dawson seemingly dismisses our relationship, but then he continues. "That's how we met, at least. I love your daughter, sir. Grey is the most amazing person I know."

Daddy clears his throat. "Nice to meet you." He has a million questions, and he doesn't like the situation, and my old Daddy is probably still in there, but he's keeping it to himself.

It's an improvement, it's a beginning, and I'll take it.

CHAPTER FIFTEEN

"…AND THE OSCAR FOR Best Actor goes to…Dawson Kellor!" Channing Tatum claps his hands, the sound too loud in the microphone, his hands hitting the envelope. Beside him, Emma Stone claps as well, holding a smile as Dawson rises to his feet and makes his way down the aisle.

As he passes me, he leans over and whispers, I *love you*, in my ear, kissing me quickly. He trots up onto the stage, gives Emma a gentle embrace, and then does the back-slapping man-hug thing with Channing. My heart is pounding, and I'm on my feet, screaming and cheering as Dawson accepts the golden statue.

I'm overwhelmed, but that's nothing new. Tom Hanks is a few rows back, Ted Danson is at the end of my row, and Jay-Z, Beyonce, and several of their friends sit directly in front of me. I see famous faces wherever I look. And then there's me.

Gone With the Wind was a box office smash, tying with *Avatar* for the highest-grossing film of all time. I wasn't even in the credits, but I couldn't care less. I worked on it, I helped make it. I sat next to Jeremy Allen Erskine during most of the shoot and watched, listened, and learned. I ran errands for Dawson and Kaz and Jeremy, and I took lots of notes. Through it all, Dawson and I worked things out. He hasn't proposed yet. I try and tell myself that I'm not in a rush. I love him, and that's all that matters but deep down, the doubts pick at me. What if he doesn't? What if he's changed his mind about marrying me?

He had his contract modified when we got back to L.A. from our trip to Macon. He would kiss Rose, but he wouldn't do any explicit love scenes, and that also went into his rider. So, even though the remake was much darker and grittier and more graphic, including a sex scene that nearly got us an NC-17 rating, it was almost entirely a body double and computer effects, after the initial kiss.

And that kiss between Dawson and Rose? I kept it together despite my stomach thinking otherwise. I had to watch it, over and over again, take after take, until Jeremy was finally satisfied. Dawson was just as upset about it as I was, which was all that really got me through it. If he has any other roles that demand a kiss, I might have to take a long vacation and not see the movie.

Except I'll probably work on all his movies.

All this runs through my head as Dawson shifts his weight in front of the podium, adjusts the mic, and clears his throat. "God, this is awesome. Thanks so much, everybody. The Academy, obviously. Jeremy, you rock. Rose, Armand, Carrie: You're the best co-stars I could ask for. Dad, for getting me into movies when I was four." He holds up the statue, and my heart is in my throat. Will he mention me? "Um, so…I know I don't have long, but I've got something else to say, and you'll just have to adjust your schedule, 'cause I've got the mic." People laugh at this, and he licks his lips, a sign of nerves.

What's he doing?

He finds me, his eyes locking on mine. "Grey? Get up here, babe." I shake my head, but I can't deny him. I get up, shake the skirt of my dress loose, and approach him. He comes to the stairs and hands me up, then takes his place by the mic, my hand still in his. He digs his free hand into his pocket, and his eyes burn into mine. "Grey, baby. You'll probably get mad at me for this but…I'm doing it anyway. I love you. So much. You've given me my life back."

The crowd is chattering, whispering laughing, *awww*-ing. I hear, but I'm not aware of them, except as background noise. I realize what's coming. I can't move, can't speak, can't breathe. I can only watch as Dawson pulls out a black box from his pants pocket, opens it, and shows me a huge, glittering diamond ring. It's got to be at least four carats, but even the brilliance of the ring can't keep my gaze from Dawson's.

"Grey? Will you marry me?" He says the words, then sinks to one knee, holding the box up to me.

I stare at the ring, then at Dawson. There's only one answer, of course. "Yes." I say it quietly, and my voice cracks at the end. I try again, louder, leaning toward the mic. "Yes, yes! Dawson, baby…you're crazy, but yes, I'll marry you."

The audience howls and cheers, and for the first time I glance out at them. It's a mistake. There are thousands of people, famous people, important people, all watching me. I've never been in front of a crowd like this, and my knees buckle. Dawson catches me as I stumble, and he laughs as I stare up at him in perplexed shock. The reality of what he just did, what just happened, is sinking in. He just proposed to me during his acceptance speech at the Academy Awards. He just proposed to me. At the Oscars. Most of the world is watching. Live.

I start to hyperventilate.

And then warm wet strong lips touch mine, and I give myself over to the kiss, to Dawson's mouth taking mine, giving me my breath back. I hold on to him, to his broad shoulders that are hard beneath his silky suit coat. He breaks the kiss, slips the ring onto my finger.

And then Morgan Freeman is beside us, tall and imposing, speaking to Dawson in that amazing voice of his. "Well, John Travolta and Rachel McAdams were supposed to be the next presenters, but you and your new fiancée here might as well do the honors."

Dawson's arm clamps me to his side, and I lean against him, trying not to look out at the crowd or the cameras. Dawson reads from the prompter, introducing the next award, for Best Actress. My head is whirling and spinning, so I hesitate when Dawson nudges me with his hand. Then I realize he wants me to read the list of names. I clear my throat and read the words on the prompter, the names of the actresses and the movies they were in, which includes Rose for her role as Scarlett.

I'm proud of myself for getting through the presentation without stumbling over my words, and then Dawson is taking an envelope from a black-clad stage hand with a headset on. He rips it open, flips the flap up, and reads.

"The Oscar for Best Actress goes to…Rose Garret!" He grins and points with his Oscar at Rose as she rises in her seat. "Rose, you're amazing. You deserve it. And now, I'll finally leave the stage. Y'all can have your program back now." Everyone laughs at him, and then he's sweeping me off-stage and into the darkness of the back-stage area. We're in a far back corner beneath a red-lit exit sign, and his features are bathed in the glow. He's deliriously happy.

And so am I.

"Are you mad?" he whispers to me, his voice in my ear, low and intimate.

I let him press me up against the door, and I plant a soft kiss to his jaw. "No, I'm not mad," I whisper. "Surprised. I was starting to wonder if you were ever—"

"I wanted it to be something you'll never forget."

"I don't think there's ever been a proposal like it." I giggle as his mouth descends to my neck, to the hollow of my throat, and then down to my cleavage. I stop him there, though. "Not here."

"No?" He glances around us, to the bustle at the entrances to the stage, the black-clad stagehands scurrying back and forth, quiet whispers in headsets. We're isolated here, but still visible.

I shake my head. "No. Too public." His mouth doesn't leave my skin, and I have to wrench myself out of his grip, laughing. "Come on, Dawson. Not here. Take me somewhere more private, and you can do whatever you want to me."

"Whatever I want?" There's a dark edge to his voice.

I take the dare. "Whatever you want."

He kisses the slope of my cleavage once more and then straightens, tugging his suit coat back into place and fixing his tie. I adjust my dress, shifting my breasts and pushing at the loose strands of my hair. When we're both presentable, he leads me out and back into the foyer area, which is bustling with reporters and men and women with cameras and microphones. We're assaulted immediately by a flood of lightbulb flashes and questions. I hold on to Dawson and smile, let them see the ring, and try not to panic. These situations always make me a little crazy, and it's usually all I can do to stay calm and let Dawson do the talking. If it was just me, I'd freak out and try to run, but Dawson is always calm and in control.

And then someone asks me a direct question. "Grey, over here, Grey. Were you surprised by Dawson's proposal? Did you feel pressured to say yes because it was so public?"

Dawson starts to answer, but stops when he sees I'm answering. "Was I surprised? Yeah, clearly. I mean, you saw my reaction. Did I feel pressured? No, not at all. I knew he was going to ask me—I just wasn't expecting it to be in the middle of the Academy Awards." I laugh at that, and the crowd of reporters laughs with me. "I said yes because I love him and I want to marry him. There was no pressure at all.

Except, I mean, having millions of people watch you in a situation like that is always scary."

And then Dawson is shutting down the questions and pulling me into a walk to our waiting limousine. Greg is behind the wheel, and I don't even know how Greg knew to pick us up, but he's here, and I'm sliding in across the seat as gracefully as it's possible to get into a low-slung limousine in an evening gown.

It's a quiet ride through L.A. Dawson's hand is on my leg, our fingers tangled together. I halfway expect him to make his move in the limo, but he doesn't. I'm tense, wondering what he's going to do to me, but it's an excited tension. I want him. I wanted to let him take me backstage, but I'm not brave enough for that kind of public display. The proposal was public enough.

Dawson rummages in a console, finds a cord of some kind, and plugs it into his phone, then pushes a few buttons in the console. After a moment, music comes over the speakers. I laugh when I hear the song: "Marry Me" by Train.

"Really? Cute, Dawson."

"Originally, I was just going to play this song while we were driving around, and I was going to pull over and propose in the car. But then I realized that just wasn't anywhere near good enough. You deserve everything. The whole world. Certainly you deserve a show-stopping proposal." He lifts my left hand and examines the ring. "It was a risk doing it that publicly. I wasn't sure how you'd react. I mean, I was 99.9 percent sure you'd say yes, but—"

"You're a public person," I say. "So if I wasn't willing to be seen by the whole world, I wouldn't be with you. It was scary, but…I think a cliché proposal at a fancy restaurant just wouldn't have been you."

"You mean the whole ring at the bottom of a glass of champagne thing?" I laugh, and he shrugs, seeming almost embarrassed. "I almost did that, too, actually. I've spent so many months trying to figure out the best way to ask you that it turned into this whole snowball thing. I was freaking out. No lie. Then when I got the Best Actor nom, I knew that was it. I just wasn't sure if you'd, like, pass out or something."

I laugh, remembering all too vividly how close I came. "I nearly fell over!"

His gaze turns to mine. "I'll never let you fall."

"I know."

He kisses me then, and, as always, I get lost in it, tumble willingly into the bliss of his mouth on mine.

And then we're under the arch and Greg is opening the door for us. Dawson sweeps me off my feet, into his arms, and Greg trots ahead to unlock the door and let us in, but he doesn't follow us. I hear the door close and the limo driving away. My heart is pounding again, because he's staring at me with moss-and-bark eyes, hot, hungry eyes. He carries me through the house, to the door that leads to his— our—garage. I hold still and wonder, wait.

He licks his lips as we pass car after car. Old, new, shiny, battered, in various stages of completion. We come to the end, the Bugatti. The mirrored finish reflects the soft white glow of the overhead lights, and our shapes as we approach. He sets me down on my feet at the hood end of the car. I stare up at him, waiting and expectant.

I've learned him, over the past year. He's never satisfied, never sated. He always wants me. He wants me seconds after he finishes inside me. He wants me in his sleep, in the shower, in his study, on the set.

And he's had me in most of those places. Including the set of Tara, during filming of Gone *With the Wind*. He brought me there late one night, to the front porch of the full-size plantation house built in the countryside near Atlanta. He took me right there on the porch, lying on a blanket he'd brought with him, stars shining and frogs singing in the warm fall night.

I went on birth control while we were in Macon, and I've come to love the feeling of him bare inside me, nothing between us.

"Anything?" he asks again.

I don't hesitate. "Anything."

There's only one thing we haven't done. I'm still not comfortable with any of the normal terms for things, and Dawson thinks my clean and proper speech is cute. I'm willing to let him do that, but I'm not sure he'd bring me to the garage for it.

He smiles, a predatory, erotic gleam in his eyes. He brushes a strand of hair away from my eyes, and then his hands glide over my shoulders, around to my back. I'm wearing a Givenchy Couture gown that Dawson surprised me with for tonight's appearance. It's both modest and sultry, showing off my curves while not revealing too much skin. Since I stopped stripping, I've found my own style, a meeting of sexiness and taste. I'm gradually finding out who I am.

I'm Grey Amundsen, and I am desired.

His hands go to the zipper between my shoulder blades and pull it down so slowly, I shiver as his knuckles brush my skin between the widening gap. He slides the thin straps off my shoulders with a flick of his hands, and the dress billows with a soft *whoosh* to the floor, pooling at my feet in a slowly settling pile of lace and chiffon. My surprise for Dawson is revealed: I'm not wearing anything under the dress. His breath leaves him in a slow sigh, and he gnaws on his upper lip as he drinks in my body.

Instead of touching me, he backs away, turning at the last second to face the wall where a built-in iPhone dock is located. Those speaker docks are in every room of the house, including the bathroom.

He sets his phone on the dock, scrolls through his songs until he finds the one he wants. A fast electronic beat fills the garage, and I immediately recognize the song. It's "Palladio" by Silent Nick, one of Dawson's favorite songs to work out to, and one of my favorite songs to dance to. He approaches me with a sway to his hips, a bounce in his step. Of course, he can dance. He can do pretty much anything.

He takes my bare hips in his hands and moves my body with his, a sensual writhing of our bodies to the music. In rhythm to the music, I reach up and pull his slim black necktie free, drape it around my neck, and then slide his coat off. I slip his buttons free, one by one, popping them loose to the beat as we dance together, and then toss the shirt to the floor on top of his coat. As we move, his hands slide up my sides, hold my ribs just beneath my swaying breasts. His eyes lock there, so I accentuate the movement of my upper body, making them jiggle and sway even more, and his lips curve in a smile. I unbuckle his belt, whip it free of his pants, toss it aside, far from the car, and then slowly work his pants open. His body ripples in time to the music, his sculpted abs shifting and tensing as he dances with me, cupping my backside, tangling his fingers in my hair, tracing the curve of my belly to hips. I let his dress slacks fall to the floor, and he steps out of them.

He's in nothing but his boxer-briefs, dark maroon
cotton molded to his taut backside, bulging where his
manhood strains at the cotton. There's a dot of moisture where his tip touches the fabric. I run my fingers
around the gray elastic waistband, gradually working
it down his hips to the beat of the music, swaying my
hips, shaking my cleavage at him, leaning in to steal a
quick kiss, and then I grow impatient and shove the
underwear off him and he steps free, kicking it away.

And now we're both naked in the garage, dancing, our bodies reflected in the mirror-finish of his
Bugatti, his darker skin blending with mine. The
song has shifted, another entrancing, quick-beat
house song. We keep swaying, keep dancing, our
bodies closer. My breasts brush his chest, and he dips
at the knees to take a nipple in his mouth. I gasp, and
he suckles until my knees flex, and then he's back
upright, dancing chest to chest with me. His hand
steals between our bodies and I shift my legs apart to
let him in. By the song's end my cheek is pressed to
his and I'm panting as we sway together, losing the
rhythm as I come apart under his touch.

Dawson turns me in his arms as I come. He's still
moving to the music and all I can do is let him hold
me as waves shock through me. He leans me forward
over the hood of the car, his erection hard against my
backside. I'm anticipating him inside me, but I'm still
not sure what his plan is.

"I've wanted to do this since the first day I met you," he growls in my ear.

"Do what?"

"Make love to you on the hood of this car." My body is pressed to the cold surface of the hood. "Open your eyes," he commands. "Look at us. Watch us."

This close, our reflections aren't distorted. My breath has fogged the mirrored surface where my cheek was pressed to the metal, but I can see him behind me, all brawny bulk, ripped stomach and massive shoulders and thick arms, and my breath is lost as it always is by how perfect he is. I see me, my face, my cheeks flushed red, my hair coming loose from the up-do Luisa, my stylist, put it in. Thick strands flutter around my cheeks and mouth. My eyes are wide and my neck is curved as I watch us, and the reflection of my breasts merging with my flesh as I'm bent over the hood.

His hands are on my shoulders, and his eyes meet mine in the reflection. He caresses my back, my spine, my shoulders, my ribs, my hips. He settles his grip on my hips and pulls me hard against him, and I can't help grinding into him, needing him inside me now. I need it. I'm as insatiable as he is. I never take the lead, though, not until we're in the moment together. When I feel him close to release, that's when I take over and bring him to climax. Otherwise, I let him take me as he will, let him decide how he wants me. I love the mystery of it, because he's always inventive and creative and always thinks of my pleasure before his. He's never come before me, unless I use my mouth on him. So now I'm still, and waiting. But I need it, so badly, and that little grinding roll of my hips is my way of telling him to hurry.

He lets go of my hips and takes the generous bubble of my bottom in both hands, and then his finger, the middle finger of his right hand, slips into the crease and finds my rear entrance. I shiver and gasp and shake, sure of what he's going to do now, and not entirely sure I'm ready for it. I want it, I do, but I'm not sure I'm ready.

His finger glides over me, back there, and I flinch. "I want you, here."

"Now?" I gasp the question.

"No, baby. Not yet. You're not ready." Even as he says this, his finger presses, just slightly, the gentlest application of pressure.

"I'm not?"

"No." He chuckles, but then quickly sobers, and his eyes narrow. "You sound…almost disappointed. You want that?"

A little more pressure, and I'm trying not to squirm away, but the pressure is gentle and relentless, and now there's an ever so slight intrusion, and I'm breathless. "I'm…oh…*god*…I'm curious."

"You'll love it. I know you will. You're so perfect, so sensual. So responsive."

"I'm loud." A little more, and those two words are all I can manage. I can't believe I'm letting him do this, but then, yes, I can, because I love anything and everything to do with him, and I trust him. And it feels…so good.

"I love that about you. I love that I can make you scream. It's a game I play with myself. To see how loud I can make you scream. When I fuck you in your ass, I might have to do it somewhere far from people, because baby, you're going to *scream*."

I moan as the intrusion becomes presence, and my hips push back, just a little, of their own accord. My eyes are closed, and I feel his other hand find my cleft and my clitoris, and I'm unable to stop the small shriek of ecstasy as he brings me to climax again. I'm out of patience now. I lift up on my toes and rub my folds against his hardness, begging him silently.

He slowly and gently withdraws his finger. "Are you ready, babe?" His voice is silk sliding over me, his mouth against my ear, his chest against my back.

"Yes…" I breathe. "Now."

"Is that an order?" His voice is amused.

I nod, my cheek against the cold hood of the Bugatti. I harden my voice and put all the command into my delivery as I can, craning my neck to meet his hot hazel gaze over my shoulder. "*Now*, Dawson."

He literally growls, and his pupils dilate. His manhood jerks and thickens. "*Fuck* me, that's hot. You should order me around more often."

I would, but he's got his erection in his hand and he's teasing my clitoris with it. His knuckles brush against my inner thighs as he moves himself, and I'm straining for stillness, waiting for him to slide into my folds.

He does, but it's glacially *s s s s l l o o o o w w w*, an oh-so-gradual merging of bodies. "I can't wait to call you my wife," he murmurs, bent over me to whisper in my ear.

I moan, both at his words and his entrance into me. "Me, too. But…you already are my husband—we just haven't said the words yet."

He slides fully into me, hips against my flexed bottom. "True."

That's all he says, because words are beyond both of us then, for a moment. He withdraws, and slides back in. My groan is a quiet breath against the hood. And then he's taking my hips in his big hands and pulling them, lifting me. I push up onto my hands and onto my toes, spine arched down, bent over fully. He pushes deep, and I'm screaming silently, mouth wide.

"Watch us, babe."

I force my eyes open and down to our reflection. My breasts hang low, swaying with our quickening rhythm, and his shape is above me, tan and huge, and my skin is flushed all over, and then I move my gaze down, and I'm hypnotized by the sight of our joining. I can see it all in the reflection of the hood, his thick shaft sliding out, my folds taut and stretched to take all of him, and then he's moving and I watch as he enters me, and my blood pumps wildly, adrenalized lust flowing through me at the erotic sight of us moving together. I squeeze with the muscles of my vagina, and he groans as my walls clamp down around his erection; I feel him swell and burgeon, and I know he's close, know my turn is coming soon.

He's losing his rhythm, his motions growing erratic. He grips my hip in one hand and jerks me roughly against him. I like the roughness. I love it. It's a tender thing, counter-intuitively. The roughness of his ardor is when I love our sex the most, when he's beyond control. His other hand cups one swaying breast and squeezes, kneads, grips, thumbs the nipple and pinches it, and he's losing it—his eyes are closing and sweat is beading on his brow and he's moving faster and faster.

Now. Now it's my turn.

I lift up on my toes, clamping down with my walls, and crash down against him. He groans, and I do it again. I start moving against him, into his thrusts. Where before I was moving with him, in sync with him, now I meet his thrusts with my own, harder and harder.

"Touch yourself," he orders, breathless.

He's watching. I brace my head on my forearm on the hood of the Bugatti, lifted up onto my toes. His hands both go to my hips, and he lifts me so I'm not touching the floor with my feet at all, my head and my chest on the hood, and he pumps into me as I slide my fingers against my slick flesh.

I start to come, and he moves harder, pulling me into his thrusts, and I'm screaming, ululating, out of control, and then I feel him start to shudder, and I find my breath, remember what he said about me giving him commands.

"Say my name when you come," I tell him. I also know he likes it when I swear, which I don't often do, so I give him that now as well. "Say my name when you fuck me."

He bellows, a roar of brute animalism, and he pushes deep into me. "Grey! Oh…god…Grey, my love." He comes apart then, no rhythm, no pattern, just motion and desperation. "I love you, fuck, I love you so much."

He fills me. I feel the release, a jetting spasm of wetness and heat inside me. He fucks me then. Out of control and forceful, and I meet him with a fuck-ing rhythm of my own, milking his release, and then I come again, feeling another spasm from him as I collapse against the car and roll my hips into him, our bodies slowing and softening and going tender once more.

I'm limp against the mirror-silver of the Bugatti, blessedly cool against my sex-hot flesh. His manhood softens inside me, aftershocks rocking us both, quakes shivering over me, spasmodic fluttering thrusts from him that make the aftershocks in me harder.

He's breathless, panting, but he pulls out of me, draws me me up and then back against his chest and kisses my temple, nibbles my earlobe, then down to my jaw and shoulder. Our skin is slick and hot and sweaty, and we're both breathing hard, and I've never in my life ever been happier than in this moment. I feel taken away by true, bone-deep joy. He gives it to me, that joy, with his love. I rest my head against his shoulder, and he twists us to kiss my lips, leaving us both more breathless than ever.

He lifts me in his arms, effortlessly, and carries me into the house, leaving his phone and the music playing and the door to the garage open. Into the living room, and he lays me gently on the couch, opens the lid of an ottoman, and pulls out a thick, soft blanket. He slides onto the couch behind me, his spine against the back of the couch. We're sweaty and sticky, and I love it. His softened manhood is against my backside, and we doze like that, thoughts of having him take me back there running through my head.

I want it.

I let the dirty thought float through my head: *I want his cock in my ass.*

I almost giggle out loud at the dirty, nasty, sensual thought, but it's too erotic to laugh at, and I'm mostly asleep, drifting and drowsing with his hand absently cupping one breast, the other wedged between us and the couch cushion.

When we wake up, I'll have him take me that way.

Or maybe, since his birthday is coming up next week, I'll wait until his birthday, and I'll make a special event of it.

He shifts in his sleep, moving against my bottom, and I wonder, as sleep takes me, how it will feel. Like everything he does, amazing, I'm sure.

I'm going to be his wife.

CHAPTER SIXTEEN

IT'S FOUR O'CLOCK on a Tuesday afternoon. Dawson is reading for a part; he's reached the level where he rarely has to audition, but apparently the casting people and the director have a few big-name actors in mind for the role, and they need to see who's right for it. I'm on Rodeo Drive, shopping for his birthday surprise tomorrow night. Of course, there's a big party tonight, a swanky, glitzy thing set up by his manager, Audrey. It's a big deal, since the who's-who of the attendee list reads like an issue of *OK Magazine*. It's going to be fun, in a role-playing sort of way. I've done a few appearances with Dawson—none as big or dramatic as the Oscars, obviously—and each time, I feel like I have to be the glamorous, confident version of me, the arm-candy, entertaining me. I have to wear shudderingly expensive gowns and jewelry and shake hands with people like Cameron Crowe and Adam Carolla and Jennifer Lawrence. Yes, it's exciting, but in a nerve-wracking sort of way. Especially since I'm in the business, a teeny-tiny little fish in a big, dangerous ocean. And those gowns? I spend my time worrying about about potentially ripping or staining a gown that costs as much as or more than most people's houses are worth.

I've gotten the manicure and the pedicure already, and after I finish shopping, Luisa is coming over to do my hair and makeup. That—having a personal stylist—is my favorite part of being with someone as wealthy as Dawson. It's shallow and horrible, I know, but it's just the honest truth. The girl in me loves having someone primp and preen my hair until it's perfect, and to do my makeup in a way that I never could. Luisa has this technique that gets my eyes just smoky enough to be sexy, but not so much that I look like someone from *Jersey Shore*, which is what I end up with if I do it myself. Luisa has tried to show me, but I just never get it right.

The mani-pedi every week is nice, too.

I won't even mention the personal massage therapist. That would just be mean.

I step into the lingerie store Agent Provocateur, and my heart is in my throat. I've always bought my underwear from somewhere like Kohl's, or, if I've got some extra money, Victoria's Secret. And it's always just basic underwear and bras. I've never even tried on real lingerie. The most daring undergarment I own is a backless, strapless bra that I bought for my first big night out with Dawson where I knew we'd be photographed.

The woman who greets me is polished and sophisticated, the picture of Rodeo Drive excellence. She's tall, lithe, and platinum blonde. She introduces herself as Violet, which is just the most apropos thing I can imagine.

"Can I help you find something?" Her voice is like silk.

"I—well…" My throat is dry, and I've got no idea what to ask for. I don't even know where to start. I decide to go for honesty; I'm embarrassing myself either way. I'll probably never be able to visit this store again. "I've never shopped for…lingerie before. It's my boyfr—my *fiancé's*— birthday tomorrow, and I want to wear something to surprise him."

She nods evenly, and her expression never changes, although I can almost smell the contempt coming from her. "I see. Buying him something extra to unwrap, hmm?"

"Something like that. He already has pretty much everything, so all I can really get him that he'll want is…well, me." I blush as I say it, but it's true.

I see her expression shift slightly, and I realize she recognizes me but can't place me. It's weird to be recognized. "Ah, I see," she says, looking me up and down, assessing. "You're very tall, even in flats. A very…generous build, as well. You're probably a D cup, but no more than a thirty-two or -four around." She paces around to the side and examines my butt. It's weird to be so thoroughly examined by a woman. "A four panty, most likely." She says this in a nearly disapproving way.

I realize, somewhat belatedly, that she's used to seeing petite women of a very particular size and shape come in here, and I'm not that. There's no obvious condescension in her tone—she's too professional for that—but there's clear judgment. I pretend I don't notice. She measures me, and then shows me several different kinds of lingerie, some that are full-body suits which leave most of me bare, others that are little more than complicated and lacy bra-and-panty sets. What catches my interest, though, is the corsets. There are all sorts of interesting and sexy numbers in this section, bustiers and basques and corsets, some that are sheer, some opaque, all providing lift and shaping. Not that I need lift or shaping, but still. That's the point of lingerie, isn't it? To accentuate and accelerate what you've already got?

I realize, as I browse, that the sizing here is weird. I'm a size four in their underwear, when normally, at every other store I've ever shopped at, I'm more of an eight or ten. I try on several different options, and settle on an item which Violet calls a "Leah corset." It's flesh-colored, pleats of soft fabric wrapping around and tied in the back, lifting and compressing and all-around providing enough oomph that even I can tell I look good. Dawson is going to combust.

After Violet has all the ties tugged tight and fastened, I examine myself in the mirror, and imagine his reaction. He's…oh, my. He's going to get that look in his eyes, the nova-hot, dangerous one, the dilated pupils and the ravenous gleam of raw lust and bone-shaking love.

"I'll take this one," I tell Violet.

I get dressed and wait by the register as she wraps the lingerie for me and rings it up. I hadn't looked at the tag, so my throat closes when I see the number on the register screen: $1,709.25. I have to remind myself to breathe, tell myself that this is fine. I can afford this.

I hand her the Chase bank card Dawson opened for me. It's in my name, drawing off his account. That's love and trust for you right there. Giving a girl a debit card with access to millions of dollars? Good thing for him I'm not a material girl. I would never go and spend a bunch of money on diamonds and clothes and shoes. I have what I need, and if there's something I want, it's more fun to tell Dawson and let him buy it for me. Don't get me wrong—I like shopping as much as the next girl, but I enjoy getting gifts from my lover more than I do buying things for myself. It's more rewarding. Plus, I then get to thank him in the way we both enjoy.

Which is why this lingerie I'm buying is really for both of us. I would never wear the corset for myself. It's stiff and uncomfortable and confining. I feel sexy as sin in it, but it's for him. It's to make him need my body more than he already does, which shouldn't be physiologically possible. And it's for me, since after he's looked his fill, he'll take it off me and make me scream until the neighbors think I'm getting murdered.

I shiver just thinking about what I'm going to ask him to do to me.

I'm lost in thoughts of his touch and kiss as I leave the store, and I don't spot the paparazzi until it's too late.

"Grey, Grey, over here, Grey! What'd you get at Agent Provocateur, can you show us?"

"Grey, how did you feel about Dawson's proposal?"

"What are you getting Dawson for his birthday? Is that what's in the bag?"

"Are there children in the future for you and Dawson?"

I blink as flashes go off, try to breathe and keep calm and ignore the flurry of questions. And then a question is shouted that makes me panic.

It comes from a man in his thirties, with a long dirty-blond ponytail and a high, pimple-dotted forehead, sharp, cruel brown eyes, and an over-hanging beer belly. "Grey, is it true you used to be a stripper?"

I can't help reacting. I know I shouldn't, that reacting gives credence to the question, but I'm not Dawson. My eyes are drawn to the reporter asking the question. "No…no comment." I'm faint with panic. It's going to come out now, and it's going to ruin Dawson's career. And mine.

"Come on, Grey, we both know the truth. We have a friend in common, you see. A certain Mr. Timothy van Dutton. He told me you were his best dancer."

"No comment." I try to push past, but they won't let me through.

His grin is lecherous, gleeful. "How about this, if it's true, say 'no comment' again. I mean, there's no sense denying it. He told me all about you. You wouldn't go topless except for on-stage." He licks his lips, and his eyes lower with obvious lust to my cleavage. "I'm sorry I never got to see you dance."

I don't answer. I step out into the street, narrowly avoid being smashed by a silver Mercedes. They follow me, bombarding me with questions.

"Grey! Is it true? Were you a stripper?"

"Grey, come back! Where did you dance? How did you get the job?"

"Can you give us a little sample of your dancing?"

"Look at me, Grey! How long were you a stripper? Did you ever perform sexual services?"

I'm not crying yet, but nearly. I'm all but running, and I know this is tantamount to confirming it, but I can't help it. I'm finally to my Rover, almost a block away from the shop, and they're crowding around me, repeating their questions, cameras flashing, held up over their heads to get a shot, microphones and recorders and flip cameras capture my flushed face, watery eyes, and trembling hands.

I know at least one of the clicking cameras captures the single tear that falls from my eye as I start the Rover. And the second one as I back up, heedless of toes I must be running over. For once, I understand the anger with which some celebrities respond to situations like this. I'm hyperventilating, each breath wheezing and fast. I'm dizzy, but I don't dare stop. Honks tell me I'm driving erratically, and I hear squealing tires and shrieking brakes, but I keep driving, letting autopilot take me home.

Dawson isn't home. I wish he was. I need him.

I end up in the gym, sitting in the middle of the dance floor, sobbing. I hear the front door open at some point, and the stiffness of my muscles tells me it's been a long time that I've been here on the floor, crying.

"Baby? What happened?" He scoops me up and sits down with me on his lap.

I bury my face in his chest and try to breathe. I start crying all over again. "They…they found—found out."

"Who? About what?"

"The reporters. The paparazzi. They found out… that I was a stripper." I choke on the word.

"Who found out?" I describe the reporter who asked the question, and what he said. Dawson curses floridly. "Fucking Larry Tominski. That guy is a fucking cunt."

"I tried to stick to 'no comment' like you told me, but…I got so upset."

"Did you verbally confirm it?" His voice is soft but sharp.

I shake my head negative. "No, of course not. But the fact that I was so upset…I ran, and I was crying. It's as much of a confirmation as saying yes."

He squeezes me. "You did great, baby. They're vultures. There was nothing you could have done differently. It's going to be fine."

"It's not, Dawson. It's not fine." I stand up, and he moves to pull me into an embrace, his lips by my jaw. "Everyone will know. They'll believe it, and no one will hire me. They'll say things about me, about you. About us. It'll affect your career. End mine."

He sighs. "Grey, please listen to me. I knew from the very beginning that they'd find out. It was inevitable. In this business, there are no secrets, not for anyone."

"You knew they'd find out?"

He nods. "Of course. You thought no one would ever know? You think Kaz didn't know what you did on the side?" He sounds almost amused. "Kaz knew, babe. You never mentioned it, so neither did he. And neither did I. And as for our careers…it doesn't matter. You think you're the only student to ever strip her way through college? That's nothing. Not in this business. It wouldn't even be a deal-breaker if you'd fucked your way through. Girls fuck their way to the top all the time. In this business and others. And so do guys. No one is innocent. Not in life, and certainly not in Hollywood. We'll ignore the articles and rumors, and eventually it'll die out. Don't answer any questions, and you'll be fine."

I go limp against him. "I don't want them to know. I'm ashamed of it. I don't…I want to pretend it never happened."

He holds me tight, supports me with his arms around my waist. "But it did, babe." He touches my chin, and I look at him. "Don't be ashamed of yourself, Grey. You survived. You took care of yourself. I'm proud of you."

"I feel so…disgusted. When I think about it, I want to throw up all over again. I hate knowing that I did that. That I was…that I let men—"

"It's over now. You'll never have to do it again." His words are a breath in my ear. "I'll always take care of you. And I'll never let anyone talk bad about you, or make you feel less. You're my lady, Grey. Mine. And that means no one will ever get to say anything shitty about you, or make you feel shitty. Not anyone, not ever. Including yourself."

"I'm sorry, Dawson, I just—"

"You have nothing to be sorry for."

"But it's your birthday, and I'm a mess."

He laughs, brushing my hair off my cheek. "I don't care, babe. The party doesn't start for a few hours yet, and even if we had a house full of people, I wouldn't give a fuck. You're my priority. If you're upset, fuck everything else—I gotta make you happy again."

"You do make me happy."

"Then smile and kiss me. In that order."

I try to smile, and nearly succeed. The memories are still cycling through my head, though. The eyes on me, the lights bathing every inch of my body, the music throbbing in the background, the hands reaching for me. Fingers stuffing greasy dollar bills in the string of my thong.

Hey, baby. I'll give you a hundred bucks to suck my cock.

I've got a thousand bucks for you if you'll come home with me.

The not-so-subtle whispers of one buddy to another. *Hey, Mike, check out that chick's ass. I could plow that shit for hours, bro.* And that was totally normal, expected. I had no right to complain. I'd asked for it, since I put my body on display for them.

"You're not there anymore." Dawson's voice brings me back to the present. "You're not there anymore. You're mine now. Only mine."

"Only yours." This truth is like a wave of light eradicating the shadows. I can't quite smile yet, but I can look at him, meet his soft hazel gaze. "Promise?"

"You wearing my ring?" he asks, by way of answer. I flatten my palm on his chest and look at the ring. It absorbs the light and refracts it like a gleaming white sun. "There you go, then. But I still need to see you smile."

I fake a smile, and Dawson rolls his eyes. I smack his chest with my palm. "It's not like I can just...be happy. It's hard. It's upsetting. It's memories I'll always have that I wish I didn't."

He just blinks at me, then leans in and touches a small kiss to the corner of my mouth. "Then I'll have to find a way to cheer you up. Make you forget."

"You're too far over. A little to the left," I breathe. He smiles against my cheek and kisses my upper lip, sucking it into his mouth. "Closer. Lower." He slides his mouth down to the hint of cleavage above my shirt, kisses and kisses. "That's way off. But…it might work. Keep going."

"Up? Or down?"

"Either…will work." He takes my shirt off and kisses my stomach just beneath the underwire of my bra.

He's tugging the cup of my bra down when the door to the gym opens and Luisa pokes her head in. "Oh, sorry, sorry. I—I'll come back, then. Sorry."

Dawson rests his head against my breasts. "Stopped by the stylist." He straightens and tugs my shirt down. "You should go get styled, then, huh?"

I shake my head. "No, I—I need you." I crush my mouth to his, take his hand in mine, and guide his touch down, down.

He gathers the fabric of my loose cotton skirt in his hands and cups my privates. "What do you need, baby? Tell me, so I can give it to you."

I won't say it, and he knows it. He's always try-ing to get me to talk dirty, but I won't unless I'm caught up in the heat of the moment. I can show him, though. I twine our fingers and push our joined touch under the elastic of my underwear, and then his fingers are inside me and my forehead is resting on his chest and I'm breathing hard. He slides my skirt off, pushes my underwear down, and I step out of them. While he touches me, brings me closer and closer to climax, I'm ripping at his belt and his button fly, freeing his erection and sliding my hands around him until his knees are dipping and he's hard and huge and leaking from the tip. I've learned to tell when he's close, and I caress his length slowly and gently until he's there. Normally, he'd have lifted me and impaled me and made me come already, but he's going along with what I'm doing this time. When he's at the edge, I press my lips to his ear and speak over my mortification.

"Now. Take me now."

"Oh, thank fuck," he growls.

He slips his hands from between my thighs and lifts me up by my backside. I wrap my legs around his waist and kiss his temple as he takes long strides to the wall. My back bumps against the wall, and he's inside me. He's kept me on the edge of orgasm this entire time, so I'm desperate. I cling to his shoulders and lift, sink, lift, sink, driving myself on his hardness, gasping as each pounding thrust brings us closer.

And then his middle finger searches the crease of my backside, finds the hot, tight center, and presses in. I bite his shoulder and moan, scraping myself up his length and then back down. His finger slips into me slowly, and I'm so tight that I feel the bulge of his first knuckle as it enters me, and I'm growling now, low noises in the bottom of my throat, embarrassingly feral noises.

"I want you here," he whispers. "Someday soon, baby."

I smile a secret smile into his shoulder. He has no idea how soon.

Thoughts aren't possible then, as we both reach the point of no return, and fall screaming over the edge. He's blasting into me, unleashing a thick wet wave inside me, and I'm clenching around him with every muscle, moving with him.

When we've both caught our breath, he leans away and stares at me. I'm grinning from ear to ear, a bright smile of sated happiness.

"There's the smile I'm looking for. And what a way to get it." He kisses each upturned corner of my mouth, and the smile he gives me is so bright and so beautiful I'm breathless, reminded how lucky I am to have this man, to have the love of this man.

He lets me down, and we both groan as he slides out of me. I gather my underwear in my hand and lean up for a long, slow kiss. "Thank you," I say.

"For what?"

"Loving me. Cheering me up. Being mine. For being you."

"I should be the one thanking you for that."

"Beat you to it," I say, then turn and leave the gym, giving my hips an extra sway for his benefit. I feel his gaze glued to my backside as I leave. All negative thoughts are banished by the force of Dawson's love.

I take a quick shower and then text Luisa to meet me in the bathroom. Yes, I have a cell phone now. It was kind of a nonnegotiable for Dawson. Luisa won't quite meet my eyes as she does my hair and makeup.

The party is long, and intense. Armando is there, charming as always, and Kaz. I corner Kaz around midnight.

"You knew?" It comes out blunt, almost angry.

He smiles at me and sips his scotch. "Of course, Grey. It's my business to know about my interns and potential employees."

"But Nina, you fired her—"

"I fired her for being a prostitute and lying about it. She wasn't a stripper, Grey. She was an escort." He sips his scotch again, and digs a long, thick cigar out of the inside pocket of his blazer, clips it, lights it in thick puffs of acrid smoke, and then glances at me through the fog. "You were doing what you had to do to stay afloat. You were quiet about it, discreet. Nina? She was basically flaunting what she did. I found out she was using my client database to contact johns. I found out, because one of them called my office to request her services again. When I confronted her about it, she denied it. I could overlook even that, if she was discreet about it, but I cannot and will not tolerate liars."

He snags a glass of white wine off the tray of a passing waiter and hands it to me. I sip it carefully, slowly, as I still rarely drink, and never enough to get drunk. "I was worried you would fire me if you knew. I never told you, and I was afraid if you found out, you would fire me for having not told you."

Kaz laughs, a kind but amused chuckle. "Oh, Grey. So naïve." He wraps his arm around my shoulder, his cigar fuming near my face, making my eyes water and my throat tickle. "I wouldn't have fired you. But I have to say I'm glad you're not doing it anymore. It didn't suit you. You're too…good…for that lifestyle."

Kaz is stolen away then by a nervous-looking young scriptwriter who worked on *Gone With the Wind*, probably hoping to pitch an idea. I float from one knot of guests to another, chatting and smiling and trying to act like I know how to be a hostess. I feel like an impostor sometimes. Like someone will see through my disguise and point at me and laugh, and say, "She doesn't belong here! She's just a hick from Georgia!"

It never happens, of course, because it's all in my head.

I'm on my third glass of wine, the most I've ever drank…drunk?…at one time in my whole life. I'm a little dizzy, a little loose. I've had amazing conversations with some of the most famous people in the world. Shaquille O'Neal is here, for some reason which I can't quite figure out. He's nice. Jack Nicholson is a lot nicer than I thought he'd be, based on most of the roles I've seen him play.

I find myself in the backyard, by the pool, surrounded by a crowd of young producers and a few sound guys, and they're talking about some project they all worked on together, and I'm able to figure out which film based on the context, which makes me feel pretty smart. I'm listening and learning, and I'm out of wine. I like this feeling, this slow, easy, loose buzzing in my head. Conversation comes easily, and the guys around me listen when I talk, and answer my questions without condescension. I feel like I'm part of the business. I'm *in*, and it feels great.

A hand takes the empty wine glass and presses a round tumbler full of square sparkling ice cubes and amber liquid into my hand. I take the glass and stare at it, uncomprehending. Why would I drink this? I don't drink liquor. I barely drink wine. I tilt my head up to look at the person who gave it to me. He's very tall and thin, good-looking in a hipster kind of way. He's wearing tight black jeans and an untucked white button-down beneath an argyle sweater vest.

A loosely-knotted tie completes the look. His hair is long and unkempt, and his eyes are glazed but intent on me. I think he may be an agent, or maybe an effects tech. I've seen him before somewhere, but I don't know where. It bothers me.

I hand the glass back to him. "I'd rather have wine, thanks."

He pushes it back at me. "It's Blue Label, baby. Some of the best whiskey there is. Just try it."

Those two words—"Blue Label"—bring back a muddled memory, which I force away. "No, really. I don't like that stuff." But I'm sipping it anyway, for some reason. I cough, but the way it burns after I've swallowed isn't unpleasant. I take another sip.

Hipster smiles happily. "See? Not so bad. I'm Pavel, by the way."

I shake his hand, and he doesn't let go right away. "Hi, Pavel. I'm—"

"Oh, I know who you are, Gracie." He holds onto my hand, seemingly oblivious to my attempts to withdraw it. His smile shifts. Darkens, somehow.

My buzz dies. I need out of this conversation, *now*. But he's still holding my hand. I pull, but he doesn't let go. I look around me, but the group I was talking to has scattered, and Pavel and I are alone by the pool. There are people on the other side, near the house, but we're on the far side, obscured from the view of the house by a huge stand of palm trees.

"I don't know what you think you've heard, but my name is *Grey*. I'm Dawson's fiancée."

He lets go of my hand, but his palm wraps around my back and forces me against him. I struggle, and he just laughs. "Oh, come on. We both know what you really are. I saw you, you know. At Exotic Nights. I was a regular. I loved watching you dance. And then you vanished and the club closed…but now here you are. Dance for me, Gracie."

I lift my knee and jam it as hard as I can into his groin, and he stumbles backward, coughing. He drops the glass he's holding and it smashes on the ground, splashing whiskey on my sandaled feet.

He lurches, then stumbles, glances up at me with hate in his eyes. "You *bitch*! You're a stripper. That's all you are. Fancy fucking dresses can't hide it." He takes a step toward me.

I drop the glass as I back away from him, and it smashes, too, and then massive hands are around my shoulders, pulling me away. I struggle, and then go still when I realize the huge paws belong to Greg. There's a flash of movement, and then Pavel is flying. He smashes into a tree, and then Dawson is there, holding him off the ground with a hand around his throat. Pavel kicks, makes a strangled gasping noise. His feet are three inches off the ground, and Dawson is keeping him aloft with one hand.

"Dawson." Kaz says calmly as he's striding up with his scotch and cigar held in the same hand. He puts his free hand on Dawson's shoulder. "Don't. Greg will escort him out, and I'll blacklist him. He's done."

Pavel shakes his head, more horrified by this pronouncement than by the thought of being brutalized into bloody hamburger by Dawson. Dawson lets go and turns away. Pavel sinks to the ground, coughing, bent over double, gasping. I think it's over, and so does Pavel, who opens his mouth, probably to plead for his career, but then Dawson whirls back around and his fist is a hammer, smashing into Pavel's face. He pitches to the side, and Dawson is about to swing again before I capture his arm. I put my hands on Dawson's face and his arms go around me.

"No. No more. I'm fine. It's over." I take his hand and rub his knuckles with my thumbs.

Dawson is on the brink, rage making him bigger and harder, a violent glint in his eyes as he stares down Pavel. "Grey, he—"

"He's nothing. It's your birthday. Just make him leave." I meet Dawson's eyes, and let him see that I'm okay.

And really, I am. In one respect, Pavel was right. The fancy dresses and expensive jewelry can't hide who I was, what I used to do. But it's the past. I'm not that person anymore, no more than I'm the innocent and naïve pastor's daughter who first moved to L.A. But both are a part of who I am and who I used to be, but it's not me anymore.

It also felt really good to knee the bastard in the balls.

I laugh at the uncharacteristic thought, and Dawson's expression shifts from anger to confusion. "What's funny?"

"Just…I was thinking how good it felt to nail that asshole in the balls."

Dawson sputters and then cracks up, and so do Kaz and Greg. "Just don't do it to me."

I reach down and cup him between the legs. "I would never. I love them too much." Kaz and Greg cough and turn away, and I realize I might be a little buzzed still, if I really just said and did that in front of them.

Dawson is shocked speechless for a moment. "Damn, Grey. You should drink more often if it makes you like this. You're sexy when you're tipsy."

I let Dawson draw me inside, and we sit in the living room on the couch. I lose count of how many glasses of wine I drink as we talk to our friends. The room fades until there are only the seven or eight of us clustered on the couch and loveseat and leather recliners, talking the night away, and I get dizzier and dizzier until Dawson is a pillar holding me up, and he's watching me, gauging me, and letting me do what I want. Kaz lights a cigar and hands it to Dawson, who puffs it, and then, with a quirky smile, puts it to my lips. I take a small puff and cough, choking. The men all laugh, so I take it from Dawson and try again, and maybe it's just the wine, but I feel sexy holding it and smoking from it, like an actress from the '40s sitting on a piano in a slinky dress.

Dawson shakes his head at me, but his eyes gleam.

I stand up unsteadily, and then have to sit back down. Dawson chuckles. "Need help, baby?"

I nod. "I've gotta pee." I sound more Georgia than ever, and I realize I've been slowly taking the accent on all night, since the incident with Pavel, which was hours and hours ago by this point. The cable box says it's 3:26 a.m. I can't believe I'm still upright.

I feel something happening to my feet, and I look down to see Dawson unstrapping the heeled sandals I'm wearing, sliding one off, and then the other. I watch him, and let him do it, and then he's half-carrying me to the bathroom. Well, not half-carrying. I'm leaning against him, my arm around his waist. I'd definitely fall over if he wasn't here, but he is, so I'm fine. He follows me into the bathroom, but he doesn't let go of me. He holds me by the shoulders as I clumsily focus on hiking my dress up, my underwear down, and sit to pee. There's two of him, for some reason. More sexy to look at, so it's okay. He has an amused grin on his face, both of them.

"What?" I ask.

"You're hammered."

I nod floppily. "Definitely kind of drunk. Is it funny?"

He laughs and helps me stay upright as I re-dress and wash my hands. "Yes, my love, it is. Very funny."

A thought occurs to me, and I turn to frown at him, or whichever one of him is the real one. I close one eye, and there's only one. I carefully enunciate my words. "I'm not embarrassing you in front of your friends, am I?" Well, that was very slurred.

Dawson's expression is priceless, amused and tender at once. "No, babe. Not even a little bit. We've all been a bit sloppy before. You're beautiful, and you're perfect. Just have fun and relax. I'll take care of you."

"But…it's your birthday. You should be having fun and getting drunk, not me."

He brushes my hair away with his thumb. "This is the best birthday party I've ever had, douchebag Pavel notwithstanding. And I'm plenty drunk, baby. It's almost four in the morning, and I've been drinking since seven."

I stare at him, kind of awed. "But…you don't seem drunk at all."

He laughs outright at this. "I've had lots and lots of practice."

I nod. This makes perfect sense. I think of something else I have to tell him. "I know…I know everyone else gave you presents today, and I didn't. But I've got a present for you. I just can't give it to you until tomorrow. Or today. Whatever. It's a surprise."

Dawson gives me that amused yet loving look again. "*You're* the present, babe. You're all I need from you."

I grin. "Oh, I'm pretty sure you'll like this. But it's a surprise." I think I already said that, but I can't remember. Suddenly, I feel drunker than ever, and very tired.

Dawson sees, and scoops me up in that effortless way of his. "You're ready for bed, aren't you?" I nod, and he kisses me softly. "Rest, then." I drowse, and I feel him set me in our bed, cover me up. He shakes my shoulder, and I wake up. He presses a glass of water into my hand, and a pair of pills into the other. "That'll help you not be so hung over in the morning. Sleep, baby. I love you."

After I wash the aspirin down, I peer at him with one eye. "You're the best thing that ever happened to me, Dawson Kellor." It's the last lucid thought I can express.

"You've got that backward, love." He kisses me, and I want to kiss him back, but I'm going under. "I think we're the best thing to happen to each other."

That's true, so true. But I'm totally numb, pleasantly loose. The room is spinning, the bed tipping and tilting underneath me. I open my eyes, but the room is still, and I realize it's me, in my head. I let go, and slide under the waves of sleep. I feel a hand go around my middle, and he's behind me. Time has passed, and birds are chirping in the gray sky, and then I'm back under with him.

CHAPTER SEVENTEEN

I HAVE LUISA COME OVER to do my hair and makeup and help me tighten the corset. She's been my stylist for a while now, and she's turning into a friend, and anyway she's the only person who I'd feel comfortable asking to tighten a corset for me. She ties the knot and then moves around in front of me and gives me an appraising stare.

"Damn, Grey. That's…you're lookin' pretty fine, girl." She grins at me. "That must be a birthday surprise for Dawson, hmm?"

I nod, smiling nervously. "Yeah. I wasn't sure what to get him, since he's, you know, got everything you could think of. Does it look okay? I've never worn anything like this before."

"I don't think 'okay' is the right word, honey." She lifts her eyebrows suggestively. "I think your man is gonna have a hard time deciding whether he wants you in that outfit or out of it. He's gonna be a mess, know what I mean?"

I laugh with her, reassured, but still nervous. I put on a robe I bought for this occasion, a light, silky thing that barely covers my thighs. I tie it loosely around me so he'll be able to get a good look at my cleavage without revealing what I'm wearing beneath it. Luisa leaves after hugging me, careful not to muss my hair. It's carefully pinned up off my neck, but she put the pins in so that Dawson will be able to pull them out easily. He likes my hair down.

An older man who vaguely resembles Michael Caine meets me at the top of the stairs. "Everything is ready downstairs."

I thank him, and the catering company leaves. I'd thought about trying to do the whole dinner thing myself, but I've not exactly had a lot of experience cooking fancy dinners. I go into the dining room, and I'm stunned. They didn't just bring food, they turned the dining room into a romantic dinner for two, complete with candles and bouquets of roses. The effect is elegant yet not too feminine. It is *his* birthday, after all. He's out golfing with Armando and a few other of his friends, which was my suggestion. I needed him out of the house so I could set this all up and get myself ready.

Right on time, I hear him come in from the garage. I arrange myself in the chair on the side of the table, leaving the place set at the head of the table for him. I'm waiting, my heart on my proverbial sleeve. I've never done anything like this, and I'm desperately hoping it makes him happy.

"Grey?" I hear him setting down his keys and the chirp as he plugs his phone in.

"In the dining room," I call.

He stops in the doorway, and his eyes widen at the flowers and candles, low-lit chandelier, the spread of all of his favorite dishes, and me. Mostly, he looks at me. "Holy shit, baby. What is all this?"

I rise and stalk toward him, feeling sultry. "Happy birthday, my love." I don't use a lot of endearments, not like he does, so when I use one, he takes note.

"What's under the robe?" He asks it with a smirk, reaching for the tie.

I stop his hands. "Your present. But you can't see it until after we eat."

His eyes darken with lust. "God, baby. You're killing me. You look…you so good I'd rather eat you."

"Soon enough," I promise. "But first, sit down."

He scoots the chair out and sits down. An expensive bottle of his favorite white wine is opened and breathing in a bucket of ice. I pour him a glass, set it in front of him. He watches me, curious. Usually, he does these things. For my birthday a few months ago, he rented out an entire restaurant, had the food made, but served me himself. Even in an everyday capacity, he does things for me. Makes me snacks, pours my wine, takes care of me. So now it's my turn to take care of him.

He sips the wine, and I slide my body between his knees and the table. He holds the glass of wine in his hand and stares up at me. "What are you doing, babe?"

I'm not nervous, not really. I don't do this super often, but it's something I want to give him. I sink to my knees, rest my hands on his thighs, and smile up at him. "This."

He's wearing the stupid clothes men wear golfing, but he looks hot even in a pair of almost-white pants and a pastel-orange collared shirt. I undo his pants, and his eyes open wide in understanding. "Grey, honey—"

I give him another thing he likes: me, acting dominant. "Shut up and drink your wine."

He smirks and sips his wine, then lifts his hips as I tug his pants down far enough to bare him for what I'm going to do next. He's already hard, and I grasp him in both hands, caress my fists up and down his considerable length, roll my palm over his head, and then rub the tip of him with my thumb. He closes his eyes briefly, then sips his wine again, meeting my eyes. I hold his gaze as I lower my mouth to his erection and wrap my lips around his thickness. He gasps out loud when I take him in until he's at my throat, and then back away. He caresses the curve of my neck with his free hand as I suck him into a bucking frenzy, and then I back away and let him subside a bit. I lick the tip of him, run my mouth down the side and back up before wrapping my lips around him again. I caress his balls with one hand, and with the other pump his base until he's groaning. When I feel him start to lose control, I slide my hand up and down him faster and faster, moving my mouth on him slowly, in contrast to the speed of my hand.

"God, I'm—" But he doesn't have time to get any more of a warning out before he's lost in groaning bliss.

I know it's coming, so a warning isn't necessary. I don't stop when he explodes in my mouth. I keep going, keep moving and suckling, and his groans are so desperately pleasure-filled that I groan, too, and either the sound or the feel of my voice buzzing makes him come again, even harder, and I keep going until he's panting and pulling at me to get up.

He tugs his pants back on as I stand up, and then pulls me against him, and I bend to kiss him.

"Part one of your present," I say.

His eyes search mine. "Baby, that was…god, that felt *so* fucking good. Thank you."

He pours me a glass of wine, and I sit down and sip it. He dishes up food for both of us before I can, and I let him, because I think it's just in his nature to do things for me. We talk as we eat a long, luxurious dinner. He got the part he was reading for, a contemporary drama about a man coping with the slow death of his father at the same time that he finds out his wife was unfaithful. It's a turn away from the action and the sex and the romance, and I think it'll be a good role for him. When we finish with dessert, I lead him by the hand up to our bedroom. He brings our wine glasses and a second chilled bottle, pours us each a new glass.

I take a sip of mine, and then set it aside as I mentally prepare for the next part of my surprise for Dawson. "Sit down on the bed," I tell him. He sits on the edge of the bed, and I stand in front of him, facing him. I hesitate with my hands on the tie of my robe. "Part two," I say.

"How many parts to this present are there?"

"Three."

I loosen the knot, let the ends of the tie fall free, and then slowly part the robe. His eyes widen as the robe opens, and then he shifts in place as I let it fall off my shoulders. He takes a casual sip of his wine, but his gaze is anything but nonchalant. He hasn't said anything, but he hasn't looked away from me, either. His breathing is deep, and his eyes betray him. I stay still as he stands up, sets his glass down on the bedside table, and then comes to stand a foot away from me.

"Jesus, babe." His hands trace the curve of my waist, come to rest on my hips. "I don't know whether to rip that thing off you as fast as I can, or leave it on so I can stare at you."

I laugh. "That's exactly what Luisa said your reaction would be when she helped me tie it."

"Smart woman."

"You really like it?"

His hands run up the backs of my thighs, cup my backside. Fire heats my core at his touch. "God... *damn*, Grey. Like it? You're so fucking gloriously gorgeous that I literally cannot stand it. I'm having to remind myself to keep breathing, because you take my breath away." He kisses the side of my neck, my shoulder, the slope of my breast. "Jesus. I don't even have words. You deserve an epic poem or something. A paean. Or no, that's not right. I don't fucking know...you're my goddess, Grey Amundsen, and I'm going to worship you."

"Do you want to know what part three is?" I ask.

He shakes his head. "Not yet, I'm still appreciating part two." He's touching me all over, praising me with his hands.

Dawson touches every inch of me from head to toe, and then starts over again with his mouth, paying homage with hot, wet kisses.

I've never in my life felt so powerful, wanted, so *loved*. When he's kissed me to his satisfaction, he's standing behind me. He unties the knot, then oh-so-slowly loosens the cords until the corset is ready to be drawn off. He does, and I'm wearing nothing but the flesh-tan briefs with the tiny bow at the top, and those are off next. I'm in his hands now, under his mercy. He's still fully clothed, but I'll take care of that at some point.

First, I let him do whatever he wants.

Which involves him kneeling in front of me, spreading my stance with gentle nudges of his hands, and pressing delicate kisses to the inside of my thighs and upward, and licking and suckling me into a moaning climax. When I've come down from the shuddering high, I draw him to his feet and peel his shirt off, caress his stomach and chest and shoulders, kissing him all over as he did me, then helping him to shed his pants and underwear.

When we're both naked, I climb onto the bed, reach into the drawer of my nightstand, and bring out the bottle of lubricant. Dawson's eyes fix on it, then shift to mine.

"Part three," I say.

He moves onto the bed with me and picks up the lube, staring at it. His expression is hesitant and hopeful. "What's part three?"

I climb onto his lap, rubbing my damp folds against him, and whisper in his ear. "I want you to fuck me in the ass."

He takes a deep breath, resting his head on my shoulder. "Grey, baby. Don't say that just because you think that's what I want—"

"It's what I want," I tell him, grinding against him, ready for more of him, needing more of him. "I said it that way for you, because you like it when I talk that way, but…I want you to do that. When you put your finger inside me like that, it feels good, and I want more."

He's caressing me, his palms skating in a circle over my shoulders and down my back, to my hips, my thighs. "You're sure?"

"Completely. I trust you, and I want you."

"Then I'll have to make you come again."

"Well, damn," I say, smiling into his mouth.

He laughs, and then we're lost in a kiss. Dawson reaches up and pulls a pin from my hair, freeing some of it, and then another pin, and another, and then all my hair is down around my shoulders in a cascading golden wave. He leans forward and lays me down on my back, not breaking the kiss, and his hand finds my cleft, caresses me, delves into my core and swirls around my clit. His kiss moves from my mouth to my nipple, and then he's lower down again, and two fingers are inside my folds and the middle finger of his other hand is seeking my tight entrance. He's slower to bring me to climax, this time, and his finger is sliding in and out of me. I'm gasping and bucking, needing a release that he won't let me find. He brings me to the edge and then slows down, and I'm mad with need.

I'm bereft when his finger leaves, and then I feel something wet and cool smeared onto me, and then again. And then again, and he's pushing in with his finger, pushing in and pulling out, and then I feel a sense of being stretched, and I realize he's added two fingers, and oh…*god*…it's too intense for words, and I'm wondering how I'll ever survive the rest of him, but it's so intense, so good, so amazing, and I can't even form words.

I let my knees fall aside and silently encourage him, and then his fingers leave me and he's pushing at one hip. I know what that means, what he wants. I roll over onto my stomach, and he gently lifts my hips, snags a pillow and tucks it beneath me, and then applies more lubricant and I hear a condom wrapper; I turn my head over my shoulder to watch, and I'm turned on even more by the sight of his hand around his thick shaft.

Oh. Oh, god.

He's touching the tip of his cock to my ass, and even in the throes of nervous excitement I'm absurdly proud of myself for using those words in my thoughts. He's using his other hand, the one he touched my folds with, to bring me to climax, bent over me and reaching between my legs to fondle me, finding my clit with his fingers and rubbing it until I'm rocking on my hands and knees into his touch, and he uses that motion, pressing the head of his erection to my rear, and then I feel stretched and too too too full, so full, and it hurts a little, but he's waiting, holding still, and I slowly grow accustomed to it.

And then he moves, just a little. "Dawson, oh, god, *Dawson*…"

"Okay, baby?" He asks the question with concern rife in his voice.

I can only nod and shift my hips a little. His fingers are inside me again, three fingers sliding into my *pussy*, as Dawson calls it—and I'm at climax and coming apart, and then he slides in a little further and I'm moaning loudly, biting the pillow and groaning low in my throat, a noise so feral I can't believe it's coming from me. It makes Dawson wild, that animal growl, and he slowly buries himself the rest of the way. For some reason, the feel of his body coming to rest against my ass, knowing he's buried deep in that place, is erotic beyond all my wildest dreams. He's had me from behind, course, but this is different.

I can't believe he's got all of his massive erection inside me without it hurting. There's an edge of pain, but not enough to even shadow the sunburst ecstasy.

And then he pulls out, so slowly, achingly slowly, and I moan all over again, every muscle shivering in response, and it causes something deep inside me to ache, to pulse and turn fiery, a blinding throb so intense I can't breathe around it. He slides in a little, and then back out, and I'm mouth-wide silent-screaming, which turns into an actual shriek, high-pitched and breathless, as he slides in.

He does it like this, slow withdrawals and careful thrusts in, until I can't bear the slowness anymore and I'm the one to push my backside into his next thrust, and harder, and then harder again. With each thrust, the shuddering ache in my core builds, and I realize it's an orgasm being built, but one unlike anything I've ever felt before.

It's going to be so intense I'm almost afraid of it.

His hands caress my back, both of them running over my soft skin, and then as our bodies meet on an in-thrust, he takes my hips in his hands, fingers digging into the skin and pulling at me. Oh, I like that. I love the feel of his hands on me like that, encouraging me, pulling at me desperately.

He's losing it, growling, his rhythm faltering as his thrusts become harder and more erratic, and I'm lost right alongside him. We're groaning together, and I have no control over the sounds I make; my screams are growing louder and more breathy, more frantic.

The throb inside me is a chasm, a crushing pressure. So much, so much.

And then it breaks open, and I'm blind, deaf, swept away by the rocket rush and earthquake shakes and chaotic intensity. I can't contain it, and I know my screams must be deafening.

I hear Dawson groan, and my orgasm is shuddering and fading, but I never felt him come. He carefully and slowly withdraws as the climax leaves me with trembling aftershocks, and when he slips out completely, I actually whimper and feel the loss. But he's not done with me. He lifts me and rolls me to my back, and I watch through blurry eyes as he strips the condom off himself. He's harder and bigger than I've ever seen him, and every muscle in his body is tensed. He kneels over me, kisses his way up my body, to my mouth, and then he's inside me, bare inside me, and I'm weeping with pleasure at the feel of him there, the familiar bliss of him gliding where he belongs.

"Grey, oh, god—"

I'm there all over again, at the edge of climax with him, but this feels more like an emotional orgasm, a sense of such blasting, overwhelming, soul-shearing love for Dawson that my entire being is shaking with it.

"Dawson…" I whisper, and then he's holding me close, almost limp on top of me except a bit of his weight supported on his forearms, the rest of his body skin to skin on mine, and I wrap my legs around his back and my arms around his neck and crush my lips to his ear and let words tumble out. "Dawson, I love you. Oh…fuck…I love you. I want you to feel you come now. Come for me, baby."

He actually whimpers in the back of his throat and lets go then. When I say the word "baby," he comes unglued, comes apart, goes completely spastic and frantic, each thrust a shuddering blast of seed inside me, and he's whispering my name, gasping *I love you* brokenly in my ear, and I come apart with him, breathing with him, each breath synced with his, each sigh breathed together, the only words uttered each other's names and *I love you.*

There's never been anything but this. The world, time, history, love, eternity; it all boils down to Dawson here, inside me, above me, with me, us together.

I press my lips to his ear. "Happy birthday, Dawson."

He just laughs and rolls with me, fits me into the nook of his arm. Sometime later, we make love again, slowly, without saying a word.

CHAPTER EIGHTEEN

A CELEBRITY WEDDING is a ridiculous thing. We spent so much money, invited so many people. There's media coverage, weeks of newspaper and magazine speculation, article after article. There was even a TV special, which we did interviews for and let the cameras follow us around during wedding planning.

Now I'm trying not to cry as I walk down the aisle with my hand on Daddy's arm. A veil hangs down my back to merge with the train of my dress, which cost somewhere north of $100,000. Kind of ridiculous, honestly, considering I'll wear it for a few hours at most. But Dawson insisted. A dress with that price tag is expected for a wedding of this scale. There are hundreds of flowers, all over the pews and scattered on the floor.

It's a traditional wedding, for all that it's a celebrity affair. In deference to my father, Dawson made sure of that.

I'm staring at Dawson, watching his face as he works to contain his emotions at the sight of me. He has never been more attractive than he is in this moment, dressed in a custom-tailored vintage tuxedo, his hair combed into a part that makes him look like he could have stepped out of a Clark Gable movie. His tuxedo is designed to enhance that look, and so is my dress. The whole wedding, in fact, is vintage, '30s-inspired, right down to the car we're going to drive away in: a 1937 Rolls Royce Phantom.

Daddy hands me off to Dawson, but before he does, he leans in to whisper to me, "I love you, Grey. I'm so proud of who you are." My eyes water as I hear the words I've wished for my entire life. Daddy sniffs and blinks hard. "Go marry him. He's a good man."

I step up to Dawson and take his hands. I barely hear the pastor but when it comes time, I repeat the vows.

"I do." Two words, and they hold so much meaning. I've been his, I've always been his, and he mine. From the first day I saw him in the VIP room of that awful place, we've belonged to each other. But now, now we're completely and officially bound together, tied and linked and made permanent.

The reception is a happy blur. I'm on cloud nine, overcome and overwhelmed by joy. And then the time comes for the first dance.

A spotlight shines on the edge of the dance floor, bathing a single figure: Lindsey Stirling. She lifts a violin to her shoulder, pauses, and then launches into "Elements." Dawson and I are off with the music, dancing a choreographed and rehearsed tango.

A boring old slow dance wasn't going to cut it for *this* wedding, after all.

I've never danced so well in all my life; dancing comes from within, and inside, I'm alight with pure happiness. I've got everything I could ever ask for, and then some.

THE END

PLAYLIST

"The Giving" by Michael W. Smith
"Ten Thousand Hours" by Macklemore
"Can't Hold Us" by Macklemore
"Just Give Me A Reason" by Pink & Nate Ruess
"More Than Miles" by Brantley Gilbert
"Don't Take the Girl" by Tim McGraw
"Our Solemn Hour" by Within Temptation
"Hibernia" by Michael W. Smith
"Marry Me" by Train
"Palladio" by Silent Nick
"Elements" by Lindsey Stirling
"David's Jig" by Natalie McMaster

I know this is kind of a short and random play-
list. I'm not going to pretend I understand how

these songs came to fit into the story, but they do. They're the songs that Dawson and Grey communicate with, and those two are eclectic people, musically. The song that Grey dances to, in Chapter 12, after Dawson opens up is "Our Solemn Hour" by Within Temptation. It's not named in the text, but I wrote the scene listening to that song on repeat, so it's important.

There was another song I wanted to use in this book. It never seemed to fit into the story, but I have a scene in my head, of Dawson and Grey dancing together. It's early morning, still gray outside. Dawson wears a pair of gym shorts and is shirtless, and the hazy morning light makes him look like he stepped out of a Greek myth. Grey is in a pair of spandex shorts and a sports bra, and they're whirling across the gym floor of Dawson's house together. "David's Jig" by Natalie McMaster plays, a skirling fiddle jig, lively and energetic and relentless, happy and joyful. Dawson's chest glistens with sweat as he dances, and a wisp of hair falls across Grey's face, and they dance as if nothing exists but the music, and each other, and motion. The scene reminds me of *Far and Away*, for some reason.

Anyway, after that random aside, I hope you enjoy listening to these songs, the brief and random, but wonderful, soundtrack to *Stripped*.

ABOUT THE AUTHOR

New York Times and *USA Today* bestselling author Jasinda Wilder is a Michigan native with a penchant for titillating tales about sexy men and strong women. When she's not writing, she's probably shopping, baking, or reading. She loves to travel, and some of her favorite vacations spots are Las Vegas, New York City, and Toledo, Ohio. You can often find Jasinda drinking sweet red wine with frozen berries.

To find out more about Jasinda and her other titles, visit her website: www.JasindaWilder.com.

CPSIA information can be obtained
at www.ICGtesting.com
Printed in the USA
LVHW04s1816180618
581091LV00003B/877/P